FALSE WITNESS

FALSE WITNESS

Veronica Heley

**SEVERN
HOUSE**

First world edition published in Great Britain and the USA in 2024
by Severn House, an imprint of Canongate Books Ltd,
14 High Street, Edinburgh EH1 1TE.

severnhouse.com

British Library Cataloguing-in-Publication Data
A CIP catalogue record for this title is available from the British Library.

ISBN-13: 978-1-4483-1256-6 (cased)
ISBN-13: 978-1-4483-1257-3 (e-book)

All Severn House titles are printed on acid-free paper.

Typeset by Palimpsest Book Production Ltd., Falkirk,
Stirlingshire, Scotland.
Printed and bound in Great Britain by TJ Books,
Padstow, Cornwall.

Praise for the Abbot Agency mysteries

About the author

Veronica Heley is actively involved in her local church and community affairs. She lives in Ealing, West London.

Veronica is the creator of the ever-popular Ellie Quicke mysteries, as well as the Abbot Agency series. *False Witness* is the seventeenth Abbot Agency novel.

www.veronicaheley.com

ONE

B ea Abbot ran a domestic agency which was doing very well, thank you. Her portrait painter husband was much in demand, and a hard winter was giving way to the first signs of spring. Bea was an optimist. She liked fairy stories in which the poor orphan boy fought against the odds to win the princess and inherit the castle. Hadn't she rescued one such orphan boy and helped to restore him to his childhood sweetheart and his inheritance?

Bea was also a realist, and understood that the young couple didn't always live happily ever after. There might well be wicked cousins plotting to regain the family estate . . .

Monday morning

To Bea's way of thinking, a last-minute invitation to lunch was either a 'please' or a 'thank you'. Either you were being thanked for something you'd done, or your host wanted you to do something for him.

When Julian rang, she couldn't think of anything she'd done recently to justify a celebration, so she decided this invitation must be a 'please'. Had something happened to make him ask for her help?

Julian and his young wife Polly had produced a bouncing baby boy; no problems there. He'd also inherited a neglected stately home in the Home Counties . . . and nothing there had gone well.

For a start, the cupboard was bare. The money that ought to have been in the bank accounts had disappeared. The roof of the Elizabethan mansion leaked and the windows didn't fit. The electrics and plumbing were eccentric at best and lethal in some places.

Julian's grandfather, old Sir Florian, died the night after his great-grandson was placed in his arms. In view of the parlous state of the building, Julian made alternative living arrangements for the remaining members of the family and closed the Hall and all its dependent businesses for much-needed refurbishment.

Julian sold his flat in London, borrowed what he could, and set about trying to save the Hall. He moved his little family into temporary quarters in the Tithe Barn behind the main building and, trained as an accountant, had seemed to be coping well.

But, when he rang to ask Bea out for lunch at short notice, she could hear the strain in his voice.

He said, 'I've a meeting in the afternoon, so could we make it noon?'

She probed a little. 'Of course. How's Polly, and your fine son? And your wonder dog, Bruno?'

'They're fine. Polly only sits down to feed the infant and Bruno guards them both when he's not with me. The boy has a yell on him to be heard in the next county.'

She risked a teasing note. 'Have you found the money stolen from the estate by the previous manager? He was some kind of uncle of yours, wasn't he?'

'Yes, Frederick. He ran the estate for my grandfather, and did it very badly in my opinion. And yes, he did clean out the Hall's bank accounts. I've got my old firm of accountants working on the matter. They've traced the money to the Cayman Islands, but Frederick's set a password on it and he's not telling what it is.'

'You'll figure it out, I'm sure. So what's the problem for today?'

'I've solicitors to the left of me and death duties to the right, competing for my attention with builders and electricians. We've just found a whole stack of paperwork shoved into an unlocked drawer. I've been summoned to a meeting at the parish hall to explain why I've thrown so many people out of work and when I plan to reopen. Under Frederick's management some were on short-term contracts, but most had no contract at all. They're unhappy with the job losses I've had to make and I can't blame them. They'll probably pelt me with rotten tomatoes.' He tried to laugh at himself. 'I don't like being unpopular. Perhaps you're the only person in the world I can say that to.'

Bea said, 'I've heard it said that the only people who should have power are those who don't want it. You fall into that category. Do you ever regret taking over the estate with all its problems? You might have put it on the market and led a comfortable life with Polly and your son in a pleasant suburb, with nothing more to worry about than whether you take the SUV or the sports car to the station on your way to work.'

He almost laughed. 'Me with a sports car? I think not. I'm Mr Safe-Rather-Than-Sorry, aren't I? Boringly keeping to the speed limit and never drinking and driving. No, I don't regret it, exactly. There are days when I feel in tune with the house and the land around it. That's a strange feeling for a man brought up to think in terms of a semi-detached in Ealing and a fortnight's holiday abroad once a year. But yes, there are days when I wake in a cold sweat, worrying about the people who used to work at the Hall, not to mention in the farm shop, the restaurant and the amusement park. They all blame me for the closures but if I hadn't made them, Health & Safety would.'

'Julian, you've been coping with all that for a while. What's really wrong?'

Silence. Then, 'I can't tell you over the phone. See you at noon.'

So, there really was a problem?

The day was chilly, so Bea wore a dress in her favourite willow green and her favourite pair of suede boots. A woman might be sixty-ish but that didn't mean she couldn't look her best.

The venue Julian had chosen had a reputation for good food in unfussy surroundings, and he was there when she arrived.

Sir Julian Marston-Lang had a presence of which he was totally unaware. Tall and spare of figure, with fair, curly hair and remarkably bright blue eyes, he might have posed for a statue of some long-ago Greek athlete, except that he wore rimless glasses and a grey business suit.

He put his arm around Bea in a rare gesture of affection. 'How are you? You look good.'

'So do you,' said Bea, with a smile.

He didn't smile. Polly said he didn't smile enough nowadays, and Bea thought that was true.

As they settled at their table and looked at the menu, Bea ran through in her mind what she knew of his background.

Julian's grandfather, Sir Florian Marston-Lang, had married twice. His first wife died after giving birth to a fair-haired son. That boy grew up in the dark shadow of Sir Florian's second venture into matrimony, and eventually left his ancestral home to make a life for himself elsewhere. He dropped the 'Marston' from his name, married someone he'd met at university, and produced a son and heir. Tragically, the young couple were killed in a car crash, and their toddler was put up for adoption.

Julian had been brought up in ignorance of his lineage. He'd been happily progressing up the ladder as an accountant in a prestigious firm, and planning to marry his childhood sweetheart, when members of Sir Florian's second family learned, to their horror, of his existence. Far from sitting pretty and expecting to inherit, Sir Florian's second wife, her son Frederick and his family discovered that they had a relative who was the heir to the Marston-Lang estate.

Several efforts were made to do away with the unsuspecting Julian, one of which brought Bea Abbot into the picture. In due course the would-be murderers had been exposed and arrested . . . and Julian had been offered the keys to Marston Hall by his grandfather, Sir Florian.

In Bea Abbot's opinion, Julian had many good qualities but one fatal flaw: he couldn't resist helping those weaker than himself. Common sense urged him to resign his title to the nearly bankrupt estate and run for the hills. Instead, he worked every hour he could keep his eyes open to save the impoverished estate.

The restaurant had an excellent reputation. They ordered and Bea waited for Julian to explain.

He didn't. He tried small talk. 'Where's your husband, and who is he painting now?'

Bea had to think. Piers was in demand internationally. 'He's in some place in the Balkans. He says the politics are diabolical but he hopes to escape unharmed. He should be back soon. What's the problem, Julian?'

He brushed that aside. 'I'm meeting British Heritage this afternoon. I've asked if I might install solar panels, which is the only sensible way to provide us with heating and lighting the complex. We really need to have double glazing for the windows at the Hall, but apparently that would be vandalism and is not allowed, though it may be permitted sometime in the future. We've agreed on installing shutters, but they'll all have to be handmade and, well . . . It would have been helpful if I'd studied woodwork at school.'

The food came. It was good.

Julian put a mouthful on his fork and laid it down on the plate again. 'It's starting again, Bea. Someone's trying to kill me, and I don't know why.'

'What? But . . . all the bad lots are in prison, aren't they?'

'Yes.'

Bea laid down her fork, too. 'Are you sure?'

'Do you think I haven't checked? They are. I'm told that, all evidence to the contrary, Lady Fleur, my grandfather's second wife, is still insisting she is as innocent as Snow White of any bad intentions towards me. She lays all the blame for the attempts on my life on her son, my step-uncle Frederick; that's the one who mismanaged the estate and subsequently ran off with the takings. In turn, he's blaming her for everything. I imagine they'll remain as guests of His Majesty's pleasure for some years to come. Which leaves Frederick's son, Bertram; that's the muscle-bound idiot who tried to run me down and ended up wrapped around a lamppost. He's currently in the prison hospital suffering from the injuries he sustained in his last attempt on my life. I don't think they'll let him out in a hurry.'

'Which leaves your two cousins, Mona and Celine? And their sister-in-law, Bertram's wife, Gerda? But those women weren't involved in any of the attempts to knock you off, were they?'

'They say they knew nothing of it. On the whole, I believe them. When I closed down the Hall, I let them have a house in the village rent-free for a year, and they're still there. The concept of having to earn your own living is new to them but, to give them credit, they're trying to adapt. Mona fancies she'd rather like to run the farm shop, though I don't think she has the slightest idea of how much work is involved. Celine is taking some kind of online course which she believes will set her up for a job for life. As for Gerda, Bertram's wife – poor creature, I feel sorry for her – she goes up to London to visit him as often as she can. She's got a cousin of hers helping out with the animal rescue centre and she spends most of her time there.'

'Then who . . .?'

'Search me. Bea, I need a good personal assistant. Can you find me one? Only archangels need apply.' He laughed as if he'd made a joke.

Bea didn't laugh. 'Why an archangel?'

'The paperwork is getting away from me.'

'Nonsense. Archangels don't do paperwork. They wield swords.'

'Yes. Someone shot at me when I was out riding the other day.'

Bea pushed her plate aside. 'Tell!'

'It never occurred to me that I could afford to keep a horse for myself, but there's a rescue centre for animals locally which needed more space. They asked if I could rent them a paddock and some stabling and said they'd provide and pay a man to look after the animals. We arranged a three-month lease to see if it would work.'

He twitched a smile. 'They had me bang to rights. They haven't paid me a penny yet. Instead, they sent along a hunter called Jack who'd been badly treated, plus an ancient groom called Mickey to look after him and a couple of really old nags. Jack took one look at me and knew I was a soft touch. I've been riding him around the estate every early morning since. He didn't like being shot at, either.'

'You reported the incident?'

'Of course. I was riding through a small wood, a mile or so from the Hall. I dismounted, soothed Jack, and searched for the bullet but failed to find it. The police think I imagined it. It was probably a poacher.'

'You weren't hurt?'

'No. All I heard was the whizz of a bullet past my head. Perhaps it was a wasp or a bee.'

'You had the wonder dog, Bruno, with you? How did he react?'

'He bounded off into the undergrowth, barking like mad. I called him back because I didn't want him to be shot at, too. I saw no one. Heard nothing else. I probably imagined it.'

He ran his fingers over his left wrist, which had been damaged in earlier attempts to kill him.

The people who'd attempted to kill him before – Lady Fleur, her son Frederick, and grandson Bertram – were now behind bars. So who was shooting at him now?

The waiter removed their half-empty plates. Neither wanted a sweet.

Coffee came. Really good, strong coffee.

He said, 'There's more. Last Friday morning a local woman was found hanged in the stables at the Hall. She was neither young nor beautiful, and the death didn't make the national papers. The groom, Mickey, found the body. He cut her down and tried resuscitation, but it was too late. When he realized that, he ran up to the barn to tell me what had happened.'

'Why didn't he ring the police?'

'Mickey's of a certain age. He has an ancient mobile but hates using it, and doesn't keep it fully charged. I was up and dressed, ready to ride out before breakfast when Mickey came in. I went with him, checked she was dead and rang the police. By that time Mickey was in tears. He's a poor sort of creature who expects to be blamed for everything. He'd recognized the corpse. I knew who she was, too, though I'd never spoken to her.'

'A local woman? Not a holiday-maker or visitor?'

'Mickey said she'd been born here but left the area many years ago, only to return recently. The police officer who came knew her, too. Apparently she had a reputation for this and that and there'd been some speculation about the child she'd brought up by herself. They said that the woman – Dora, that was her name – had had a rough time, and had probably decided to return to her roots to end it all.

'I gave a statement, as did Mickey. They removed the body. End of. I thought. I went back to the house, told Polly what had happened, tried to shift my appointment for that morning, was told it would create difficulties if I did, so changed back into a suit, collected my laptop and went off to work.'

There was a thoughtful pause while Bea digested the facts. He had recognized but hadn't had any dealings with the woman. She'd had a sad life and ended it. 'So . . .?'

He said, 'My meeting took most of the day. Permits to do this and that. Paperwork. Budgets. I did wonder about a connection between the dead woman and the Marston-Langs. If what Mickey and the police had implied was correct, then it sounded possible that Dora had had an affair with a Marston-Lang in the past. Did people think that one of them had been responsible for siring her child? I reviewed what I knew of them. I didn't think it was my grandfather who might have had a fling with her. Why not? Because he was pretty strait-laced. He'd have acknowledged the child and paid for its upkeep. And clearly, the boy's parentage was not generally acknowledged.

'I considered my step-uncle Frederick, who'd mismanaged the estate so badly for so many years. He'd had three children of his own – Mona, Celine and Bertram – and I'm told his wife left him many years ago. Or maybe his son, Bertram, had been responsible? The one who's ended up in hospital?

'Yesterday morning two police officers arrived to see me. They'd found one of my business cards in the pocket of the top Dora had been wearing when she died. They wanted to know when I'd met her and what we'd talked about. They said that the man she'd been living with had told them she and I had had a falling-out over my intention to raise the rent on her cottage.

'I told them that couldn't be true. I hadn't spoken to her or anyone else in the village about raising the rents and, in any case, I'd been told that Dora had her cottage rent-free for life . . . which was why the rumour had started about her son being sired by a Marston-Lang. I'd heard that Frederick had been threatening to raise the rents in the village but I hadn't got around to it. I explained that I'd intended having a survey of the houses in the village to see what repairs needed doing and to review the rents, but I haven't scheduled that yet.'

'They found your business card?'

A shrug. 'I've no idea how she got hold of it. Yes, I do give them out to people who ask how to contact me. Anyone could have got hold of one. The police officers didn't like my answers. They said the woman hadn't hanged herself; she'd been strangled and then hung up in the stables. They wanted me to account for my movements the night she died.

'I told them that I'd slept beside my wife, that both of us had got up when the boy wanted his feed. I thought that was about four o'clock, maybe half past, but I hadn't taken any particular notice. Some nights he sleeps longer than others. We have a routine. Polly hears him first, she gets up, rouses me, I make a hot drink for both of us, and we get back into bed together when the boy's had enough. I get up for good about half seven, preparatory to riding out with Jack, before I start the day proper. Polly gets up about then, too. She makes breakfast, timing it for my return from my ride. There wasn't anything different about our movements that night.

'The police took another statement from me, and then went in search of Polly, who was up a ladder rehanging a chandelier, if you please. She had my faithful hound Bruno with her and the boy in his bouncer. Bruno got very sniffy about the police, the boy didn't like them very much either, and it took me a while to calm everyone down.

'So the police left, saying they'd be seeing me again soon, and that I was not to think of going anywhere. Apparently I'm under suspicion of murdering a woman I've never spoken to. I don't think I'm imagining it, but everywhere I go now I can hear people whispering behind my back. I can feel the ill will in the air, thick as custard. I smell danger, but I can't see why or how.

'I asked Polly if I were imagining it, and she said I was to ask you for help. Only, once I'd got you here it all seemed so crazy that I couldn't imagine you taking it seriously. Tell me I'm making a mountain out of a molehill.'

'Describe the woman.'

He looked off into the distance. 'I understand she was supposed to be a real Delilah, but on the odd occasion I'd seen her in the distance in the village, I'd thought she was mutton dressed as lamb. When I saw her hanging there . . . ugh! No, I must try. Her face was swollen but . . . No, you don't need to know that. Well, she had a frizz of dyed yellow hair with darker roots. Black eyebrows, tattooed. One earring, cheap and glitzy. Bright lipstick. Garish. Smudged. Rather too much make-up, too strong a colour for this time of the year when we're all looking pasty. One false eyelash, the other missing. Is that enough?'

'Cheap clothing or pricey?'

'Fake fur, dyed pink for a gilet. My card was in the pocket of the gilet. Several gold chains long, droopy. Probably not gold. White T-shirt, polyester, stained, not new. Jeans, none too clean but slashed over the knees. One shoe on and one shoe off.' He quoted, '"Diddle diddle dumpling, my son John; one shoe off and one shoe on". Where did that come from? Some nursery rhyme or other.'

'You're in shock,' said Bea. 'What was the one shoe like, and were the other shoe and the other earring still there?'

'The second shoe? Yes, I think so. I think it was on the floor beneath where she'd been hanging. Polly says you can tell a lot of a person from the shoes they wear. She wanted me to describe her shoes, too. I couldn't. I could see her face and . . . I wish I couldn't.'

'The sort of woman whom I think you mean might not have had shoes which matched the environment in which she was found. Was she wearing riding boots or sandals? Was she wearing stiletto heels or strong walking shoes?'

'Ah, got it. Not stiletto. Wedgies? Is that what they're called? Black satin with a rhinestone decorated bow on the front. Peep toe, I think they call them?'

'Was she taller than Polly?' Julian's young wife was neat and curvaceous but not tall.

He stared at her. 'I've no idea.' He rubbed his eyes. 'Sorry. I'm not being very helpful, am I? Mickey had cut her down, so I did see her, lying on the ground. She looked . . . grotesque. Her head at an angle. She was well-built, her figure thickened with age. Maybe in her early fifties? My head tells me it's a tragic death but nothing to do with me.'

'But your gut reaction is . . .'

'That it has everything to do with the family. Do you remember the saying, "Something wicked this way comes?"' He rubbed his left wrist. 'I feel like a small child.'

'Your instincts are fine. Something is very wrong. You have no idea what it is or how it relates to you, but you smell danger. Off the top of your head, in which direction is the danger coming from?'

'Not sure. Not sure of anything. Black cloud waiting on the periphery of my vision. No idea why. You don't think I'm off my rocker, then?'

She shook her head.

He said, 'I am grateful to you for so many things, not least for believing in me when others didn't. I hardly dare ask—'

'Yes, of course. I'll find you a good PA, too. Even if she's not exactly an archangel.'

Bea mentally reorganized her work schedule. Her office manageress was perfectly capable of running the agency for a few days and any emergencies could be dealt with by email or phone. She ran over a card index file in her mind and came up with the name of an archangel. Well, an angel of sorts. She was a freelance nowadays and might be available.

Piers was due back . . . this weekend, or next? He'd long agreed to paint Julian and Polly when he could fit it into his schedule, and this would be a good excuse to do so.

She said, 'I'll see if I can set up an interview with a woman to help with the paperwork, and I'll be down on Wednesday morning.'

He looked worried. 'I can't pay much.'

The woman Bea had thought about could charge anything she liked and was well worth it. If Julian couldn't pay her going rate, then Bea would offer to make up the difference. Only, Julian's pride would probably not allow that. There was only one way to ensure he took the girl on.

'I'm afraid she's been through a bad time lately. A spell in a quiet country house dealing with paperwork would be just the thing for her. By the way, she wouldn't need accommodation because she gets around in a big motorhome. It's part of her wanting to be safe from, well, everyone.'

It worked. Julian said, 'Oh, poor thing. Yes, of course. Tell her she can park in the yard at the back of the Hall. Let's hope she likes us.'

'I'm sure she will,' said Bea, crossing fingers under the tablecloth. 'Now, would you like to say that my arrival is for a long-arranged visit for Piers to paint you and Polly? Piers should be back soon. You can say I'm coming down early to set everything up for him. Now, can we sleep in your quarters in the barn or do you want us to move into one of the rooms in the Hall?'

A real smile flickered and vanished. 'You have a choice: a four-poster bed in an unheated bedroom with an uneven floor, no electricity and no plumbing? That's in the Hall. Or mod-cons in the Tithe Barn where Polly and I are playing Happy Families.'

TWO

Several phone calls and two days later, Bea drove down to Marston Hall and parked on the gravel before it. She stepped out of the car and breathed in the country air. There was a haze of yellow and green over the trees that lined the avenue as they began to shift from winter to spring. She could hear a cawing of rooks nearby, and a cuckoo's notes penetrated the cacophony of sound which country people took for granted.

At least, she supposed it was a cuckoo but she couldn't be sure. Country life was not something she'd come into contact with much.

After the rumble and clatter of London, this was paradise . . . except for the grinding noise of a tractor not far off. Bea sniffed, recognizing the scent of manure which was being laid on a field. Perhaps that was the field which the animal rescue charity was renting? But no, there were no animals in sight.

Instead, there was scenery straight out of one of Capability Brown's notebooks. The avenue by which she'd come curved around clumps of mature trees until it disappeared into the distance.

From where she stood, she couldn't see the closed and silent amusement park which she knew was there, just out of sight. The tree-top rides, the carousel, the miniature train and the bouncy castles were in such a bad state and needed so much money spent on them that they would have to stay closed for the time being. However, Julian said that the Hall itself, the farm shop and restaurant might, with luck, reopen for Easter.

Bea surveyed the half-timbered Elizabethan house with interest. She thought it looked good enough to feature on a calendar, with its myriad of windows freshly cleaned and twinkling. Bea checked to see if the gutters were now cleared of the weeds which had been growing there when she'd first visited some months ago. The gutters were clear, and the missing slates had been replaced on the roof. All the previous signs of poor management, all the litter and damaged signs, had disappeared.

The prospect pleased though it was, perhaps, a trifle lifeless? Town-bred Bea would have preferred some movement but there were no human beings, no horses or cattle to be seen. No cars, either, except for hers.

Over the phone the previous day, Julian had said, 'I must warn you that we now have a housekeeper, name of Mrs Maggs. She used to work for the family years ago, has recently returned to the neighbourhood, heard what we were trying to do at the Hall and moved in to take over where she left off. Amazing woman! She knows which key works which lock and where the trapdoor into the wine cellar is.'

Did Bea hear a reservation in his voice. 'And . . .?'

'She's inclined to tell Polly how things were done in the old days and believes they should continue to be done that way. Poor tactics on her part. Polly tells me at least once a day that the woman means no harm, but I await the inevitable explosion with interest.'

Bea reflected that such a large and important house certainly needed a housekeeper, but perhaps not one who expected everything to be done her way?

The front door behind Bea opened and a sharp voice said, 'Mrs Abbot?'

A slight burr in the voice. Black hair, medium length; not a bad cut. Gold studs in ears, make-up non-existent. Black top, rather smart. Black jeans and comfortable shoes. Keys hanging from a good leather belt.

This must be the housekeeper about whom Polly had conflicting emotions.

Mrs Maggs said, 'I expected you earlier.'

Bea recognized she was being told she was late and therefore, implicitly, had made life more difficult for everyone. She knew that tactic as she'd used it herself on occasion with uppity clients who thought they could impress her with their wealth or connections. It didn't work when played on Bea.

She turned to the housekeeper with a smile. 'Mrs . . .?' And pretended she'd forgotten the name.

'Maggs. Mrs. There's been Maggses in these parts for I don't know how many years. I worked for the old family till I married my cousin, as was another Maggs, and we moved north till he died. So now I'm doing my best to bring this old house back to what it should be, but that's an uphill task as you can well imagine. I told

Sir Julian that having visitors at the moment was impossible, with not one of the bedrooms in the Hall available for occupation, what with there being no heating or lighting or water there. I have only occasional help in the house and not a single one of them knows how things should be done.'

'How very difficult for you,' said Bea, being oh-so-understanding. 'I'm sure my husband and I will be perfectly happy in the barn.'

Bea didn't say so, but she and Piers valued a comfortable bed and access to an en suite far above the pomp and circumstance of Ye Olde Stately Home. A horsehair mattress, for instance, was nowhere on their wish list for a weekend visit.

Perhaps Mrs Maggs had hoped Bea would turn tail and go back to London? With a sour face, she said, 'I was told your husband would be with you.'

'My husband is currently in the Balkans painting some politician or other, but he'll be down in a couple of days' time. Now, where would you like me to park?'

'If you take your car round the house to the tradesmen's entrance, you can park there, out of sight. We don't wish to spoil the look of the place, do we? And watch out for that dog of Sir Julian's. He's a menace.'

The tradesman's entrance. Yes, of course! Mrs Maggs was doing her best to make Bea feel unwelcome, wasn't she? And naturally, she'd think Julian's dog a nuisance.

Bea continued to smile. 'I'm to go round the house, past the entrance to the stables and park in front of the Tithe Barn?'

Mrs Maggs narrowed her eyes. 'You've been here before, then?'

'Only once. We knew Sir Julian and Lady Polly before they inherited.'

Mrs Maggs drew in her breath. 'Sir Julian and Lady *Paula* . . .' with an emphasis on *Paula*, rather than the *Polly* which was the nickname by which she'd always been known, '. . . seem content to occupy an outbuilding for the time being. No doubt they will move into more appropriate accommodation when the house is finished.'

Bea didn't comment. She'd interviewed many women of this type over the years, and recognized their strengths and weaknesses. In Bea's opinion, Mrs Maggs would be intensely loyal to her employer if she decided that it was in her best interests to do so; she would be hard-working and a perfectionist who would talk non-stop and either drive her staff crazy or blend them into a highly efficient unit.

Which would she be? Difficult to say.

Bea drove round the corner of the house and on, past the entrance to the stables, to park in a cobbled yard between the huge old Tithe Barn and the kitchen quarters of the Hall. A miscellany of cars and vans was already there. Belonging to workmen? Where was Julian's own car?

The doors and windows of the back of the old house were all open to the elements. The cheerful sounds of workmen dropping pipes and yelling at one another were punctuated by the pop music blaring out from an unattended ghetto blaster. The back of the house was alive, in a way.

The Tithe Barn wasn't. These enormous old barns had been built in the early Middle Ages to house the harvest collected every year by the lord of the manor's tenants. This one had been built of stone with a lime rendering. No thatch, but shingles. A primitive-looking outside staircase of stone accessed the first floor but lacked a balustrade. There were only a few tiny apertures and no windows in the original structure, and access was by two huge wooden doors in the middle of the barn, which were currently propped open.

In the last century the barn had probably housed farm vehicles, plus the family's carriages and carts. Later still a procession of cars would have been parked there. And now? Full of junk, probably.

According to Julian, his uncle Frederick – the one who'd mismanaged the estate so badly – had intended to divide the barn up into a number of units which could be used for holiday lets. Scaffolding had been put up and a Portaloo stood nearby, but there was only one finished door and a glazed window at the far end.

A superb Alsatian was lying down outside the door at the end of the barn. He recognized Bea and got to his feet with a 'wuff' of welcome, wagging his tail and ducking his head.

She fondled his ears. 'Still on guard, Bruno?'

He wuffed again, looking back at the closed door of the end house.

She said, 'Watch my car for me?'

He lay down again, this time closer to her car.

She tapped on the closed door. Getting no response, she opened it only to stop short on the threshold.

She was looking into a large, bright room with windows on three sides. No curtains, no blinds. This was an all-purpose living room – part office, part living room – with an assortment of furniture from different centuries, probably selected from cast-offs stored in the attic of the Hall. An open stair on the inner wall climbed to the floor above.

Julian was sitting with his head in his hands on a big armchair, which looked comfortable but showed signs of wear. His laptop and a slew of paperwork was on a low coffee table in front of him.

An ancient but practical wooden baby's crib, newly furnished with a quilt, sat waiting for the boy, who was nowhere apparent. And neither was his mother. So where were they and what was wrong with Julian?

He looked up when he heard Bea came in. A bruise was colouring up on one cheek. He was wearing a good shirt and jeans. One of his shoes was off and his foot was wrapped in a tea towel and propped up on a low table in front of him. A broken riding helmet was on the floor beside him together with a stout walking stick.

He'd had another 'accident'?

Bea was angry with herself. She ought to have come as soon as Julian had told her of his unease. She shouldn't have wasted a whole day in town. 'What's wrong?'

He tried to get up but didn't make it and fell back on to his chair. 'Sorry. I was miles away. Had a good journey? I'm afraid I'm not very mobile. I fell off my horse, would you believe?'

And pigs might fly. He had an excellent seat on a horse. 'What happened?'

He rubbed his eyes and resettled his glasses on his nose, not looking at her. 'Jack was fidgety this morning, eyes rolling, telling me he wasn't happy. I got into the saddle and he shot off like a rocket. I tried to pull him up, but he went round and round the paddock, head down and . . . well, I fell off. Won't Polly laugh when I tell her! Banged my head, sprained my ankle. I managed to get to my meeting in time, but I had to take taxis there and back because I couldn't drive. It was an accident. It has to be. It can't have anything to do with . . . anything.'

'Have you had yourself checked out in hospital?'

'No, no. It's not that bad. The taxi driver offered to take me, but no, I'm all right. Just shocked. Need to be quiet for a bit. Everything comes at once, doesn't it? When I took this place on, I thought I could wave a magic wand and everything would fall into place. The sin of pride, I suppose.'

He tried a smile, which didn't work. 'Someone spat at me in the village yesterday. I understand their problem. Closing things down has meant putting people out of work, so . . . pay no attention. I was just thinking I'd better take some painkillers. More to the point, how are you, and when is Piers getting back? Did you have a good journey down?'

Bea thought of the dozens of people who had worked on the house and park in the old days. The wages bill must have been horrendous! Now, everyone and everything depended on this man's shoulders. He'd beggared himself to try to save his ancestral home and it didn't look as if he were winning.

She said, 'I'm fine. Piers will probably be here at the weekend. Where do you keep the painkillers?'

He wasn't listening. He flicked at a pile of papers on the table. 'How many times do I tell other people to check and check, and check again? And I didn't. I suppose I ought to have known that my wicked uncle would have started the alterations here in the barn without getting permission.

'I'd been getting on so well, too, with British Heritage. You remember I was meeting with them the day I saw you? I mentioned that we were now ready to start work on dividing the Tithe Barn up and that I'd moved into this end section. They went into shock/horror mode. They wouldn't hear of converting the barn into accommodation to let. They say it's important to maintain the original appearance, and I do, reluctantly, agree. So I had to tell the builders to stop what they were doing till I could think what to do.

'The meeting this morning was with the council, who want to increase council tax but don't want me to increase the size of the old car park. When I got back from that meeting, I found a bill for the rewiring of the house, which should have been completed last week. They've run across this problem and that, but want their bonus now, and . . . My grandfather recommended the firm, which is local, but I'm beginning to think it was a mistake. They're nowhere near finished and their bill is double what I'd allowed for.'

'Piers and I can help you with a loan. Piers never spends half of what he earns.'

'I'm not taking money from you. You've done enough.' Again, he tried to stand and again didn't make it. 'What a welcome! Give me a minute and I'll be right with you.'

She looked around. There was a slight disorder of newspapers and coffee cups in the room. Behind the staircase on the inner wall she could see a small but workable kitchen which showed signs of use.

Making her way there, she said, 'Where's Polly? And the boy?'

Painkillers? Women usually kept them close to hand. In one of the kitchen cupboards? Yes, but there was only aspirin, which was probably not strong enough. Well, it would have to do. She ran a glass of water and stood over him till he'd taken the pills.

He said, 'Polly's father's been causing ructions. He says his retirement home is not looking after him properly. Polly took the boy down there yesterday to see what could be done and is staying a couple of nights. What he really wants is to come and live here, in the Hall. He says it's Polly's duty to take him in and look after him now. If the Hall were up and running, I suppose we could find him some place, but . . .'

He raised his hands and let them drop. 'Polly's trying to find an alternative retirement home for him. I haven't told her about my accident. She'd only worry.'

Polly's father was an old curmudgeon who had never wanted his daughter to marry Julian when he was a nameless foundling, but now was all over his son-in-law because he'd inherited an estate. Bea had heard stories about Polly's father and didn't like what she'd heard. She wondered if he'd made himself so disliked in his retirement home that he'd been asked to leave.

Julian managed a real smile. 'I'm so glad to see you. Do you think you can take your bag upstairs yourself? Back bedroom. You'll have to share a bathroom with us, I'm afraid.'

Bea collected her bag and laptop from the car and carried them up the stairs. Everything was beautifully clean. The back bedroom was furnished in the same eclectic mix as the living room; a double bed with brass knobs on the finials, a wardrobe whose door was held closed with a twist of wire, and a dressing table which looked as if it had once graced an Edwardian lady's boudoir. A Turkish carpet was on the floor, worn but clean towels had been thrown over a wooden stand, and there was a modern electric blanket on top of the attractive but somewhat threadbare counterpane.

In short, it was as pleasant a place to spend the night as you could imagine, and the next-door bathroom, though lacking a shower, did have all the usual 'cons', even if they were not 'mod'.

Bea unpacked, visited the bathroom, and brushed out her short-cut ash-blonde hair. If Julian's pride wouldn't allow him to accept any money from her, she could at least make sure he ate properly and nursed his ankle while Polly was away.

Downstairs again, she found Julian hopping about in the kitchen with the aid of his walking stick. He was trying to make himself a coffee and not getting on very well. The upright line between his eyes was deeper than usual, and his colour was poor. He was in pain? Yes, of course he was.

She told him to sit down, donned an apron hanging on a hook, and asked when he'd eaten last.

'Breakfast, I think. Or did I? I remember I had a cup of coffee while I waited for the taxi to take me to my meeting. I meant to eat afterwards, but . . .'

'I'll make you something to eat. Now, to basics: can you get up the stairs? If not, you'd better use the Portaloo outside.'

'Yes, Granny.' Julian pretended to grovel.

She flicked a tea towel at him. He ducked, smiling, and hobbled out to use the Portaloo, leaning heavily on his stick.

Now, food. What was there for him to eat straight away? Fridge: Polly had left a casserole for them to heat up. The freezer was well stocked, as was the fridge. Eggs and bacon would do him for now, and some tinned soup. Bea didn't think much of tinned soup normally, but this was an emergency.

She fed and watered Julian, cleared up in the kitchen, and was on the point of demanding to look at his ankle when she heard Bruno bark, twice. Sharply. A heavyweight of a car had driven into the yard and parked.

Julian pulled himself upright in his chair, looking exhausted. 'Whatever's the matter with me? I forgot; that'll be the builders, wanting to know what's going to happen next.'

Bea opened the door and a youngish, skinny man danced in, followed by a much older, hulking great brute, with greying bristle all over his head and chin. Builder and plumber's mate?

Bea was still wearing Polly's apron, so the newcomers ignored her as being hired help and of no importance.

Julian said, 'Ah, Bea, may I introduce—'

Skinny interrupted. 'Well, Sir Julian! Had a good meeting?' His tone was one of relish, a torturer about to apply the thumbscrew.

'My apologies for not ringing you back this morning, but—'

Bea retired to the kitchen from which she could see and hear everything that happened, and started preparing some vegetables for supper.

Skinny interrupted again. 'The police are asking everyone if they'd seen Her What Got Herself Done In, and a squeaky little bird's telling everyone that she saw you with her the other night.'

'But I never set eyes on—!'

'An eyewitness, no less. The police will have to act on that, won't they? Dora only wanted her rights, didn't she? Not for her but for her son, Craig, right? Everyone knows he's family. One of those open secrets. Opinion is divided as to which member of the family was responsible for the boy: the old man, your grandfather, or your uncle Frederick. I suppose it doesn't matter too much because the lad's family and you can't get away from that. The word is that young Craig's on the warpath, wants to revenge his sainted mum's death – not that she was all that saintly from what I've heard – and, of course, he wants his rights. What do you say to that, eh?'

Julian frowned. 'I did hear a story to the effect that this Dora had a son by someone in the family, but she never approached me about it.'

The painkillers didn't seem to be having much effect, and he was not coping well with this attack.

Skinny seemed to be enjoying himself. 'Gossip says young Craig wants the lot, the whole estate; lock, stock and barrel, so it doesn't look like you're going to be here for long. Good thing, too. You haven't made yourself popular, have you? Sacking everyone that worked here before. Not a true Marston-Lang. They had their faults, but they looked after their own. And you fell off your horse this morning, I hear? Typical. That's what comes of trying on boots too big for you.'

Julian said, 'I'm aware that—'

Skinny ignored him. 'Now, to business. My brother wants to give you the benefit of the doubt, but what about British Heritage, eh? You've been told to put everything back to what it was, eh? Which includes this cosy little hideaway in the barn, right? And where are you going to sleep then, eh? Back in the big house, which is uninhabitable at the moment, so they say.'

'Well, you're partially right, but—'

'So I suppose you'll be down on your knees begging us to start back tomorrow.' He paced – or rather danced – around, eyes everywhere. 'First thing, we'll have to tear these doors and windows out and fill in the holes we've made and, before I forget – brain like a sieve – this is really why I came, we're not doing another hour of work till you settle up for what you owe us already. We don't want you running off to live in luxury in a tax haven somewhere before you've paid us what we're due.'

He slapped a piece of paper down on the table in front of Julian. 'That's for work done already, and what Frederick owed us from before. And no nonsense about post-dated cheques.'

Julian said, very quietly, 'I'm not running anywhere. You know perfectly well that Frederick stripped the estate of everything he could lay his hands on. The coffers are empty and death duties due. I sold my flat to keep this place afloat and start the repairs which were needed. If I fail, then I'll have lost my flat and will have to start again from nothing.

'It's an attractive thought to walk away from this mess, which was none of my making. But you must realize that if I do fail, the estate will have to be sold, and that's unlikely to benefit anyone hereabouts. The Hall would probably be bought by some Middle Eastern tycoon who would employ security guards to keep the place private. Such a buyer is not likely to need local people in any capacity whatever.

'As for paying your bill; yes, we have to talk about that. If we can't come to some sensible payment and I go bankrupt, then your bill will have to wait its turn to be dealt with . . . in which case, I doubt you'd get the full amount. You'd come a long way down the line of creditors, way after His Majesty's Revenue and Customs. You'll be lucky if you get twopence in the pound. That's the future for you, if I fail.'

Skinny said, 'Three choruses of hearts and flowers. And we'll need half what's due us, tomorrow, when we'll start on tearing this place apart again, right? Any idea where you'll sleep then?'

Julian rubbed his forehead. Looked at the paper. And, instead of looking at Skinny, he addressed himself to the one with the bristly beard. 'Yes, it was my fault. I didn't check that we had all the right permits. Frederick did have permission to turn this end part into an estate office, though not into living accommodation. As you guessed, he hadn't requested permission to turn the rest into holiday lets either.

'I've negotiated an agreement whereby I can use this section for temporary living quarters for six months, when it will become the new estate office. It means we can keep the new door and windows that we've already done.'

The bristly one spoke for the first time, and his accent was pure Oxbridge. 'That's not a bad idea. Frederick had to leave the old estate office when the ceiling fell in. He'd been warned about it but took no notice. He shifted his papers over here and had a woman come up twice a week to pay bills and that. You do need an office.'

Julian nodded. 'Thank you. We also agreed on some other work we can do. I'll explain that in a minute. I know I owe you for work done, and I agree that you are also owed payment for work you did for Frederick. I have enough at the moment to pay you for a third of the total. I'll pay another third when I get the next lot of rents in at Easter and the remainder four months later.'

'Oh, come on!' said Skinny. 'Everyone knows this Hall is a little gold mine.'

'It was,' said Julian, 'and it could be again, once the rotten apples have been removed. That takes time and money.' He was still looking at the big man, and not at Skinny.

Bristles said, 'I've seen you out riding. You ride well. That Jack . . .' He shook his big head.

Julian looked worried. 'I know. Not like him. Before I left, I asked Mickey to get the vet to have a look at him. That's something else I must check.'

'Aye, there's lots to think about when you take on a place like this. We all knew Frederick was cutting corners. We should have warned you.'

'Thank you for that, but it was my responsibility. I should have checked.'

The big man nodded. Bea noticed that he had large, capable-looking hands. And sharp brown eyes. Perhaps it wasn't a question of master and servant, but two men with equal authority?

Bruno barked out an alert and someone thundered on the door. Mrs Maggs, the housekeeper, burst in.

'Sir Julian, this is the outside of enough! You didn't tell me you were expecting guests, even though the lad's family in a way.'

Julian tried to heave himself out of the chair and failed. His colour was poor. He said, 'What lad?'

'That No Good Craig, that's who! Drives up in a taxi, bold as brass. I've known him since he was born, and a nasty, sneaking child he was in those days, and I don't suppose he's changed since then. He says he's moving in and he's dumped a whole pile of stuff in the Hall. What am I supposed to do about it, eh?'

THREE

Wednesday afternoon

J ulian fell back in his chair. 'He wants to move in? But . . . no!'
Skinny clicked his fingers. 'Craig's here? Didn't waste much
time, did he? Now we'll see some fireworks!'

He was enjoying this, wasn't he?

Bristles rubbed his chin, looking at Julian. Bristles wasn't amused.
He said, 'He was nothing but trouble in the old days. I don't suppose
he's changed.'

Mrs Maggs nodded. 'Trouble, yes. Petty stuff. But Dora always
made excuses, didn't she? And now he's got reason to make trouble,
hasn't he? What with his mother being killed and all.' She looked
worried.

Julian closed his eyes. Bea thought he'd very much like to walk
away from the whole situation. Perhaps by pleading his injuries?

But no. He heaved himself to his feet, took a step forward and
almost fell.

Bristles caught him. 'I've got you. You'll not be walking on that
ankle for a while yet, I'm thinking.' He put Julian back in his chair.

Julian's face went blank as he fought to control his pain.

Bea scolded, 'You should go to the hospital to be checked over.'

Julian said, 'No. I must see Craig.'

Mrs Maggs looked dubious. 'How you going to do that? You
can't walk, even. And there's Bernie, the taxi driver; he wants
paying.'

Bea realized that all three of them – Mrs Maggs, Bristles and
Skinny – not only knew one another, but they also knew Craig.
Unlike Julian.

Julian was breathing lightly. His various aches and pains needed
more than aspirin.

Bea had an moment of inspiration. 'Wheelchair! Did Julian's
grandfather have one when he got so frail, and if so, where is it?'

Bristles shot out of the door. 'Everything ends up in the barn.'

Mrs Maggs was all of a dither. She ran to the door and then ran back again. 'That Craig! I don't like leaving him alone for so long. Goodness knows what he'd be up to . . .'

Bristles burst back through the door, half carrying and half pushing an ancient bath chair, the sort one's great-great-aunt used in the days of a long-deceased queen; Victoria, not Elizabeth. It was dusty but functional. Bristles walloped the seat, wiped the handles and helped Julian into it.

Julian attempted a laugh. 'A museum piece. Remind me to get an ear trumpet to complete the picture.'

He drew his arm across his forehead to wipe the sweat away and said to Bristles, 'Thank you. Sorry to interrupt our meeting. I have some news, but it will have to wait. May I trouble you to wheel me into the Hall?'

And to Bea, 'Apologies, Bea. I'm afraid I'll have to deal with this. Back shortly. Make yourself at home. Mrs Maggs, I think I should go into the house the back way. No steps.'

Skinny rubbed his hands. 'I can't wait!'

Bristles set off. The wheels creaked. One of them looked as if it would like to wobble off, but didn't. The basket-weave of the bath chair squeaked. Everyone trailed out after the chair. No one wanted to miss whatever was going to happen next.

Including Bea, who followed on their heels.

Bruno rose when he saw Julian in the chair. Julian clicked his fingers, and Bruno fell in at his side.

Mrs Maggs leaped ahead to pull open the door to the kitchen quarters and they all went in. This was a working kitchen, which meant that anyone who was working at the Hall gravitated here for tea breaks. The table was littered with used mugs, plates and sandwich wrappings. There might not be any electricity elsewhere in the building, but someone had rigged up a temporary connection so that here at least there was hot and cold water, power for a kettle and a microwave.

Bristles manoeuvred the chair into a corridor which ended in a solid door. Mrs Maggs stepped ahead to open it and they passed through into a spacious entrance hall.

Here there were voices raised in argument. 'You owe me for—!'

'I told you, put it on the tab for the Hall.'

Two men turned to face Julian and his entourage. One was a large man with an acne-scarred face and workaday clothes. He would be Bernie, the taxi-driver?

The other was a man in his late twenties who could do with losing a pound or two. His eyes were bold, suggesting to Bea that he probably enjoyed pinching women's bottoms. He was dressed in clothes which said, 'Look at me! Designer wear!' Flowered shirt, waistcoat and cinnamon-coloured jeans.

He had suspiciously bright yellow hair and his nose was a mere blob; unlike Julian's, which was growing more hawklike every day. Bea thought of the pictures of Julian's ancestors in the gallery of the Hall and almost laughed. Julian's nose was in all the pictures. Craig's wasn't.

The taxi driver appealed to Julian. 'Look, guv'nor. Is it right what Craig says? He summons me to Dora's place, says he's family – which he might be, or so I've heard, though not the right side of the blanket if you get my meaning – anyway, he says he's moving in and you'll pay for the fare to the Hall. But you're not taking in folk yet, are you?'

The newcomer bestowed a wide smile on everyone. 'Yes, I'm Craig and I'm family. Apologies for the delay in making myself known. Been working in Tenerife. Got back to hear the news. What a terrible thing, eh? But good to meet you at last. And yes, I've come to stay.'

Bea noted the newcomer had a light tenor voice which affected an upper-class accent far more 'precious' than Julian's. And to her mind, that bright yellow hair of his had been permed and dyed.

Julian's colour was poor, but he held his head high. He said, 'I regret that the Hall is closed to visitors for the time being.'

'Ah, but not to family.'

Julian said, 'I am unable to make exceptions. Even the remaining members of the family have had to move out while the house is rewired and new plumbing installed. Now, I'm in the middle of a business meeting with—'

'That pair of odd-job men? I know them both of old. I'd heard you were spending your days scratching around in the gutter for pennies to pay the bills, but if you're relying on this pair, it's no wonder you're in financial trouble. They'll skin you alive.'

Julian held on to his patience. 'Thank you for your advice. I'm sure Bernie will be happy to return you to the village.'

Craig held on to his smile. 'You don't understand. You need to get rid of these people and then we can have a nice little talk, just the two of us.'

The two builders, the taxi driver and Mrs Maggs were all round-eyed with excitement. And, judging from their interested expressions, had no intention of moving.

The dog Bruno looked from his master to Craig. Somehow he made it clear that he didn't like Craig. He sat upright at Julian's side, ready for action.

Julian dropped his hand to Bruno's neck. 'Down, boy!'

Rather reluctantly, Bruno dropped to the floor, his nose on his paws but his eyes still fixed on Craig.

Bernie, the taxi driver, said to Julian, 'Shall I start shifting his stuff back to the village, guv'nor?'

Craig waved his arms about. 'Now, now. I'm not going anywhere. Why don't you take yourself off, Bernie? And the two brothers Grimm? Mrs Maggs, too; always poking her nose in where it isn't wanted. And that woman, whoever she is, standing behind you like a death's head at the feast. We can do without all of them, can't we, Julian? Keeping it in the family, as they say.'

Bea recognized the threat behind the pleasant-seeming words.

Mrs Maggs's lips thinned and she folded her arms at the intruder. She wasn't moving.

The taxi driver scratched the back of his neck. 'If someone will pay me?'

Skinny was amused. His brother, Bristles, was not.

Julian sighed sharply. He said, 'Craig, I am asking you to leave. If you refuse to go, then you'll be trespassing.'

Craig said, 'Oh, dearie me! You mustn't talk to me like that, you know! I've every right to be here. I'm family, that's what I am.'

Bea noticed their audience was taking this in various ways. Skinny was grinning. Bristles looked thunderous. Bernie was embarrassed and uneasy.

Mrs Maggs was seriously displeased. 'Now what are you after, Craig? Bringing up that old tale about Frederick being your father? Everyone knows Dora used to spread herself around, but he never acknowledged you and you look nothing like him.'

'I've evidence of the connection – the very, very close connection to the family.'

Julian held back a sigh. 'There is no mention of you in my grandfather's will. I do not believe that Frederick was your father. If you wish to know more, then you'd best contact our solicitor.

The Hall is not open for visitors, and for the second time I am asking you to leave.'

'Oh, come now!' An easy smile. He was used to getting his own way, wasn't he? 'Frederick's not the only Marston-Lang who spread himself around.'

'You think my grandfather sired you? Really?' Julian repeated, in exactly the same courteous tone of voice, 'I don't think we need to take that claim too seriously, do you?'

'Now, now! We don't want a full-scale scandal, do we? Let's do this nice and quietly. You and me in a room without all these people interrupting.'

Julian raised his eyebrows. 'You have something you want to say to me in private? I can't think what.'

'On your own head be it,' said Craig, clapping his hands together. 'It was in my mind to spare you grief by keeping the matter between us two.'

By way of answer, Julian got out his phone and held it up. 'Out of here, or I ring the police and ask them to remove you.'

Craig flicked his fingers. 'You think it was Frederick who sired me? Or the old man, your grandfather? There's another candidate, isn't there?'

A thick silence spread over the hall as everyone tried to work out what Craig meant.

Bea got it first. And drew in her breath.

Julian got it next and stiffened in his chair.

Bea put her hand on his shoulder.

Was it possible that Craig was right, and if so . . .?

Bea did a quick recap of what she knew.

Old Sir Florian Marston-Lang had married twice. His first wife died young, leaving a boy child called Julian, who was fair of hair and blue of eye. The boy thrived but his father went to pieces.

Sir Florian's second venture into matrimony was with Lady Fleur, a woman who could have played the evil stepmother in all the fairy stories. She produced a dark-haired, bully of a boy called Frederick, and encouraged him to fight with his half-brother Julian. Sir Florian either would not, or could not, interfere, and in consequence the young heir found himself thwarted at every turn. The situation worsened when his pet Labrador and favourite horse were shot by Frederick in separate 'accidents'.

*Wait a minute! His horse AND his dog were shot . . .? Oh, no!
I need to think about that . . . but not now!*

After a series of blistering rows the young heir left, got a job
teaching, married a girl he'd met at university and dropped the
Marston from his name. The young couple produced a fair-haired,
blue-eyed son, also called Julian. On holiday, their car was driven
off the road and both parents died.

Lacking the 'Marston' part of his father's name, the baby's family
was not traced and he was put up for adoption. He grew up knowing
nothing of his antecedents and caring less. He became an accountant
with a firm who appreciated him.

He might never have discovered his lineage if his future father-in-
law, old Mr Colston, hadn't had a phobia about his daughter marrying
bad blood. It was he who caused Julian's DNA to be sent off for
identification . . . which alerted the Marston-Lang family to the fact
that a child whose existence they'd never known about was alive and
heir to the estate. They'd set about wiping him off the face of the
earth, somewhat inefficiently because, with Bea's help, he'd survived.

The instigators of the plots against Julian – Fleur, Frederick and
Frederick's son, Bertram – were handed over to the rigours of the
law, while old Sir Florian Marston-Lang acknowledged his grandson
Julian as his heir and asked him to take over an estate which was
heading for bankruptcy.

True to form, Julian had been unable to dismiss an appeal for
help. He turned his back on a lucrative career in his old firm and
taken on the equivalent of the Seven Labours of Hercules.

So which members of the family qualified as a possible sire for
Craig?

Craig hugged himself with glee. 'Could it have been Sir Florian
himself? He'd have been about sixty at the time of my conception,
so it was possible.'

'No,' said Julian, without hesitation.

No, thought Bea. Sir Florian was as straight as his grandson,
Julian. He'd never have refused to recognize a child he'd sired.

Craig almost giggled. 'Was it his son, Frederick? Oh, go on!
Have a guess, do!'

Bristles said, 'I suppose Frederick would have been about the
right age to have sired Craig. His wife divorced him years ago but
not before he'd fathered Bertram and the two girls. Frederick would
have been capable of it. My bet's on him.'

Craig was grinning. 'You're all wrong. So now we come to the third possibility, which is Sir Florian's eldest son, this Julian's father. The fair-haired, blue-eyed one. He fits the brief nicely, doesn't he? He quarrelled with everyone and then dropped out of sight.'

Bea's mind was in a whirl. Could Julian's father have sired a child by Dora before he left? He did marry and sire a child *after* he'd stormed out of the Hall, but before that . . .?

Doubt ruled everywhere Bea looked. What did this announcement, if true, mean to them, and to the Hall?

Bernie the taxi driver leaned against the wall. 'That'd be a turn-up for the books. You think . . .?'

Bristles was muttering to himself. 'Could be. But, no; not the man I knew.'

Skinny was smiling. 'I knew it! This Julian is an incomer, who can't even pay our bills. He's an imposter. What do we know of him? Nothing. But we all know Craig. We all knew what Dora was like, been at it like a rabbit for years, way before my time, not that she was my cup of tea ever, but there was always talk. It stands to reason she had it off with the son and heir, too. Then he ran away. We know the estate goes to the old man's heirs by his first wife. So it passes down to his son Julian and then . . . to Craig!'

Mrs Maggs said, almost to herself, 'The timing's about right. But I knew him, and he'd never have left Dora to fend for herself if he'd given her a child.'

Bristles was doubtful. 'Maybe he didn't know. He went off sharpish after Frederick killed his horse and dog?'

Bea was horrified. It was *Frederick* who'd killed his half-brother's horse and his dog?

Craig was a happy bunny. 'Come on, come on! You're getting there. My mother was quite a beauty when she was younger, wasn't she? Naturally she caught the eye of the son and heir, and yes, she had a boy by him. Which means . . . come on! You can do it?'

Bea felt Julian's hand reach up and clasp hers, but he did not speak.

Craig gave Skinny a high five. 'Bravo! It took you a while, but you've got there at long last. I was born in September and he in June the following year. I'm the eldest son of the eldest son, and so under the terms of Sir Florian's will, I inherit everything.'

Julian made an effort. And everyone could see it was an effort.

He said, 'Are you trying to say that my father married Dora before he left the Hall? I don't believe it.'

'I'm the first born and that's what counts.'

'No, it doesn't. Do you have a birth certificate naming your father? Or a marriage certificate? What proof do you have that would stand up in a court of law? Have you had a DNA test done?'

Craig shrugged. 'I don't need it to confirm that I am who I am. I have all the proof I need.'

'That I'd like to see.'

'It's the money she was given to live on, see. She told me someone in the family was looking after her up at the Hall, and that she had her cottage rent-free for life.'

'She didn't say why?'

A smirk. 'She told me it was because she'd done some work up there when she was young, but we both know that was a lie, don't we?'

'She didn't give you any proof of who your father might have been?'

'She said he'd moved on to other interests, but she didn't care. I had everything I wanted: clothes, games, money for treats. She told me I was special, and I was.'

He scowled. 'Only when I was thirteen she fell for this travelling salesman who said he'd invest her money for her and then disappeared. She lost the lot. That's when she rented out the cottage and we went to live in London. She got a job in a pub, and I went to a big school which had a great art section. If I'd stayed down here, I'd never have become a famous interior designer.

'I've done all right, got my own space in a friend's house in London, and I was learning my business, travelling all over. She did all right, too, with a businessman she met up there. Moved in with him, enjoyed herself till he died and left everything to his wife that he'd never bothered to divorce. So she had nowhere to go and came back down here, moved in with the guy who was renting her cottage.

'I did suggest visiting her this last Christmas, thinking she might help me with . . . well, that doesn't matter now. But she said the guy renting her cottage objected and she couldn't afford to upset him. She said things were bad, that he'd lost his job when the amusement park was closed and she didn't know how she was going to make ends meet because he'd stopped paying her rent. I said that

I thought she had somebody looking out for her at the Hall and she said that was all water under the bridge and promises got conveniently forgotten as time went by.

'So I said to her that I'd have a go at getting her some more money when I got back from my next job abroad, and off I went to Tenerife, only to be called back when my friend here' – indicating Skinny – 'sent me a text to say I should get back pronto because she'd copped it. And now I'm back, I'm claiming what's mine, right?'

Julian repeated, 'Dora told you she had someone looking after her at the Hall?'

'That's what she said. She told me the money came as a lump sum through the family's solicitor. To get it, she'd had to swear she'd never tell why she'd been given it, that it was a one-off and she was never to ask for more. And she hadn't. But she hadn't promised for me, had she? She said there wasn't any paperwork but I know there must be. So now I'm getting copies of her bank records from that time which will show where the money came from.'

Julian said, 'You asked the bank for evidence, they said they needed your mother's signature and . . . I see. She didn't leave a will so you're having to apply for probate and the banks won't play ball till they're sure you're entitled to the records.'

'It's so inconvenient. But time is on my side. I'm going to get a solicitor to sort it for me. I know they're all sharks and I can't afford them, but in this case his bill can come out of my inheritance.'

Julian said, 'I doubt if one will give you the time of day if your mother was given a one-off payment and agreed not to talk about it.'

'He can't hide behind that, not now my mother's been murdered. If he won't tell me, the police will force him to reveal the truth. And then it'll be clear who is the rightful heir to the estate.'

Julian lifted his hands and let them drop. 'Craig, I know nothing of the arrangement by which your mother received money from the family. DNA tests should give you the proof that we are, or are not, related, but you don't even have that. If it's proved that you are my half-brother, born before me, then to inherit, you would have to prove there was a ceremony of marriage between your mother and father.'

Craig reddened. 'I'm getting the proof! You're out, and I'm in!'

'If what you say is true and the solicitors agree with your construction of events, then I will walk away from this place and you will never see me again.'

'No, no,' said Craig, much annoyed. 'That's not the idea at all. I wouldn't dream of turning a member of the family out into the cold. My friend here' – and here he waved at Skinny – 'tells me you have a certain flair for management, that you can make the figures dance, and rake in money from this and that. I haven't the slightest interest in taking over the day-to-day running of the place. You can go on doing that for me. I expect I can even find you some sort of cottage on the estate that you can have, rent-free. Or practically rent-free. Never say that I treated you badly.'

Mrs Maggs looked into the future according to Craig and didn't like it. 'The nerve of you . . .! I suppose you'll want us all to start calling you "Sir Craig"!'

FOUR

Craig spread his hands. 'Naturally. I am Sir Craig.'

Mrs Maggs struggled with herself. 'And you want me to carry on as housekeeper? Or have you got someone else you'd prefer to bring in?'

'No, no, Mrs Maggs. All will go on as before, except that I will be in charge. You were never particularly vile to me as a child, not like your old father whom I trust has now passed away?'

Julian took a deep breath. 'I see. Well, nothing changes for the time being. Craig, your claim may be upheld and you may be recognized as the new owner of the estate, but until that happens, I will continue to do my best to run the place. Let me make myself clear: you cannot move in here until the law approves. You cannot issue orders. You cannot access the bank accounts or make any changes to personnel or indeed anything on the estate. Legally, you have no standing here unless and until the courts say so.'

It was the right thing to say and do. Bristles, Bernie the taxi driver and Mrs Maggs considered what Julian had said, and nodded.

Julian lifted his hand. 'I give you my word that if the courts decide in your favour, I will resign everything into your hands and walk away.'

Craig said, 'Careful! Careful! You can't do that. You heard that someone saw you with my mother the night she was killed? The police don't know who that was, but I do. So if you don't play ball, all I have to do is tell them who it was. Now do you understand your position?'

Julian blinked. 'Blackmail? But as I didn't meet your mother that night or any other night, you can say what you like to the police or anyone else and I still wouldn't go along with what you suggest. Are you ready to leave now, or shall I call the police to have you evicted?'

Craig's voice rose. 'You don't dare!'

Bruno sat up and growled. Julian said, 'Try me.' He produced his smartphone again and began to press numbers.

Bernie the taxi driver came to life. He picked up two of Craig's cases and took them to the front door. 'Craig, do you want to go to your mother's cottage, or back up to London?'

Julian spoke into the phone. 'Is that the police?'

Craig shook with rage. 'You . . . I'll make you squirm for this!'

Julian lifted his eyebrows.

Craig rounded on the others. 'Are you going to let him . . .?'

Mrs Maggs looked everywhere but at him.

Bristles stared back at Craig.

Skinny yelped. 'You lot don't know what you're doing!' He grabbed another case and followed Bernie out of the door.

Julian held Craig's eye, holding up his phone, from which came a voice asking which service he wanted.

Craig's nerve broke. 'I'll be at my mother's cottage till you're ready to see sense.' He followed Skinny and Bernie out of the door, taking the last of his packages with him.

Julian made his apologies to whoever was on the other end of the line, and put his phone away. He leaned back and closed his eyes. He was ashen with exhaustion and pain.

Bea groped for something to sit on. There wasn't a stick of furniture in the room. She leaned against a panelled wall, and tried to make sense of what she'd heard. That had been some scene!

After a while she was able to lift her head and look around.

Julian's head was bowed and his eyes closed. She could just imagine how agonizing it must be to think that his father had had a child outside marriage and abandoned it. That, on top of being thrown from his horse . . .

And what was that about his father's horse and dog being shot by Frederick?

But what if Craig's 'proof' were confirmed?

Julian's right to the estate had been called into question and everyone would now have to decide what attitude they should take to him – especially if their jobs were at risk.

Take the taxi driver, Bernie. He'd removed Craig without getting his fee but Bea didn't think he was anti-Julian. Bernie would come down in favour of whoever won out.

Mrs Maggs was in a similar position. She didn't like Craig much, she hadn't made up her mind about Julian yet, but she needed the job at the Hall. So she'd also sit on the fence. Yes, here she goes!

Mrs Maggs exclaimed, 'Just look at the time! Those idle, good-for-nothing workmen, drinking tea at all hours . . .' She bustled out, letting the door slam to behind her.

Bristles was another matter. He had brains and seemed secure in himself. He would sift the arguments. He had to bear in mind that the estate owed him money for work done, and was probably also good for more work in the future . . . but only if he could be sure that the estate could pay him.

Bristles had seen how Julian operated in these difficult circumstances. He had Julian's promise of money to be paid as and when it came in. Would Bristles accept that?

Well, Bea reasoned, that depended on a number of things, not least of which was what Bristles felt about Craig. Would Bristles think Craig would make a better go at running the place than Julian?

No, of course not. Even Bea could see that Craig hadn't the know-how nor the flair to manage the estate, which meant he'd run it into the ground and it would have to be sold off. And that would mean Bristles would be paid very little – if anything – for work done.

If Craig managed to oust Julian . . .? No, Bristles didn't think Julian would continue to work for the Hall.

Mind you, thought Bea, if Julian thought it was his duty to continue running the estate, he might well be persuaded to do so, even though it would mean a life in straitened circumstances and a poorer outlook for the future. Polly wouldn't be pleased, and they wouldn't be able to give their little boy the education he would have had as a scion of the Hall, or if Julian were still working in the City.

So Bristles would vote for backing Julian, who probably was the only hope they all had of rescuing the estate from financial disaster.

Besides which, Bea thought that Bristles actually had some regard for Julian, whom she noticed was looking increasingly ill.

Bristles said to Julian, 'I was much younger, of course, but I knew your father. Yes, Dora smiled at him. All the local girls did. But he wasn't interested. He had a girlfriend up at university, brought her down here a couple of times, was teaching her to ride. Pretty little thing with a real spark to her. Rose, her name was.'

Julian said, 'Thank you. I can't remember them. Perhaps you can tell me about them some time?'

Bristles gave an emphatic nod. 'My young brother hasn't the sense he was born with. If my father hadn't begged me to look after him . . .'

Julian closed his eyes, exhausted. 'I understand.'

'If Craig takes over, he'll run the place even further into the ground than it already is. He'll have it up for sale within the year and devil take the hindmost.'

Julian nodded. He tried to make himself more comfortable in the chair but the movement must have set his ankle aflame, because he gasped out loud, and then made himself become still.

Bea decided it was time for her to take a hand in proceedings. She said, 'Julian, you need that ankle looked at. Now. You need it X-rayed and dealt with. And that bump on your head. I'd better take you to the hospital. That is, can you direct me to the nearest Accident and Emergency?'

Julian exhaled, tried to relax. 'No, no. I'll get a taxi. Polly's away and I can't leave Bruno.'

Bristles stood up. He stamped his feet to ensure his circulation was working properly. 'I'll take you. I know the nearest A and E. My brother was always there, growing up. My father said they should have named a ward after him.' He looked at Bea. 'You want to come?'

Julian reached out his hand to Bea. 'This is Mrs Abbot, whom I trust with my life. Bea, this is Lance, expert on the restoration of old buildings, who has done so much to help rescue the Hall. If he takes me to hospital, can you stay here and look after things for me? If they keep me in overnight, help yourself to food.'

Bea nodded, her mind whirling with possibilities.

Julian laid his hand on Bruno's head. 'Bruno, stay with Bea. Look after her and the house till I get back.'

Bruno whined with reluctance, but accepted the order.

Bea clicked her fingers at the dog, and he went to her side though he continued to keep an eye on his master.

Lance-cum-Bristles – now revealed to be a wonder-working expert on old buildings – took the wheelchair out of the hall, with Bea and Bruno following in its wake.

Julian called back to Bea. 'There's a dozen things I should be doing. I'll pick up my laptop on the way but can you find out how my horse Jack is doing?'

'Will do.'

In the kitchen, Mrs Maggs was busying herself with clearing the table.

Julian said to her, 'Mrs Maggs, I have to go to the hospital to get my ankle checked out. Lance is going to take me. I'm leaving Mrs Abbot in your capable hands. She'll liaise with me.'

The wheelchair was manoeuvred out into the yard, and the back door slammed shut.

Bea was left alone with Mrs Maggs.

Now what?

Mrs Maggs said, 'Well!' And squared up to Bea. This was her kitchen, and Bea was an intruder. Mrs Maggs recognized a business-woman when she saw one, but Bea was an unknown quantity. A lady who might need waiting on? Mrs Maggs said, in a voice which signalled she didn't want Bea in her kitchen. 'You're his friend from London?'

'Yes, I run a domestic agency in Kensington. I fell over him outside my garage one winter's day. He'd been roughed up by certain people who'd discovered he stood in their way of inheriting this place. He hadn't a clue why. It took some sorting out.'

Mrs Maggs started putting used crockery into the dishwasher.

Bruno pawed at the handle of the back door and let himself out.

Bea said, 'Does Bruno normally go out by himself?'

Mrs Maggs nodded. 'He makes the rounds of the estate every day about this time. He'll let us know if anything's amiss.' She swabbed down the tabletop with a disinfectant spray.

Bea tried to get through to Mrs Maggs. 'I could murder a cuppa.'

Mrs Maggs softened. 'A cuppa? Yes. So could I.' She bustled about to fill and switch the kettle on.

This was a signal that Bea might take a seat; so she did. 'Thank you. I don't know about you, but I'm not sure whether I'm on my head or my heels.'

Mrs Maggs concentrated on making tea. 'So you're the one who helped Sir Julian get rid of them rotten apples: Lady Fleur, that bully Frederick, and that waste of space, Bertram. As they're all out of the picture now, we thought it would be plain sailing from now on. Bar the hole in the finances, that is. But who'd have thought . . .?'

Her voice tailed away. She made a pot of tea and produced tea cups and saucers instead of dunking a couple of tea bags in mugs.

Milk was poured into a small jug and an ancient biscuit tin was pushed in Bea's direction. 'Sugar?'

Bea shook her head, graciously accepting what she recognized to be an olive branch. She added milk to her tea, and chose a chocolate digestive biscuit. 'Thank you. Just how I like it.' She had to remember that this was Mrs Maggs's territory and Bea was an uninvited guest.

Mrs Maggs took two chocolate digestive biscuits, placed the chocolate sides together, and bit a segment out of them. Mrs Maggs was trying to work out what position she should take.

Bea waited.

'Thing is,' said Mrs Maggs, 'Sir Julian has made himself unpopular hereabouts, shutting everything down. Putting people out of a job. Making those idle, lazy girl cousins of his move out of here. People don't like change. Mind you, they didn't like the old lot either. La-di-dah Lady Fleur and her brood. But they were used to them.'

She finished her doubled-up biscuit, and considered another. Shook her head at herself. Sipped tea, looking into the distance.

Bea waited.

Mrs Maggs said, 'Mind you, I got nothing against Sir Julian. He's all right. Chip off the old block, and I don't mean Lady Fleur and her lot. Sir Florian was all right, too, though he lived in his own world. Would hardly know who you were if he came across you unexpectedly.'

'And his son, the first Julian?'

'Nice lad. Gave no trouble, except for his dog; great soppy thing, tracking mud all over the floors. He'd ask how you were and listen to what you said. He never gave no trouble to the girls. He'd plans for the estate which he was working on when he came down from university. Brought a pretty little thing with him a coupla times. Rose, her name was. She adored him, and he had eyes for no one but her.'

'So you don't think that what Craig was hinting at . . .? That the first Julian would have played around with Dora?'

'Oh, she tried it on. She was quite something in a gypsyish way, if you know what I mean. But no; he liked little blondes, something with a bit of snap, crackle and pop.'

Someone more like Polly?

'So who do you think was Craig's father?'

A shrug. 'Frederick, maybe. He liked a bit of slap and tickle and thought he had every right to jump on us girls. I was lucky; got him in the whatsits first time he tried it. I told my father, who was Sir Florian's tenant at the Hilltop Farm – that's the one that my brother runs now – and he told Sir Florian there'd be trouble if Frederick tried it again, and Lady Fleur went ballistic and wanted to sack me for telling lies.

'I was dead worried because I'd only just started going out with my young man and if I'd lost the job here I'd have had to leave home to find something else. Only, my father had a word with the old man and I was kept on with a warning. To give her credit, Lady Fleur did have a word with Frederick and he went looking for his fun elsewhere. Only, his eye was always on me, if you know what I mean. If he'd have caught me in a dark corner I don't know what would have happened.

'Luckily, soon as we got married, my man found himself a good job up in the Docklands and we moved up to London. I went to work in a big hotel, and we had our two girls, both married and with their own kids now. My man passed on last year and I didn't want to move in with either of my daughters, so when I heard the news about the old guard being thrown out, I thought I might as well come back and apply for a job here.

'I know what I'm doing in the house, and Sir Julian respects that. A cottage comes with the job, the girls bring the grandkids down once a month. My brother and his family are still up at the old farm, my niece lives two doors away and I'm busy from morning to night. I don't fancy going back on to the labour market.'

Bea said, 'No, I can see that. With your knowledge of the family, you could probably put a name to whoever it was who sired Craig? Not this Julian's father, I presume?'

'Not him, no. That Craig's gone and blonded his hair. I'm sure it was never that fair before. I suppose he thinks it makes him look like the Julian who left. But no. I can't see it. That Julian wouldn't have bothered with Dora.'

A heavy sigh. 'It could have been Frederick, but . . . I dunno. Say what you like, Frederick had something about him and I don't see it in Craig. Dora went with anyone who took her fancy. She took after her mother that went the same way. And her grandmother, too, if what I've heard is true. Not a marriage certificate between them, but they knew enough not to have too many kids.'

Bea said, 'But if Craig has got it right, the money his mother lived on came from the Hall, which means from Sir Florian. Surely Sir Florian wouldn't have settled money on Dora unless it was a member of his family who'd given Dora a child?'

Mrs Maggs said, 'Do you think we haven't worked that out? And yet . . . I can't see it.'

Bea looked around her. The kitchen was spotless, the units not of the latest, but perfectly adequate. Everything worked. Water and electricity had been supplied to the kitchen if nowhere else.

She said, thinking it through, 'Infrastructure. You're right, Mrs Maggs. Julian's dealing with the infrastructure because without it, nothing works. He's made sure this kitchen works and there's a portable loo outside, which means the workmen can get on with the job, which they wouldn't do if they didn't have all their mod cons.'

Mrs Maggs poured them a second cup of tea each. 'I told him, I said I need running water and electricity in my kitchen. I must have a microwave, a dishwasher and a kettle. There are workmen coming and going at all hours, and they need looking after; not to mention the men in suits with their clipboards and laptops. The place is never quiet, but we wouldn't be so far along with the repairs if it weren't for his putting this lot right first.'

'He said the house was in a bad way.'

'It's like the old guard was living in the last century but the cracks were showing. Everything broke and nothing got mended. Lady Fleur had money of her own but she wasn't for spending it here. Had everything delivered and to hell with the bills. Diamonds for dinner and rats behind the skirting board. She gets taken away, Sir Florian dies and Sir Julian takes over. The next day it's empty rooms with scaffolding and workmen everywhere. It all takes a bit of getting used to.

'I never thought to see the family moving into the barn, and Lady Paula down on her hands and knees scrubbing! But within days I could see they were right. The old days have gone. We'd got used to not noticing when a floorboard went soft, or a tile fell off the roof. The wiring here was dangerous, lights flickering on and off, could have set the place on fire.'

Bea mused, 'It's probably because Julian wasn't brought up in a place like this that he sees the problems so clearly.'

Mrs Maggs eyed the biscuit tin. Should she have another? She decided against it. She said, 'He doesn't really like being called "Sir" Julian, though he's getting used to it. Lady Paula's the same. Now, don't get me wrong; I've always voted Labour and I always will, but I don't want to get rid of the privileged. I can see we need them if we want to keep the old places going. On the other hand, I'm no Commie. We're not all born equal, in height or weight, or in wealth or poverty. Some of us have brains to manage things, and some work hard and make it anyway. We need both. With respect on both sides.'

'Julian and Polly have earned your respect?'

'I suppose.' Reluctantly, she continued, 'It's been hard for some people hereabouts to understand that he had to shut everything down and start afresh, but I reckon he's done the right thing. The amusement park was a disgrace, as was the farm shop. And the restaurant? There were rats there, as well, and not just four-legged ones. I'm surprised they were able to operate as long as they did. I reckon Sir Florian had given up and let it rot because he thought Frederick and Bertram would take over after him. He perked up after they left and Julian came, but it was almost too late to save the house.'

'Cleaning gutters, replacing tiles, tracing leaks in the plumbing, rewiring; all that's necessary stuff but the punters don't see it. Infrastructure; out of sight, out of mind but necessary. When we get the place open again, well, that's the future and that's what we're all counting on.'

Bea risked an awkward question. 'But he's not there yet, is he? What do you think about his being shot at in the woods the other day? And what about his accident this morning?'

FIVE

Mrs Maggs didn't want to answer that. Instead, she looked at her watch and started to clear the table.

Bea said, 'Julian's father lost his dog and his horse. Our own Julian has been shot at. He's been thrown off his horse and could have been killed. And Bruno is free to run wild.'

Mrs Maggs said, 'That horse is dangerous. Everyone knows that. Sir Julian has trained Bruno not to start eating anything till he's given permission. The butcher lets me have a bone for him every now and then and there's one in the fridge now that he can have later.'

Mrs Maggs wasn't going to answer Bea's question, but it had disturbed her so much that she was clashing china around like nobody's business. Like Bea, Mrs Maggs suspected someone was attempting to make history repeat itself. But who? Someone local?

Bea recalled that Mrs Maggs had family roots in the community.

Bea said, choosing her words with care, 'I understand that people thrown out of their jobs might well be unhappy with what's happened.'

Mrs Maggs tossed her head but didn't reply.

Bea continued, 'Julian has borrowed money from all sides and sold his flat in an effort to save the Hall.'

Mrs Maggs dropped the last of the cutlery into the dishwasher. 'I'm sure he knows where money is to be found. Folk around here think he should have put them on board wages for the winter.'

'He couldn't afford that. Also, you and I both know he needed to get rid of some of those who ran various businesses in the park. He might prefer to bring in new blood.'

'Immigrants? I don't mind them, if they know how to do the job. It's those young ones on their phones all the time that I can't be doing with. They don't know how to think or add up for themselves because it's all done on their phones. What good is that when you have to watch the pennies?'

Bea chanced her arm. 'What do you think of Craig?'

Mrs Maggs began to wipe down the table. 'Sorry for him, in a way. Dora did put herself about and everyone knew it, but he was her only. He went to the school here with the rest. He could talk the hind leg off a donkey so he had a certain following. Not the serious ones like Lance, but that stupid young brother of his, he thought the sun shone, know what I mean? I never thought Craig would make anything of himself, but going up to London didn't do him any harm, did it? Interior decorating, is it? Well, I've seen some of that on the telly and maybe he's found something he can earn a living at. As for taking over here, he wouldn't think about the infrastructure, would he? He'd be all for pasting gold leaf on rotten wood.'

Bea thought that was an interesting summing-up of Craig's character, and very likely correct.

Mrs Maggs looked at her watch. 'I must be getting on and so must you. I want to start on the linen cupboard, see what's what and what needs replacing. You'll be all right at the barn, won't you? Let me know if you need anything. I'm here till six. I see the men off the premises for the night and go round the house with Bruno, checking they haven't left windows open, which has happened before now.'

Bea understood she was being dismissed. She stood up. 'Thank you for looking after me so well. I appreciate it.'

Bea went out of the back door, and into the open air. The sunlight was losing its dazzle and beginning to fade. She hoped there was some form of heating at the barn, because it was going to be a chilly night.

There was no sign of Julian. He would ring her on his smartphone if he was held up at the hospital, wouldn't he? Or might he have left a message on the landline at the barn? Uh-oh. There might not be a landline there.

And where was Bruno?

She let herself into the barn. There was a landline and the light on it was blinking. She listened to the messages. The time of starting for the meeting at the parish hall had been changed, and something he'd ordered would be available on Monday.

She checked her own smartphone. Something from her office manager. A query quickly dealt with. There was also a message from her husband, Piers, which she played twice.

'Bea, you won't believe this. My sitting today has been cancelled because – wait for it – my client's being interviewed by the police. Some tax fiddle or other? A strong hint of corruption. He says it's all a smear by his opponent and he can prove the charges are false. I said I'd postpone our sittings but he won't have it so I'm here for another couple of days. I've never knowingly painted a criminal before. Can't make up my mind if he is one or not. How are you getting on? Cream teas and country scenes? Give me a ring when you can.'

She tried his number, but it went to voicemail. She'd try again later.

A 'wuff' at the door, and there was Bruno, reporting for duty. He lapped up the water in his dish and settled down for a nap. Presumably he hadn't found anything amiss on his perambulations?

A click. Something had switched itself on. Heating or hot water? Yes, there were a couple of radiators and they were beginning to warm up. Good. There were no curtains on the windows but that didn't matter, since they were so far out in the country.

Bea's smartphone rang.

It was Polly, anxious and upset. 'What's happened, Bea? Julian rang me to say he'd had a mishap and was at the hospital being checked out. What happened? Is he all right?'

'It's not serious. His horse, Jack, went crazy. Julian jumped off and hurt his ankle. The builder – Lance or whatever his name is – took him to hospital to have it looked at.'

'Really? He's not making out it's nothing when it is? You know what he's like. He'd walk around on a broken leg rather than inconvenience anyone else.'

'No, it's just what I said. He said I'm to stay to look after things. How are you getting on?'

'My father is . . . How can I put it? He's the most—'

'Selfish? Inconsiderate?'

'For starters, yes. He tried to stop me marrying Julian when he was a nobody and now he thinks that because we've inherited the Hall we should house him and feed him and cosset him like a two-year-old, and I could scream! I keep telling him the Hall is not habitable and that we haven't two pennies to rub together, and he keeps saying that it's my duty to look after him and he's sure I can arrange something considering that he brought me up and saw me through university. I could spit, I really could!'

Bea wondered if she ought to tell Polly about Craig and the new threats to Julian. She decided not to do so. Polly had enough on her plate at the moment.

Besides which, Polly hadn't stopped talking. 'And you'll never guess! He's made himself so unpleasant at the home that they want me to remove him. To make matters worse, the boy pulls a face every time he sees my father, and oh, I don't know whether to laugh or cry. The two of them compete for my attention.

'I was sitting with my father in his room, which is a really nice room overlooking the garden and everything, and the boy wanted feeding and it was the right time for it, so I said I had to attend to him. My father wobbled around until he fell over and lay there yelling for me to help him get up and . . .' Polly started to laugh, but there were tears in with the laughter.

Bea said, 'I am in awe of your father's ability to get his own way. Do tell me how you settled the matter.'

'I picked up the boy and walked out of my father's room. Found a chair outside and fed the boy. My father yelled for a bit but no one came, so he picked himself up and came after me, saying he had to go to the hospital to be checked out. And I said that was fine by me but I couldn't come and he'd have to get the people at the Home to arrange it. It was a toss-up whether he'd phone for an ambulance or not. But he didn't, though he has a nice bruise coming up on his forehead. It would be unkind of me to think he'd given it to himself, wouldn't it?'

'Very. But true. You're staying there another night?'

'I'll have to. Tell Julian to ring me when he gets back, will you? Perhaps he can think what to do with my father.'

'Move him to a really cheap Home with a shared room and poor food? Then he'll appreciate what he's got now.'

'Machiavelli. I like that idea. Actually, I think he's bored stiff. His brain's still fizzing and he's got nothing to do but find fault with everything. The boy's beginning to fuss. I'd better go.'

Bea sat down to think about everything she'd learned that day. In particular she considered all that Mrs Maggs had said, or implied. Or not spoken of.

Bea wondered about Dora's death. Nobody seemed to be sorry about it. Certainly not Craig. The attempt to throw suspicion on to Julian was almost laughable. It might cause him some inconvenience, but surely it couldn't be taken seriously?

Again and again, Bea came back to the deaths of Julian's father's dog and his horse, which seemed to have been the trigger to his departure.

It must have been hard for a man who'd been brought up to inherit an estate to turn his back on it and move away, but it was understandable if Lady Fleur had worked against him from the moment he was born and his father never backed him up.

Perhaps the young heir hadn't intended his exile to be for ever? Perhaps he'd thought that his leaving would force Sir Florian to get his wife to back off and that then he'd be able to return? Perhaps Sir Florian, too, had thought that if he gave them time, the hot heads would calm down and see sense.

Perhaps that would have happened. But young Julian had found himself a job, married his sweetheart, and sired a baby boy. Perhaps he'd dreamed of having another horse and another dog but hadn't been able to afford it in his new life. If he'd lived . . . but there! Lady Fleur and Frederick had monitored his movements and made sure they wiped out the competition. It was pure luck that the baby in the back of the car had survived.

So now we move forward. This Julian had acquired a dog and married his childhood sweetheart before he'd learned of his legacy. The other day he'd been riding a horse with an unreliable temper when he'd been thrown and suffered an injury. He'd been riding that horse daily for weeks, if not months. So why had it suddenly become unreliable? Was it ill, or had it been 'nobbled'?

Bea knew very little about horses, which was a disadvantage in this instance.

Julian knew about horses. And dogs. Julian had feared Bruno might have been tempted with poisoned food thrown in his way and trained him not to eat anything unless given permission to do so.

Throw in Dora's death, add Craig and his intention to let others work while he played, and what did you get? Something nasty in the undergrowth.

Was Dora collateral damage in a struggle between the local people who relied on the Hall for their livelihood, and the new owner with his sweeping reforms? In which case the answer was to be found in considering how local people thought and acted.

Bea sighed. She told herself she was imagining things. Julian had been thrown from his horse and hurt his foot. It was an accident.

Dora had managed to get across someone from her past and been killed for it. The two events were not connected.

Except that Julian said he'd been shot at in the woods. And everyone said Julian rode well and had had a rapport with his difficult horse.

Julian had told Bea he wanted to know what had happened to Jack. She could at least do that for him.

She collected Bruno and together they trekked the length of the barn till they came to the turning off into the stable yard. This was a paved area lined with boxes on either side.

An odd little man, all grey and brown, was drawing water from an outside tap. He heard Bea coming, and nearly dropped his bucket. Julian had said that Mickey was of a certain age and a nervous disposition. He was also wizened of face and bowed of legs. Age? Between fifty and sixty? Possibly even older. Some teeth missing. Ancient clothing but serviceable.

Take this slowly and carefully. Julian implied Mickey wasn't up to much in the brains department.

Bea said, 'I'm looking for Mickey. I'm staying at the barn for a few days and Sir Julian asked me to enquire after his horse. You called the vet to him this morning?'

Mickey made some inarticulate sounds approximating to speech. 'Jack weren't himself. Not his fault.'

Bea said, 'I know. Sir Julian asked me to check. What did the vet say?'

Mickey bent to put a second bucket under the tap and turned it on. 'I sorted it.'

Patience, Bea!

'What did you sort?'

'Nowt. Got work to do.' He turned the tap on, and the gush of water drowned out any words he might have spoken. He turned his back on Bea.

Bea said, 'Is your family from around here, Mickey?'

A hunched shoulder. A muddle of words. 'Jack's all right. Not his fault.'

'Then whose fault was it, Mickey? Sir Julian could have been badly injured, even killed.'

Mickey turned off the tap, picked up both buckets – he must be stronger than he looked – and disappeared into one of the boxes.

Bea walked around the stable yard. The doors of the end box

were shut and festooned with police tape. Was that where they'd found Dora?

Bruno hung at her heel, head lowered, as they passed the site of the murder. There hadn't been any blood, had there? Could the dog pick up traces of the fear and the anger which had surrounded Dora's death? Or was he merely reacting to Bea's own feelings?

The other boxes were all clean. Four had their doors wide open, meaning that four horses were normally kept there? Where were they? Out to grass?

She reached the end of the yard, where a gate shut them off from a rutted, unpaved lane and within a few feet gave access to a large paddock where three horses grazed. One was big and black and sleek. That would be Jack? The other two were ancient horses which looked as if they might fall over if they weren't careful how they took their next step.

Beyond the paddock were a couple of fields surrounded by high wire fences. They contained prefabricated sheds to house hens and possibly pigs as well. Clucks and oink noises drifted over to her.

She looked down at Bruno, sitting at her feet. He was also looking at the paddock. She said, 'What do you think of that lot, then?'

He looked at her, and then turned his head to look back at the stables. Two of the boxes had tack hanging up inside. One didn't. So where were Jack's saddle and reins?

She called out, 'Mickey? Where are you?'

No reply, except for a cock crowing in the distance.

Returning through the stable yard Bruno halted, peering into the box nearest the house. Bea stopped and looked inside. This box was clearly used by Mickey for his own comfort. Bea saw an empty flask, a tin of biscuits, a flattened cushion on an ancient armchair. Odd tools – whose use she could only guess at – hung on the walls.

She went in. A wooden staircase ran up the wall to the left and debouched into an upper room. Did Mickey sleep up there? She noted there was a central light bulb hanging from the ceiling though it was not yet dark enough to be switched on.

A saddle had been slung over a saw-horse, spread out so that someone could work on a dark stain on the leather. Judging by the rag and bowl of water nearby, Mickey had been trying to clean the stain from the underneath of the saddle. The water in the bowl was reddish. Bea considered wetting a finger and tasting the result to see if she could identify what had made that stain, but couldn't quite bring herself to do it.

Bruno stiffened.

The light changed. Mickey was standing between her and the door. He knew what she was thinking, all right. He said, 'Not Jack's fault.'

He held out his hand, palm uppermost, and Bea caught her breath. Mickey was showing her what had caused the stain on the saddle.

A burr. A sharp, many-pointed teasel head, the kind which grew in abundance where verges of lanes are left uncut. An innocuous-looking plant but its burrs can be caught in an animal's fur and cling. If placed under a saddle it might irritate, but if a man then leaped into the saddle, the horse would be stung beyond endurance, would try to fight it off, to run away, to scrape its rider off . . .

In short, the placement of a burr under Jack's saddle argued the intention to kill.

'N-not Jack's fault,' repeated Mickey. And let the burr drop to the floor.

Bea said, 'Mickey? Did *you* put it there for a joke?'

'N-n-not me. I wouldn't.' He shifted on his feet uneasily. 'Honest!' He meant it.

No, he wouldn't have put Jack in harm's way.

Bea pressed on. 'Then who? You must know.'

'Don't know nothing.' He turned to go. 'Must get on.' He vanished into the yard outside.

Bea picked up the burr. On one side the spikes were flattened and dark with what must be blood. Ugh. Nasty.

What to do now? Return to base.

Her smartphone sounded off as she ushered Bruno back into the barn. It was Julian, ringing from the hospital. He sounded tired. 'Sorry to bother you, Bea. You're not having the perfect weekend I promised you, are you?'

'You're still in the hospital?'

'Lance got me here in good time. He wanted to stay with me, but I sent him home after a while. I have to wait for X-rays. Hopefully the ankle's not broken but there's some talk about keeping me in overnight. Concussion. I thought I had a hard head but must admit it's been pounding a bit today. Hope I'm making sense.'

Bruno was looking up at her. He could hear His Master's Voice.

Bea held her phone down to Bruno. 'Say "Hello".'

Bruno obliged. 'Wuff!'

Bea said, 'Bruno's looking after me beautifully. And Mrs Maggs asked me to tell her if there's anything I need.'

'Ah, thank you. You're a lifesaver, Bea.'

Was there any point in alarming Julian?

He solved that worry for her. 'What about Jack. What did the vet say?'

'More to the point, what did Mickey do? Someone placed a burr under your saddle so that it drove into Jack's side when you mounted him. Jack's OK, out in the meadow. Mickey's in a state of nervous exhaustion. He says he didn't put the burr there, and he says he doesn't know who did.'

'Ah. It did occur to me that something out of the ordinary had upset Jack. Did you tell Polly?'

'She's got enough on her plate. Perhaps she and the boy had better stay down there for a couple of days? To get her father resettled somewhere new.'

'You mean, out of harm's way. So you think I'm in danger? Again? How very . . . boring.'

'Yes.' Bea smiled. He was taking this well. Had probably thought it all out before he left the Hall for the hospital.

He said, 'Right. Don't tell Polly, yet. She'd want to come straight back. I may not be thinking straight, but I think the police will want to question me again tomorrow.'

'Why? Oh. You think Craig is going to produce a witness who says you were seen with Dora? But surely he's waiting to see if you'll cave into his demands before he plays that card?'

'I've been wondering who that false witness might be. Craig was born here and he knows everyone in the village. I'm not the most popular person around here at the moment, so he might well have some local people rooting for him. Such as the man Dora had shacked up with, who lost his job at the amusement park and had stopped paying her rent. He might well be holding a grudge against me.'

'Does Craig get the cottage now?'

'I'll have to check with the solicitor, but I don't think so. She had it for life and now she's dead, I think it reverts back to the estate.'

'Do you think Craig understands that? He talked the talk, but I get the impression he's not doing as well with his interior decorating as he would like to have us think. You noticed he said he'd wanted his mother to do this or that for him at Christmas?'

'I did.' Julian's voice was beginning to drag. 'I can't think straight. I keep going over it in my mind that all the people who tried to kill me before are accounted for and out of harm's way, so they can't be behind this. My old firm are trying to find out what happened to the money Frederick stole' – there came the sound of a yawn – 'and the remaining cousins seem to have accepted . . . Sorry, Bea. Not making much sense now.'

He was silent. But he hadn't switched off.

Bea thought over what he'd said. He was right. Lady Fleur and her son Frederick had both been charged with attempted murder and were currently incarcerated at His Majesty's pleasure.

Frederick's son, Bertram, had also been active in trying to kill Julian but his last attempt, when he'd tried to run him over on his motorbike, had resulted in him injuring himself so badly, it was thought he might never walk again.

His pale wife, Gerda, and his two sisters, Mona and Celine, were still hanging around, but they didn't seem to be very active in local matters. Or were they?

Bea said, 'What about the three witches, your cousins? When you closed the Hall and made them leave, they didn't take it well, did they? I mean, they'd expected to live the life of Riley for good and in you come and turf them out. Have they been doing something about it?'

A long sigh. 'Mona, Celine and Gerda, in order of seniority. I agree they weren't happy about being turned out of the Hall but the plumbing and the wiring had been condemned and we couldn't risk anyone staying there till they were fixed. If Lady Fleur and Frederick had had their way, when my grandfather died the Hall would have been put up for sale and they would have had to leave it anyway. And, in that case, I doubt very much that they'd each have got enough out of the proceeds of the sale to ensure they could live in comfort for the rest of their lives.'

'But they're still living in the village. Do you think they could be stirring up trouble for you?'

'I got the impression they'd other fish to fry. Mona – that's the one who's been married and divorced. Rumour says she's got a new man in tow, someone from the City. He appears to be supportive of her, which is good. She thinks she might like to run the farm shop. In a weak moment I agreed she should study the market and let me have a business proposition as to how it could be done. I suppose she might be helpful if she put her mind to it.'

Of course he'd give the woman the benefit of the doubt.

Julian said, 'I haven't seen any written proposition yet. She said she needed transport to get around the place and wanted me to buy her a car, but there was an old SUV in the barn which I said she could use for now. If it works out and makes a profit, the farm shop would be one less problem off my hands.'

'And her sister, Celine?'

'She's taking this course. Don't know what for. Says it's going to sort out her future, which would be a blessing. Gerda – that's Bertram's wife – helps out at the rescue centre and for the rest seems to live from one visit to another to visit her husband in prison. I've let the three of them have a sizeable house in the village for free for a year so that they have somewhere to live till they work out what they want to do in future. It's better than they might have expected, so why would they want to kill the golden goose?'

'Hate doesn't co-exist with common sense. How was Wonder Dog Bruno on the night Dora was killed?'

'You're thinking that whoever it was who killed Dora would have been known to the dog, because he'd have raised the alarm if a stranger got into the stables? I've been keeping him in at night lately because . . . well, I told myself it was because he's not used to country life and goes mad at the sight of an owl or a bat . . . In truth, I suppose I was afraid he might be . . . Bea, realistically, if he was indoors with us I don't think he'd have heard anything. It's quite a way to the stables and Dora was killed at the far end of the block. Mickey, the groom, says he didn't hear anything, either.

'The electricity supply should have been connected up to the stables some days ago, with security lights timed to switch on should anything larger than a fox appear. But I don't think the system was working then. Which reminds me, that's another thing I must check. Those electricians . . . .! A nightmare. They should have been finished long ago. I must have a chat with them tomorrow.'

Bea cut across his chatter. 'Shall I put Bruno into kennels until you can get back?'

'No. I'll be back in the morning. I'm wondering what to do about Mickey. He has the brains of a snail, but he can sense a change in the weather before the birds know of it. He must know who nobbled

Jack. Or guess. I can't make him out. I should be able to . . . I'm
good with figures, but do I understand people as well?' His voice
faded away.

She said, 'You've had enough. I'll keep Bruno in tonight. Let me
know when the doctors decide what to do with you.'

'Did I tell you where to find spare keys to this and that? In the
kitchen, first cupboard on the left. Must go . . .'

He switched off, and she drifted over to the big picture window
at the back, overlooking the paddock in which she'd seen the three
horses that afternoon. They were no longer there. The landscape
seemed empty without them.

She checked her smartphone for messages. She'd missed one
from Piers, who said he was going out for supper somewhere and
would update her in the morning. He said that if his sitter was going
to be arrested, he'd come straight back to London and then on to
join her.

She found herself speaking aloud. 'Dear Lord, such a tangle. So
many people wanting so many different things. It looks like you've
dumped me in the middle of it for some reason, but how can I tell
what to do? Please, look after Julian and Polly and the boy and
everyone. Including Bruno and Jack. And, if I'm on the right track,
perhaps you'd like to give me some sort of sign . . .?'

Bruno said 'Wuff,' telling her that a friend was approaching. That
someone duly knocked on the door.

Bruno barked an alarm which said, *Strangers!*

SIX

Bea opened the door to find Mrs Maggs standing there, with her fist raised to knock again. She was alone but behind her was a car with two police officers standing beside it.

Bruno came to Bea's side. She put her hand on his head to restrain him.

Mrs Maggs said, 'They want himself. I said he's been taken to hospital. He's not back yet, is he?'

'No,' said Bea, speaking to the police officers. 'It's serious. They didn't wait for the ambulance but took him in someone's car.'

'Which hospital?'

Bea said, 'Sorry. I don't know. I'm just visiting.'

Mrs Maggs said, 'Dunno. Southampton, maybe? Or maybe somewhere up in London?'

The police turned to Bea. 'Who took him?'

'Some businessman who was here. I don't know his name.' Well, that was the truth, more or less, wasn't it?

'You got a mobile phone number for Sir Julian?'

Bea had it on her phone, of course, but now she looked blank as Mrs Maggs reeled off a number which Bea didn't recognize.

'So where's his wife, then?'

Mrs Maggs said, 'Down seeing to her father somewhere on the South Coast. One of those places where old people go to die. She did say as she'd give me her number, but if she did, I don't know where I've put it.'

Muttering to themselves, the police officers got back in their car and drove away.

'Hmm,' said Mrs Maggs, giving Bea a sideways look.

'Hmm,' said Bea. They'd both lied to the police, by omission and commission, and both knew it. Was this going to form a bond between them?

Bea decided that it would. She said, 'Sir Julian's OK, rang me just now. They think the ankle is broken but they're waiting on

X-rays. He's woozy with painkillers and they're keeping him in tonight. He's worried about Jack and Bruno. It might be best if Polly and the boy stay down south for the moment . . . out of the way of the workmen, if you see what I mean? She's got her own problems. Her father is being, well, difficult.'

Mrs Maggs nodded. 'Old folk. My husband's old dad's still living in the village. Used to be able to fix anything for anyone. Used to be nice and calm but since the Alzheimer's hit he's had a total personality change. Foul-mouthed. Won't do this and won't do that. The only way to get him to have a bath is to anaesthetize him first. No, I tell a lie. Not quite as bad as that, but if it wasn't for my sister-in-law, who's next door to a saint, I don't know what he'd do. Her daughter, my niece, she's had enough of him, but there . . . he's family, isn't he?'

Mrs Maggs was talking a blue streak to cover the fact that she, too, was uneasy. She narrowed her eyes at Bea. 'You're fond of Sir Julian, eh?'

'Yes. We've both proved that, haven't we? Lying for him.'

'He didn't kill that Dora. I dunno who did, but it wasn't him.'

But you suspect someone, don't you? Why aren't you saying who it is you think killed Dora?

Mrs Maggs looked at her watch. 'Time to knock off for the day. The workmen have gone. Drat them, they leave more dust behind than the wind from the Sahara. You all right for tonight?'

'Yes, thank you.'

Mrs Maggs returned to the Hall, and Bea went to see what she could find to eat for supper. She didn't fancy heating up the big casserole Polly had left in the fridge. What she did fancy was a nice portion of fish and chips.

She was a little shocked at herself. She'd always considered such food fattening if not directly leading to a heart attack. But there it was. Once the idea was lodged in her mind, it wouldn't let go.

She told herself bread and cheese would do. She tidied up the living room. And still wanted fish and chips.

She could get some at the pub in the village. Surely, they must do fish and chips? It was getting dark. She wouldn't walk, but take the car. And Bruno? No, perhaps better not. She didn't know if the local pub approved of dogs or not, and she wasn't at all sure of being able to control Bruno if he were given offence by a dog belonging to someone who lived locally.

She fed him, explained that she'd be out for a little while, and left him in his basket, looking reproachfully after her. Honestly, how guilty can a dog make you feel! Then to find a door key . . . ah, yes. There's the spare keys, all neatly labelled. Take the one you need, leave a security light on? No. No need, out here in the country.

The pub was all right though not spectacular. The clientele had once been purely local; men and women who worked on the land and didn't expect expense-account meals. Now, with a drift from town to country of youngish people working from home, it was a mixture of those who expected a gastropub and locals who still wanted a pint or three. There wasn't enough passing trade to justify employing a first-class chef, and the paper of the menu felt limp and overused. The fish and chips were cooked from frozen and served on a table with one wobbly leg, but the shandy that went with it was fine.

When she arrived, the bar was sparsely occupied by local people but soon were joined by a small group of noisy youngsters who settled in one corner. More people kept coming in all the time.

As Bea finished her drink, the back of her neck prickled. One moment she'd been thinking about ringing her husband for an update and the next . . . she was aware that someone had their beady eyes on her.

She kept very still for a count of five, and then made herself look around. Nobody seemed particularly interested in her. Only, her senses were telling her that someone in the now busy pub was very interested indeed. What about that group of youngsters at the far end? Was that Craig in the middle? It looked rather like it. Well, so what?

She told herself that she must stick out like a sore thumb. She was wearing rather good clothes and – a particular weakness of hers – a pair of beautiful tan leather boots which had cost a small fortune. Someone who knew about boots might well be interested in the person who wore them. Nothing to worry about.

The rowdy group shifted. The one in the middle whom she'd thought might have been Craig . . . wasn't. That was a relief. Or was it? There was another bar round the corner. He might be there. No, she was not going to explore.

Her smartphone rang. It was Julian, saying the X-ray showed he hadn't broken anything, but they were keeping him in overnight because of his concussion.

After some thought, Bea rang the girl she'd thought of recom-
mending to Julian as an archangel-cum-assistant. Outlining what
had been happening, Bea asked if Rosemary were free to trundle
into the country for the weekend. Rosemary agreed, which made
Bea feel a whole lot better.

Now, what could she do till the girl arrived? Answer: ask
questions.

Bea went to the bar to pay. She told the girl behind the counter
that she was visiting the area and would like to look up a couple
of old friends who'd moved out of the big house, and were renting
somewhere in the village. But, she'd mislaid the precise address.

Was there a hush in the conversation behind Bea?

The girl looked at Bea with a stone face. 'You mean them three
from the Hall?'

'Yes,' said Bea, telling herself she was imagining that she had
become the focus of attention in the bar. Probably any stranger
entering the pub would be of interest. The girl seemed to think the
less of Bea for being friendly with the people from the Hall, but
she did give Bea instructions as to where to find them.

Bea felt the prickle return to the back of her neck as she left the
pub. So whoever had been watching her, had remained in the bar?
Of course, gossip must be rife, what with the changes at the Hall,
Dora's death, and Craig's arrival. Now Bea had left the pub, they
were probably all at it, speculating, wondering . . . but not out loud
in front of strangers.

Bea left her car at the pub and walked along the main street to
where the houses ceased and the countryside took over. The last
house along was a pseudo-black-and-white, substantial building
built, perhaps, in the 1920s? Fake Tudor but the windows probably
fitted and, with any luck, there'd be adequate central heating.

The small strip of garden in front contained herbaceous plants
which were still alive but could do with some tender loving care.
A gravelled patch of land at the side housed a middle-aged SUV
which needed a wash and brush-up. Was this the car which Julian
had lent Mona? What did Celine do for transport?

Bea stepped inside the porch and rang the doorbell.

Celine, who was the younger of the two sisters, opened the door.
She looked at Bea without recognition. Then light dawned. 'You!
What do you want?'

They'd only met once before, on the day that Sir Florian had thrown out his scheming second wife and her son Frederick in order to welcome his long-lost grandson to the Hall. At that point it had been made clear to Mona, Celine and Gerda that their days of living off the land were over.

Celine was not a pretty picture. Her dark hair could have done with a wash, discontent ruled her expression, and her somewhat clumsy body was clad in a black sweatshirt with a food stain on it, and jeans. Also, the blueish lipstick she'd chosen was all wrong for her complexion.

Bea tried to sound humble. 'I apologize for intruding. Julian invited me down for a few days. I heard you were living in the village while the Hall is uninhabitable, but . . . you've heard what happened to him this morning?'

A tiny smile of satisfaction. 'Thrown from his horse? The horse should have tried harder.'

Bea ignored that. 'A dreadful accident. Most upsetting. What do you think about Dora being found dead in the stables? You must have known her.'

'Dora? By sight, yes, of course. She worked at the Hall when she was young but left under a cloud, overstepped the mark with Frederick. Silly girl. As if that could ever come to anything. Went to work in a pub in London, didn't she? I really don't know why she ever came back. And look what happened!'

Bea said, 'I heard that—'

Celine threw the door wide. 'You might as well come in. I'm all on my own. Mona's out, of course. Her new man's very demanding. As for Gerda, she's over at the rescue centre with her friends as usual. Anyway, the television's better company than she is.'

So Celine was feeling lonely? Bea stepped inside the square, panelled hall. It was warm and there were some pleasant watercolours on the walls.

Bea said, 'It's getting cold outside. I hear Mona intends to settle down and run the farm shop here.'

'Well, yes and no. She will if she doesn't get a better offer. Come on through.' Celine led the way into a sitting room, also panelled. Here were pieces of heavy, old furniture of the kind built to last. Cretonne curtains. On a low coffee table was an empty coffee mug, a glass half full of wine, and a laptop which was open and running. The screen showed it was paused on an old film.

Celine plumped herself down on an outsize armchair and indicated that Bea took a seat, too. She said, 'Mona's been thinking about running the farm shop through a website that supplies everything they need, but she's got other irons in the fire. Her latest wants her to move in with him. He's ancient, but she says he's still "gagging" for it. How she can bear to have him paw all over her, I don't know. 'Well, I do know of course. He's got money, that's what. She's out with him now. Chauffeur-driven limo, manservant on tap, penthouse in the Barbican, doesn't use hotels because he owns property all round the world. I tell her, it won't last. He'll insist on a pre-nup and then they'll divorce and she'll get nothing. But she says he fancies living at the Hall so maybe it'll stick. Money isn't everything, you know.'

That was jealousy speaking, wasn't it?

Bea said, 'No, indeed.'

Celine turned the laptop off. 'I can't offer you anything to drink. That's the last of the booze.'

Bea said, 'It's lovely and warm in here. I suppose this house must seem rather poky after the Hall, but at least you have electricity and water. The Hall's in pieces. Have you been up there recently?'

'I did try one day last week, but that . . . that viper, Maggs! Stopped me from going up to my own room! I can't find my black silk scarf anywhere and thought I might have left it there, but she said, no, everything's been packed up and sent on, and I'd probably lost it. The nerve of the woman! She'd never have been allowed to set foot outside the kitchen in the old days. She's just a jumped-up scullery maid, giving herself airs.'

'You say Dora got the sack for flirting with your father?'

'There was a rumour; someone said my father fancied her at one time! Honestly! As if he would!'

'But you were away at boarding school then?'

'Of course. And we didn't mix with the local children in the holidays. Naturally. Craig was the worst. Dora let him do what he liked because she was busy working at the pub, getting her kicks from holiday-makers and the like. Then one day she took him off up to London and good riddance.'

'She only came back recently?'

'Turned up again like a bad penny, without Craig. Said he was working somewhere abroad. She'd rented her cottage out to this man who used to work in the amusement park, so she moved in with him. That's like her. Paid her way with you know what.'

'And then she died and Craig returned?'

'I hear he's shooting his mouth off, saying he's the true heir and is going to move into the Hall. Don't get me wrong; I've no love for this Julian that's been foisted on us, but Craig . . . save the mark!'

'What do you think of Craig now he's grown up?'

A shrug. 'He used to try to catch me alone behind the stables or in the barn. He's a bit creepy, know what I mean? He's dyed his hair, thinks he looks fab. He says he's earning a fortune with his designs for living, but I doubt it. I think he works the passing trade, like his mother.'

Bea said, 'Who do you think killed her?'

'Well, some say it's Julian because she was supposed to be blackmailing him over being the heir, but it doesn't seem likely to me. Julian's quite ruthless, of course, throwing us all out of the Hall, and so mean, refusing to buy me a car, though he lets Mona use that old SUV, which is pretty clapped out. But . . . I dunno. I suppose he's right about closing down the Hall to fix the roof and the electrics and that. And, what was going on at the restaurant and the farm shop, you wouldn't want to know! Also, it's going to take money to rebuild the rides at the amusement park. You wouldn't catch me going on any of them. Total suicide, what! My father had big ideas, but he wasn't great on detail.'

That was putting it mildly!

Bea said, 'I heard somebody saw Julian with Dora. Who was that, do you know?'

A shrug. 'I don't get it. I mean, Julian's besotted with that wife of his, Polly or Paula or whatever her name is. Dora wasn't his type, not to mention she was old enough to be his mother. It would be convenient for the rest of us if he had killed her, but I can't get my head around it. You only had to look at Dora to see what she was.'

'What happened to her, do you think?'

'She'd have picked up some low-life who was passing through and stopped at the pub for a quick half. Or she could have been having a tussle with one of those young louts that hang around the pub. No jobs, no-hopers. Scum they are, and she'd gravitate to them, wouldn't she? I expect she was playing fast and loose and tried it on with the wrong person. He lost his temper and strangled her.'

'But why would she meet him in the stables at the Hall?'

'It would be like her to arrange to meet someone up at the Hall,

cocking a snook at those who'd got money and gave her the old
heave-ho all those years ago. She had some nerve, that one. And
don't ask me to pretend to be sorry about her death because, to be
honest, she probably deserved what she got.'

'I do understand.' Bea looked around. She really did sympathize
with the girl, brought up to believe she was a princess, only to be
reduced to the role of poor relation. She said, 'These are very pleasant
quarters, but it must be hard to have to leave your home at the Hall.
Have you any idea what you are going to do with yourself?'

'Oh, that.' Celine preened, sitting up straighter. 'I'm writing a
bestseller, and it's going to make me famous.' She indicated an
untidy stack of paper, crisscrossed with notes and diagrams in
different-coloured inks.

'Really? Tell me.'

'It's a stunner. I've been taking an online creative writing work-
shop and they tell me that I have a real talent. I've been working
on my plot for over a week now, and it's really coming together.
It's about a beautiful girl with a lovely nature, who's been brought
up in a mansion by her multi-millionaire father, only to be cruelly
turned out without a penny when he's shot by the Mafia and—'

'The Mafia?' Bea murmured, trying to keep up.

'Of course, the Mafia. She finds some buried treasure, but the
wicked cousin who ought to have looked after her interest has forged
papers to make it seem he's the heir to everything, whereas really
he's illegitimate but he's not all bad. You understand that nowadays
you have to make the villains believable, so you give them a background which explains why they're like that. Some people on the
course say I should make him turn out to be the one who shot her
father, and I'm thinking about that. I'm really not sure. What do
you think?'

'I don't know,' said Bea, feeling rather faint. Mafia? Buried
treasure? Forgery? Could such a plot possibly work? Well, it might,
for a certain readership but . . . could Celine write well enough to
sell such a plot? 'Go on.'

'I mustn't give away everything that happens, must I?'

'No, indeed,' said Bea, somewhat stunned. 'I assume everything
ends happily for the girl?'

'Yes, of course. And there's going to be lots and lots of sex.
You're probably too old to enjoy books with sex in nowadays, but
I'm told it sells.'

Bea swallowed a sharp retort. Actually, the girl was probably right, although she and Piers still liked to . . . Don't think about that now or you'll get overheated. No, on second thoughts, Bea wasn't at all sure Celine knew what she was talking about. She was far too buttoned up to be having sex on a regular basis . . . if at all! Was she, perhaps, incredibly, still a virgin?

Bea said, 'You have a contract with a publisher?'

'No, no. You're way out of date, aren't you? Nowadays everyone self-publishes. That way I keep all the money from the sales. It'll be the book everyone will want to read, and then I'll be out of this miserable house, sunning myself on a Greek island, and writing when I feel like it.'

Do I warn her it's not that easy? Has she any talent? Has she the work ethic? Oh, dear.

Bea said, 'I wish you well. Now, tell me—'

Someone leant on the doorbell. Celine started. 'Who's that? I'm not expecting anyone.' She heaved herself out of her chair, saying, 'I won't be a moment.' The door swung shut as she left but Bea could hear her speak to whoever was on the doorstep. 'What do you want?'

And the smarmy tones of Craig, replying. 'All alone, cousin? Won't you invite me in?' Was he drunk?

'No, I—'

The front door shut on Celine's protest.

Bea sat up straight. What was happening?

There was the sound of a tussle in the hallway.

'Oh, come on, now!' Craig's voice. 'I know how much you've always fancied me. We couldn't do nothing about it years ago when we were young, you being all posh and supposed to be making a match with a Hooray Henry. Not like your sister, were you? I mean, she knew how get her kicks even when she was in her school uniform. But not you. No, you were the one who looked but didn't do anything about it, right?'

'No, that's not . . .! Craig, please! Go.'

'But everything's different now, isn't it? I'm not just Dora's son, but the rightful owner of the Hall, with power to decide what happens to you and your slag of a sister. So let's pick up where—'

A confusion of sounds, ending with a squawk from Celine, cut short with a long moment of silence. And then Craig laughed. 'That's just for starters!'

Celine said, 'How dare—!'

The protest was swiftly muffled.

Bea strode to the door and tried to throw it open. It didn't shift. Not one bit. Now what?

'Come on, now, girl. It's time we got together, right? I mean, you and I, together? Cousins living at the Hall? You'd like that, wouldn't you? You, lady of the manor, with the title and all. And your tart of a sister can go hang, right?'

Bea banged on the door. It was a solid door. She tried the handle again, It still didn't shift.

'No, Craig! No! Get off me!'

'Come on, now. What have you got to lose? Except, possibly, your virginity, though I'm finding it hard to believe that you haven't . . .' A slightly tipsy laugh. 'Go on! Don't tell me you're still a virgin! Well, well. You've always been a right little tight-arse, butter wouldn't melt and all that. I know your kind. You want it, really. Now don't you try pushing me away. I've got you tight, and I'm not letting go.'

'No, Craig. You've got the wrong—'

'Come on! Come on!' Heavy breathing.

'No!' Celine screamed, and Bea tried the windows. Sash windows, well made. Not been opened in years. They didn't shift, no matter how much force she exerted.

There was the sound of a slap . . . from Celine? Followed by a thud which meant Craig had retaliated.

Then his voice, 'I see I'm going to have to teach you some manners, my girl. You're not in any position to turn me down, and if you scream again, I'll make you sorry for it.'

Bea decided she'd have to smash a window . . . but with what? There was no helpful poker and shovel set at the side of the fire-place. Could she lift one of the chairs? She tried. No, she couldn't.

Celine was reduced to pleading. 'My sister will be back—'

'She's been collected by that little runt in his chauffeur-driven car. I saw them go. And your prissy sister-in-law is off making love to the animals, so let's have you in a better position to—'

Back to the door. Frustrated, she shook the handle and the door opened . . . towards her! Into the room! Not out. How embarrassing. She threw the door wide open and said, 'Oh. Am I interrupting something?'

Craig had Celine in a clinch. He'd pulled her sweatshirt up to show her bra and her jeans were around her knees. She was trying desperately to hold him at arm's length, and failing. Her jaw was already looking puffy where he'd hit her, and her eyes were wild.

Craig's jeans were also round his knees. The scent of alcohol hung over them.

At first he didn't recognize Bea and, when he did, he couldn't work out if she were a threat or not. But he did relax his hold on Celine, who sank to the floor at his feet, sobbing convulsively.

Bea said, 'Out! Now!' She held up her smartphone. 'Or I ring the police.'

'You and who else!' The jeer was half-hearted. He'd thought Celine was alone. He'd been drinking to give himself Dutch courage. Perhaps she might have sent him an interested glance or two in the past, but she wasn't anxious to take matters any further now, was she?

Bea raised her eyebrows at Craig. 'Which is it to be? Police? I'll happily testify to hearing you trying to rape Celine, or—'

'Stupid cow! She was begging for it!' He zipped up his jeans and slammed his way out of the house.

SEVEN

B ea felt somewhat limp. She wanted to join Celine on the floor
and wail. But she couldn't do that. She said, 'Celine! Listen
to me! Do you want to press charges?'

The damp squib on the floor stilled her sobs for a moment.
Thinking about it. She gulped air, then said, 'No.' She even pushed
herself up into a seated position. 'No, I don't. He'd tell everyone
that I . . . no. No police.'

Did she mean it? She did now, but tomorrow morning it might
be a different matter. Bea pulled the girl up on to her feet, and
helped her refasten her jeans.

Bea said, 'You must tell, or he'll try again when I'm not around.'

'No! I couldn't bear people thinking that I encouraged him!'

'He hit you,' said Bea. 'Get him for assault.'

'He'd say I liked it! Oh, no! What do I look like!'

Bea would very much liked to have walked out, but accepted that
she couldn't leave the girl in such a state. 'Cold water?' she said.
And, 'Arnica for the bruise?'

Celine flapped her hand, leading the way to a large, somewhat
old-fashioned kitchen. Bea picked up a clean tea towel, ran the cold
tap and got it wet. She wrung the towel out and applied it to Celine's
swelling cheek. 'Arnica? Aspirin? Tea?'

Celine responded by bursting into tears again. Most helpful.

Bea opened various cupboards. Someone was into vegetarian
food. Not much evidence of cooking. The freezer was well stocked
with ready meals.

Bea put the kettle on, while Celine wept.

Bea said, 'If you like, I'll come with you to the police station to
tell them what I saw and heard. Then he can't pretend you were
asking for it.'

Celine shook her head.

Bea considered the usual remedies for shock: sweetened tea or a snifter. Celine had said there was no more booze in the house but that might have been a lie.

No, no booze. Three empty bottles in the dustbin.

Bea made a mug of tea with plenty of sugar in it, and dumped it on the table in front of Celine, who sat, or rather, crouched, giving the appearance of one who'd pass out if shouted at.

Celine sipped tea. At least her tears had ceased to flow. 'If he's going to inherit everything . . . You must see . . .'

'I heard him hint that he'd marry you, and make you Lady Celine.'

Celine shuddered. 'As if I ever thought of him that way! It's just too horrid to think about.'

Bea thought that Celine might indeed have cast eyes on Craig when she was a teen but she was not going to admit it now. Her behaviour, in fact, was typical of an unloved, unattractive girl who'd never been noticed by boys, and who suffered by comparison with a sister who was a honeypot for the male sex. Celine was probably still a virgin, afraid of and yet attracted to the idea of sex. The plot of her novel underlined that. Poor little rich girl, innocent but dreaming of wild sex.

Celine emptied her mug, and set it back on the table. She straightened her back. 'I could get him to give me a nice pot of money in exchange for not pressing charges. Or . . . my tutor says we have to use our own experiences in order to draw the reader into our story. I could use what's happened, what I felt, what he did . . . it would be quite powerful, wouldn't it?'

Bea absorbed that. Perhaps Celine really did have the makings of a bestseller writer?

Celine tried out this new scenario, 'I could make my readers feel my fear and smell his smell. I'll put what he did into a book under an assumed name and I'll tell him that unless he promises to respect me in future, I'll let everyone know who it was. And if he succeeds in getting Julian out and getting back to the Hall why, we'll talk on equal terms. Right?'

Bea told herself she should never be surprised by what greed could do to someone. What could she say but, 'I stand by my offer to go with you to the police.'

Celine went to the sink to renew her cold compress. 'I want to start writing, now it's all fresh in my mind. The only thing is Mona's out tonight and so is Gerda. What if Craig comes back?'

'You lock the door and don't let him in. Keep your phone handy and ring the police if he tries anything.'

Celine tried for pathos. 'You could stay with me?'

'No, I have to get back to look after Bruno. Surely there's someone you can ring to sit with you?'

'I've no real friends around here. I don't go slumming to the pub. I know Mona did, but she's . . . well, she's different. If he'd tried it on with her, she'd have knocked him to the ground, and kicked his head in. I wish I'd kicked his head in. Or not his head, but . . . Not that I could, really. But I wish I were the sort of person who could. But . . . No, I know what I'll do.'

Celine had thought of something, or somebody who could help her? Yes, she had. She stood up, saying, like a nicely brought-up girl, 'Thank you for calling. I'll be all right now.' She led the way to the hall and opened the front door to let Bea out.

Celine was going to phone someone for help the moment Bea left?

Well, that absolved Bea from worrying about her. Bea zipped up her jacket and left. She collected her car from the pub, and drove back to the Hall in the dusk, thinking the days were getting longer all the time. She let herself into the living room at the end of the barn and was greeted by a Bruno who had clearly been getting anxious at being abandoned by everyone.

He'd need a run before bedtime, wouldn't he? Well, why not take him out for a short walk around the place now? The sky was darkening into what Bea thought of as 'gloaming'. Or perhaps the right word would be 'glooming'?

'Off we go,' said Bea, leading him out.

Bruno stepped out at her side, ears pricked, nose quivering. Bea wondered what he could see and hear that she could not? He was uneasy, looking down the courtyard to . . . what? Shadows were lengthening, softening the outline of buildings.

It was very quiet. Not just country quiet. This was a waiting-and-watching quiet.

She said, 'Bruno?'

As if he'd been waiting for her to give him an order, he nosed forward, following a scent that only he could detect. He led her past the gaping entrance to the middle of the barn, and on. He paused once, looking back to make sure she was following him.

He led the way into the stable yard and stopped, stiffening. Pointing.

There were no lights on in the stable yard, but some movement in the shadows. Horses, in their boxes, putting their heads out over the half-doors, to see who had intruded into their world. There was no sign of Mickey. No lights in the box which he had made his own.

Bea counted: one, two horses. Both elderly.

Bruno looked up at her, and led her to the third box. No head poked out to see if a visitor might be good for a carrot or two. The bottom half door was closed. Bruno sat, waiting for her to get the message.

She said, 'I'm not good at foreign languages, Bruno.'

He shot her a look of sheer irritation. He wasn't moving till she'd done whatever it was he thought she ought to do.

She sighed. She did. Not. Want. To. Look.

On the other hand, Bruno was going to wait her out.

She needed a torch. And surely there should be lights? Hadn't Julian said he'd been installing a security lights system? He'd been going to check on it, hadn't he? Now, if there was a switch somewhere . . .? She didn't know where that switch might be. She must retrace her steps to the box Mickey had made his own and see if he had a torch she could borrow.

Before she could move there was a flash, and lights sprang to life all over the stable yard. They must be on a time switch and triggered by her moving down the yard?

She stepped up to the half-closed third door and peered within. A horse was lying down inside. Jack, by the look of him. Horses lie down to die, don't they? She called his name but he didn't stir. Was she going to have to go in and touch him to make sure? Would she even know if he were dead, even if she did touch him?

Julian was going to be heartbroken if what she suspected was true. She sought for her phone in the pocket of her jacket. She must ring him and break the news.

No, not yet. She couldn't be sure, she didn't know how to make sure . . . and, where was Mickey?

Bruno would know if Mickey were still around.

Bruno was now on his feet, head lowered, looking back the way they'd come. He was growling softly. Because he'd smelled death? Or was someone else lurking in the shadows?

She said, 'Where's Mickey, Bruno? Can we find him? Does he sleep here or back in the village?'

Bruno led her back to Mickey's quarters. The doors, both top and bottom, were shut.

Had they been shut a few minutes ago when she'd walked past them to Jack's stable? She couldn't remember. She didn't like the thought that someone had shut them during the few minutes it had taken her to walk down the row of boxes and back again.

Bea thought of her car, parked outside the barn. She wanted to get into it and flee back to London. And knew she couldn't.

She told herself that if Bruno were not in a state of fear, then she had no reason to be so, either.

Bruno gave a sharp bark, requesting whoever was in Mickey's box to let him in. Nothing happened.

Bea called out, 'Mickey, are you there?' She heard her voice quaver and tried again. 'Mickey, one of your horses is in trouble.'

Nothing. A listening stillness.

Mickey was hiding? In a panic? Or . . . might he be dead?

Bruno sniffed at the door, and sneezed.

Could the doors be opened from the inside? Um, no. Horses couldn't open and close doors, could they?

Use your common sense, girl!

Bea was way out of her comfort zone. Give her a teenager on an e-scooter trying to rob passers-by of their phones, and she knew exactly what to do. But horses? She'd never been so close to one before in her whole life.

She told Bruno to stand aside, and investigated. The lighting in the yard was not wonderful. All she could think of was the tune that went: 'By the light, Of the silvery moon, I'll sit and croon . . .' which didn't help at all. She thought she could see . . . yes. This bolt went this away and that bit went that away and . . . Bingo, she pulled at the top door and nearly knocked herself over backwards.

Into the gap leaped Bruno, landing on the far side to a flurry of sounds and a voice gasping something unintelligible.

So Mickey was there? Hiding? Was Bruno going to attack him?

Bea, struggling with the bottom door, said, 'Bruno, heel. Don't hurt him.'

She got the lower door open, and light flooded in. Well, didn't flood, exactly. It was more like switching on a low-level torch. It helped but didn't make things particularly clear.

But at least she could make out that Mickey was on the floor, with Bruno standing over him. Bruno wasn't going to hurt Mickey, but he was going to make sure he didn't move, either.

Bea, in her flustered state, had a feeling she ought to sit down before she fell down. And she wouldn't object to a brandy, either. A large one. Or even the half-glass of wine that Celine had been drinking earlier.

Lacking anyone else's helping arm, she staggered to the saddle-horse, chucked Julian's saddle off it, and took a seat. Only then did she say, 'Good dog, Bruno. Well done. Now, let the man get up.'

Bruno looked up at her to see if she really meant it. Apparently she did, so he removed himself to one side and sat on his haunches, waiting to see what was going to happen next.

What happened next was that Mickey curled himself into a ball, crying, 'Don't hurt me!'

As if she would. Well, actually, she did rather feel like kicking some sense into him, but refrained. The miserable little man was in a bad way, now shuffling himself backwards out of the light and into a corner.

Someone had bolted Mickey into his bolt-hole while they did . . . something . . . to Jack? And after they'd done something to Jack, they'd gone away and left Mickey imprisoned in his box.

Bruno stiffened. He turned his head to the entrance and gave a single bark. A warning bark. An intruder?

A flurry of movement, and Mickey sprang to his feet and was up the ladder into the dark void above.

Bea decided that there was no way she was going to climb that ladder after him. Not in those boots.

How annoying! Bea forced herself to her feet and made for the doorway. Bruno accompanied her. He looked up at her, looked out of the stables towards the house and looked back at her. Had she got the message?

She had. Someone was lurking out there. No one else was meant to be at the Hall tonight.

Bea wanted to shut herself into the horse box and dial the police for help.

She looked around for something she could use as a weapon. A golf club would be handy. No golf club. A riding whip? What on earth would she do with a riding whip?

The lights in the yard went out.

A scream rose in her throat. She stifled it.

She tried to work it out. The lights were on a time switch. Once a certain hour of the night had been reached, they were triggered by movement in the yard. They'd gone off now because she'd disappeared into Mickey's box. Would they come on again if she stepped outside?

She did not, definitely did not want to step outside. No way.

Bruno moved restlessly at her side. She felt for his collar and found it. He moved closer to her, so that she could feel his smooth coat touching her leg. He sniffed the air, and pulled her forward out into the yard. He could see and wanted to explore whoever was out there . . . Someone who would be up to no good. They – whoever they were – would be waiting out there in the dark to clobber anyone who rounded the corner of the yard and went towards the house.

She didn't know what to do. The lights didn't come on again.

Which meant that whoever it was who'd been out there was long gone . . . or had turned off the switch so that any move she made would not register?

Bruno reached the end of the stable yard, taking her with him, and turned left toward the barn.

The lights came on again. Yes, they were on a switch which responded to movement after dark. The sudden brightness made her bring her arm up to shield her eyes. She stepped out alongside Bruno, who kindly adapted his pace to hers.

Shadows loomed in every direction.

They passed the gaping hole of the entrance to the centre of the barn. And on . . . Bruno was anxious, nervous, wanting to be free of her hand on his collar, wanting to chase whoever was out there . . . somewhere . . . in the shadow of the back door to the Hall, perhaps?

Bruno didn't look at the Hall, but went straight for his master's new living quarters. The windows there were all dark, which must have informed the intruder that no one was home.

Bea told herself she ought to be grateful for that. Suppose the man – or whoever it was – had happened to come across Polly carrying the boy into the house, all by herself? It didn't bear thinking about.

So she thought about it.

They reached the front door to Julian's quarters and Bruno lost interest in going inside, but nosed around the doorstep. Why?

Uh-oh! She could just about make out that a package had been left there, one with a strong, meaty scent to it. It hadn't been there earlier.

Bea grabbed at Bruno's collar. 'No, Bruno! No!'

He whined a protest.

'Sit!'

He sat, but kept his eyes on the delectable treat which had been left for him.

Bea felt her knees wobble, but managed to get the front door open, locate the switch inside and turn the light on. Forcing herself to be brave, she peered out into the yard from the doorway. Nothing moved. She dragged a reluctant Bruno inside, and slammed the door. And locked it. Leaving the parcel outside.

No, that was no good. She needed the parcel. It was evidence. She did not want to open the door again, in case someone pounced on her but, yes, she would have to do so if she wanted to get the parcel.

She remembered that losing his horse and dog, on top of everything else, had caused Julian the First to leave the Hall for good. Was the same thing happening now? Julian's horse, Jack, was lying motionless in his box, and someone had just left a tempting meal for Bruno to eat.

Thankfully, Julian had been training Bruno not to eat until given permission to do so.

Bea got some rubber gloves from the kitchen and opened the door just enough to retrieve that tempting bundle which smelled so delectably of raw meat. She closed and double-locked the front door. Bruno followed her every move, drooling. Bruno was restraining himself but he couldn't understand why she wasn't letting him have the tasty present which someone had so kindly left for him. She double-wrapped the package in a large plastic bag and shoved it in the freezer. The rubber gloves she put into a plastic bag and disposed of them in the same way.

It was possible, of course, that the 'present' was harmless. But the odds were not likely. She checked the windows, deploring the lack of curtains.

She gave Bruno some more food from a tin. She considered the possibility that someone could have entered the living room while she was out and substituted something poisonous for the food Polly had left behind for her and the dog.

But no. The meat had been left on the doorstep, which argued the intruder hadn't actually set foot inside, and the food she'd given Bruno had come from unopened tins.

Was it Craig? Had he had time enough to prepare and leave a tasty meal for Bruno? Probably not. Now there's a puzzle. Who'd dunnit?

She should ring the cops. She lifted the receiver and dialled 999. Which service did she want? Police.

Name, please. Address, please. Nature of problem.

She gave her name. And the address of the tithe barn . . . which didn't seem to ring any bells at the other end of the line. Her problem was of small importance, she realized that. Mickey had been shut into his own quarters; he'd been scared, not hurt. The dog had not eaten the dicey meat in the parcel. She hadn't caught sight of any interlopers. Honestly, it was small beer, not to be compared to the mayhem that was probably going on in sundry places around town centres. Late-night brawls outside pubs. Gangs clashing over disputed territory. Knife crime. Drug pushers wreaking havoc.

The voice on the other end of the phone said someone would be in touch in due course.

What had she expected? Police cars with sirens blaring, arriving from all directions to disgorge armed officers who would surround the place, demanding through loudhailers that the miscreants – whoever they were – should come out and give themselves up.

It was not going to happen, was it?

Meanwhile, Bruno had polished off his supper and happily settled down in his basket for a nap. He was telling her, without words, that the coast was clear, the danger over, and she could help herself to food, switch on the telly, and settle down to enjoy the rest of the night.

And ring Piers? No, he'd been going out for the evening, hadn't he?

Her smartphone rang.

It was Polly. 'How are you doing? I've been chatting to Julian, poor lamb. He's still got a headache but they won't give him anything for it, because of his concussion. Hopefully they'll let him go tomorrow. He's putting a good face on it, of course. He always does. He says it would be an extra worry for him if I came back now, and if I can get Dad sorted, then that'll be one problem solved. I suppose he's right, though how I'm going to . . . But you don't need to know all that.'

'How is your father?'

'Appalling. Rude to everyone. Says the manageress at the rest home is a homicidal maniac, and the doctor who visits is a quack paid by the Chinese to try out various drugs. In reality, he's at a loose end for the first time in his life, with nothing to do and no one to boss about. He says he'll recover when he can be looked after by me with his own quarters at the Hall. Which is not going to happen. How are you coping? Have you enough food, and is Bruno all right?'

She'll be asking after Jack next. Diversion needed.

'Bruno's fine, I've just come back from giving him a run and he's in his basket. Tell you what, though. I called in on Celine in the village, and interrupted Craig trying to get his leg over her. She refused to press charges.'

'Oh, no! Oh, that's horrible!'

'Yes, it is. I feel guilty. I ought to have stayed with her but there was Bruno to think of and she bobbed up all of a sudden and said she'd be all right. I got the impression that she'd someone in mind to look after her, so—'

'She probably yanked Mona's chain. Celine acts hard done by, but usually gets someone to look after her.'

'Did you know she's planning to be a bestseller writer?'

'Celine? Really? Can she even spell? I mean . . . *really*?'

'Yes, really. Her heroine is young and beautiful and is turned out of her stately home when her father is killed by the Mafia—'

'The Mafia!'

'And then there's some buried treasure and . . . Sorry, Polly, I can't remember the rest. Except that there's going to be lots and lots of sex.'

Stunned silence from Polly. Then she giggled. And so did Bea.

'Sorry!' gasped Polly. 'But I've always thought Celine was—'

'Yes,' said Bea. 'I think she probably is still a virgin. I'm sorry for her, really I am. Oh dear! We shouldn't laugh.'

Polly blew her nose. 'I can't wait to tell Julian. Is she going to describe the Hall in her book? Would that be actionable? There is some mention in the guidebook, some rumour about treasure being buried at the Hall. No details, naturally. Well, that's given me something else to think about. Goodnight, Bea. And thanks for looking after everything for us.'

Bea didn't know if she'd handled the phone call well or not.

Ought she to have told Polly everything? But then, the girl might think she ought to rush back home and, to be honest, what could she do to help?

Tomorrow Bea would do something. She didn't know what, but something. Definitely.

On the plus side, the archangel Rosemary would be arriving at some point, and hopefully Julian would take to her. And he'd be released from hospital tomorrow. *If* he were released from hospital. *If* the concussion cleared, or whatever concussion did. It would help if Piers were able to fly to her side, but that seemed to depend upon police action in another country.

Please, Lord? A spot of help, here? And look after Julian and Polly and . . . oh, everyone. You know who I mean. I'm too tired to go through the lot, name by name.

She got herself a hot drink, watched some cops-and-robber show without caring who shot who, and went up to bed.

Bruno went with her. There were no curtains upstairs, either, which ensured she didn't sleep well.

EIGHT

A nice sunny morning. Heavy-headed, Bea breakfasted on toast and coffee. That fish and chips she'd had in the pub last night had been a mistake, hadn't it?

She thought she'd heard a van draw up and park outside at some point. When she looked out, she saw that a couple of vehicles had arrived. No doubt they'd brought workmen to the Hall to do this and that.

She wondered what time they'd get news of Julian. The nurses got patients up early in hospital, but then they had to wait for doctors' rounds to learn if they were to be discharged or not.

Bruno was bright-eyed and anxious to get on with the day. She let him out into the yard while keeping an eye on him from the doorway. He stopped to nose into odd corners before pointing his nose in the direction of the stables. He didn't show any signs of distress, or interest in anything but enjoying a good romp.

Somewhat unwillingly, she pulled on her jacket – it was a chilly morning – and went after him.

The doors to Mickey's lair were open as well . . . and empty of humans. Where was Mickey? He'd been frightened and hidden from her the night before. Had he scarpered? And what did that mean? Who was to look after the other horses?

She noted that Jack's stable doors were open. There was no horse inside, dead or alive. No doubt Mickey had arranged for his body to be removed. Oh dear, oh dear. What a shame that such a beautiful horse should have been sacrificed for a family dispute.

She asked Bruno what he thought but he didn't seem interested. In fact, he seemed rather bored, if anything.

The two ancient horses had already been turned out into the paddock. Not Jack. No. Never again. She must break the news about Jack to Julian, if he were well enough to be discharged. But, how soon would that be?

Should she offer to collect him?

Worried and upset, she returned to the barn to find Mrs Maggs knocking on the door. 'Mrs Abbot? Oh, there you are. Is Sir Julian back yet? He's not? Oh. In that case, I think you ought to see what the electricians have found. They don't know what to do about it. It's holding them up, see.'

Bea chirruped to Bruno, who followed them back into the Hall. They went through to the main hall and up the stairs. Their footsteps echoed and shadows grew in the corners as clouds gathered overhead. Angry voices came from above. Two or three men, arguing?

Mrs Maggs closed her mouth like a trap and shook her head. 'You can't blame them. It puts their bonus at risk, see.'

She ushered Bea into what must surely be the master bedroom, currently occupied by three men who looked as if they'd take a swing at one another any minute.

Mrs Maggs raised her voice to gain their attention. 'This is Mrs Abbot, a businesswoman staying with Sir Julian. He's in hospital overnight, having his ankle fixed.'

'It's our bonus, see!' blustered the largest, who had the word 'Boss' written all over him.

A whine of a voice said, 'But it might well be worth—'

Expletives deleted from the boss.

Well, Bea had heard worse. She said, 'Gentlemen?' in an enquiring but steely tone. That calmed them down.

Boss Man had a high colour and a strident voice. 'Sir Julian promised us a bonus if we finished by the end of the month, and if this holds us up, then what happens to our money, eh? We're going to board it up again and say nothing!'

The other two shifted on their feet. One was a fine-boned, handsome young man, possibly from a Pakistani background. Neat of dress and probably a good workman but clearly not going to argue with Boss Man.

The third member of the team was older than the other two. His face was deeply lined, his shoulders stooped and his knees sagged. He had the look of a drinker and his hands were knotted with arthritis, but he had a row of pens and pencils adorning his breast pocket, and possibly knew more about electric installations than either of the others. His voice was a whine, which would make him the most disliked man on a building site, but also the one most likely to be right.

'All I'm saying is, we ought to have a look. They used to bury treasure in their hidey-holes, didn't they?'

A hidey-hole? Where? Bea looked around for the hole. They were in a large, panelled bedroom lit partly by daylight, but also by a large spotlight. Cabling snaked along the floor. An enormous four-poster bed, devoid of bedding and curtains but with a plastic sheet spread over its horsehair mattress, had been shifted some way from the wall. Bea thought it must have taken the combined efforts of all three to shift that bed. Tudor magnificence required that large amounts of timber were used in the framework.

Mrs Maggs gestured to the wall. 'They were scheduled to put power points in on either side of the bed but this gap had opened up between the skirting and the wall, so they tried nailing it back in place and it sounded hollow, so they pushed and pulled and this bit of panelling fell in and one of them nearly followed it and had to be hauled out backward.'

A section of the panelling about four foot high had fallen into nothingness or, rather, into a sort of cupboard which had been boarded up between this room and the next.

'It's a hidey-hole,' said Whiny. 'Frit the life out of me, it did. I've heard on such holes afore. They find skeletons and skulls and treasure in them, don't they? There's always been talk of treasure up here in the Hall, so we gotta have a look, right?'

The workmen had trained the spotlight into it, but it didn't help much. Bea switched on the light on her smartphone and ducked down to have a look. The air inside the hole didn't smell bad so there must be some kind of vent to the outside world. She was looking into a triangular space, wider towards the outside wall, and narrowing at her end. Crammed into this was a small prie-dieu, on which a man or a woman would once have knelt to pray, the remains of a rush mattress and an ancient wooden chest. Everything was grey with dust.

Given its position, it was . . .

'A priest hole?' said Bea. 'I've seen one before, but not this shape.'

'Told you!' said the whiny one. 'It's a hidey-hole. That chest there will be full of treasure.'

Bea tried to remember what she knew of priests' holes. In Tudor and early Stuart days, Catholics were persecuted and fined for practising their religion, and a visiting priest might well need a safe place in which to hide from those searching for him. Some of the priest holes were like pits; you dropped down into the space, and floorboards were fitted into place above you. Some were just big enough to hold a man. Others might accommodate several people.

She said, 'Were the Marston-Langs Catholic?'

'Dunno.'

'Afore my day.'

Bea said, 'It looks as though they might have been once. I suppose the family forgot about this place over time.'

Whiny said, 'What about that there chest, then? That's where they hid their treasure, innit? We should take a look, right?'

Boss Man firmed his jaw. 'Have a look, maybe. But we can't waste no more time on this. A quick look round, and we board the place up again.'

Bruno nosed past Bea and jumped into the cupboard. He turned round once, sniffed here and there, sneezed and leaped out again, making it clear that there was nothing in the hole to interest him.

Bea considered that the discovery of a priest hole in an old house would make news in certain quarters. Historical societies and tourists would flock to examine it, and it would be written up in learned journals . . . but not if treasure seekers were going to snuffle around looking for treasure first. She didn't trust the whiny one to keep his hands off that chest for one minute.

What to do? The ideal would be to keep the discovery a secret till the authorities had been informed and the contents removed to a safe place. How to do that? Difficult. The find could easily be kept a secret if only one person knew about it, but not if five did. In Bea's opinion, Whiny wasn't going to keep quiet about it any longer than it took to get his hands on a pint.

Bea looked at Mrs Maggs, who folded her arms and looked out of the window. Mrs Maggs didn't know what to do. Bea wasn't sure, either. If only Julian were here!

Bea gestured the workmen away from the gaping hole in the panelling. 'We need to think this through carefully. Yes, it's important that you complete the rewiring as soon as possible, but I think Sir Julian would take an unexpected delay like this into consideration when it comes to paying your bill.

'Finding a priest hole is going to add enormous value to the Hall as a tourist attraction, but news of its location and contents have to be handled with care. We can't have kids breaking into the place to look for buried treasure.'

Mumble, mumble from Whiny, but a reluctant nod from the boss man.

'First off,' said Bea, 'we photograph everything. There may well be some important family documents in that chest, though not rubies and diamonds, I fear.'

The third man gave Bea a look which told her he hadn't been born yesterday and could see what she was trying to do.

She said, 'Has anyone got some plastic gloves, so that we don't disturb anything while we take the photos? We mustn't touch or open the chest. We have to leave that for the experts. And then, mister . . . Sorry, I don't know your name?'

'I'm Lennie,' said Boss Man.

'Well, Lennie, let's you and I put our heads together. I'll ring Sir Julian and let him know what you've found as soon as he's able to take calls on his phone. He may not be able to come home straight away, so . . . How can we best make sure no one gets to hear about this until he can notify the right people? Mrs Maggs, do please feel free to come in on this.'

Whiny wasn't finished. 'First we look for treasure, right?'

Bea hesitated. She was pretty sure there wouldn't be any treasure, but suppose there was, and she didn't secure it in a safe place? And then someone stole it?

Third Man produced gloves, donned them and held up his phone, eyebrows raised. Should he do the photographing?

'No, you don't,' said Bea, handing over her own phone. 'Only one lot of photos gets taken now. Let me have your phone while you use mine.'

Third Man twitched a smile, understanding perfectly what she meant. He disappeared into the 'hole'. The camera flashed again and again.

A hollow-sounding voice came back to them. 'The chest's falling apart. One side's broken away. I can see some papers inside. That's all.' A pleasant voice. Education at a good comprehensive? Dust rose in a cloud and he started to cough.

Whiny just couldn't give up. 'But there's a coupla gold pieces, right? One for each of us?'

'Can't see any.'

There was a general sigh. Hopes dashed, and all that.

Third Man reappeared from the hidey-hole, returned Bea's phone and retrieved his own. He coughed again, and dusted himself down.

Bea said, 'We'll have to leave it to the experts to make sense of what's in there. Now, how can we secure the site?'

Lennie, the boss, reluctantly accepted the inevitable. 'We can bypass this room for the time being, I suppose. Fit the panelling in again. Push the bed back like we found it, and take the cables and the light out of here. We'll have to come back and do this room later.'

Bea said, 'Sir Julian will be most grateful to you all for making this important find for him. I'm sure you won't be the losers by it.'

Lennie's chest expanded as he began to realize the future might promise a bigger bonus. 'He treats us fair.'

Whiny muttered. 'What, not even one gold coin? On the telly, they get rewards for finding—'

Lennie turned on him. 'Idiot! It wouldn't belong to us, even if there were any treasure. And treasure there ain't.'

'Who you calling an idiot? I got every right to—'

Bea said hastily, 'You've got every right to bring up legitimate concerns. We have to keep this secret for the time being or we'll have tourists demanding entry and wrecking the place to find some non-existent hoard or other. This find is going to be big news and you're all going to be in the limelight. There'll be journalists around, wanting to know all the details. You might get to feature on the local telly. Might make the national news, even. We're all going to have to be extra careful what we say until we go on air.'

Whiny's mouth dropped open. It had taken some time for him to get the message, but finally the penny had dropped. He tapped his mouth. 'Understood. Over and out. Mum's the word.'

Bea didn't believe him for a minute, but didn't know what to do about it. She stepped outside the room to ring Julian, while keeping an eye on what was happening within. Had the doctors been on their rounds yet? Was his X-ray clear? Ring, ring. Ring, ring. Straight to voicemail.

Mrs Maggs had also got her phone out and, with her back turned, was happily giving orders to someone . . . hopefully not telling the world what they'd found. No, it was a very short call.

Meanwhile Third Man had got on with the job. Bea thought it would be a good idea to keep an eye on Third Man. He seemed to be the one who actually got things done, whereas the other two talked a lot but did nothing much.

Mrs Maggs returned to watch the workmen fitting everything back again. She said, 'This was the master's bedroom in the old days, until he moved out and left it to Lady Fleur. Her perfume took me a while to get rid of, I can tell you. Sir Florian moved to the other side of the house.'

Bea thought the workmen would probably know all that already. So Mrs Maggs was directing information at Bea?

Lennie directed operations. 'You take this side and I'll take that.' It took the combined forces of the three men plus Bea and Mrs Maggs to shift the old bed back where it had stood for centuries.

Panting, Bea propped herself against the wall. 'However, did you manage to get it away from the wall in the first place?'

'Teddy was here. He could almost shift it by himself. But he had to go to the dentist in town. He's a martyr to his teeth, is Teddy.'

Someone smothered a laugh. Who? Mrs Maggs and Third Man both had straight faces and avoided her eye. Bea knew all about people who left the job early because of toothache. It was one of the oldest excuses in the book. Very occasionally, it might be true. She asked, 'Was this Teddy here when you discovered the panel was loose?'

Lennie nodded. 'Ah. Maybe. But Teddy's all right. I'll tell him to keep quiet about it.'

Mrs Maggs intervened. 'Teddy's like that Samson that my gran used to go on about. A giant of a man, not very bright. His weak point is his teeth, not his hair. He says he's going to have a full set of new teeth, and then he'll be able to get a girl.'

Bea sighed. Teddy was clearly a bit of a dimwit. If Lennie told him not to talk about something, he'd probably obey, but the odds were he'd already told his dentist all about it.

Working together, they managed to remove the cables and the light, and shut the bedroom door. There was no key to the lock, so they did some more heaving to get a huge old chest in front of the door.

Bea stubbed her toe, and hoped her back wasn't going to go out of sync. Occasional floorboards were up along the landing, forming traps for the unwary.

Bruno paced up and down the passage, waiting for normal service to be resumed.

'Phew!' Lennie looked at his watch. 'Lunchtime! We're ten minutes late. We'll take it off the end of the day.'

He collected Whiny and made for the stairs.

Mrs Maggs stayed put. She seemed to be listening to something

above. 'Is that rats, again? Drat them. Someone had better check.'
She flicked a glance at Bea, saying, 'Want to have a look around?'

Bea realized this was an invitation she couldn't refuse. 'I'd be delighted.'

Third Man dumped his toolbox at the head of the stairs and looked at Mrs Maggs, eyebrows raised.

Mrs Maggs nodded. 'All right, Imran. Thank you. You take the dog and do the rounds upstairs and I'll do the rest. Lennie and his lot are not supposed to have been up top today but you know what they're like. They left a window banging to and fro last week and the rain got in.'

Third Man flicked his fingers and Bruno, who was clearly accustomed to doing this, joined him in heading for the next flight of stairs up.

Mrs Maggs opened the door to the next room along, considered the panelled wall which must form the other side of the hidey-hole, and pounded on it. It sounded dead.

Bea said, 'The carpenters doubled the thickness of the panelling on this side when they created the priest hole? Clever.'

They measured distances with their eyes. Mrs Maggs said, 'They took a bit out of this room and a bit out of the next, to make the hole. I've been in here hundreds of times and never seen it, but now, yes! Look, there's less space between the window and the wall than there should be. Same as next door, I suppose. You'd never know unless you measured it, and even then, you wouldn't be sure.'

Mrs Maggs skirted the void where a floorboard had been prised out and left leaning against the bedframe. She checked the windows were shut. She said, 'This was Frederick's room. Good riddance to bad rubbish.'

From above them came the bark of a dog. Bruno, enjoying himself.

Mrs Maggs said, 'I hate rats. Imran makes the rounds for me when he can.'

As Bea left the room with Mrs Maggs . . . Whoops! She just saved herself from tripping over an unevenly secured floorboard. Ouch! Julian's comments about the electricians' slipshod work came vividly to mind.

Mrs Maggs moved along the corridor, giving information over her shoulder. 'Imran's Pakistani parents came over nigh on thirty years ago, settled in nicely. Well thought of. Took over the village shop, busy from morning to night. Mind that gap.'

They avoided another mantrap and went into another bedroom.

Mrs Maggs said, 'Imran's been to university. In his family they bring up their children to look after their parents and not go looking for pots of gold at the end of the rainbow. He didn't get much name-calling when he was growing up, but it didn't help that he's probably cleverer than most of the village kids. He's a good workman, can turn his hand to anything, and is worth keeping. But there's not much in the way of jobs around here until the Hall reopens.'

Another room with windows on two sides. Were they at the end of the house here? This room contained dust-sheeted mounds of furniture but no bed. Had it been an upstairs sitting room? Windows were checked and banged shut.

Back the way they'd come and turn right. Or was it left? Bea was getting dizzy.

Mrs Maggs noticed Bea's confusion. 'The original house was built in the shape of an E for Queen Elizabeth I, with wings at either end. Under here is the gallery with all those Marston portraits in it. The wing at the other end houses the library. In between there's servants' quarters up top, this floor for the family to sleep in, and down below the entrance hall and some rooms that have got nothing in them but dust-sheeted furniture. Over the generations, there's been bits added on here and there. My kitchen quarters and sitting room are newish. You'll soon get used to it.'

She led the way into another room with a bare, skeletonized bed; this time with the framework of a canopy over it. Windows were checked and banged shut. 'Mona's room. Cracked window, broken mirror. Bit of a slut. Married once, lasted six months. Attracts men like flies. Thinks she's a cut above but doesn't change her undies every day which they do need, if you get my meaning. *And* leaves everything on the floor for someone else to pick up. She's going around telling everyone she's going to be the new farm shop manager.'

Mrs Maggs checked to see that Bea was listening and passed on. Another room, another canopied single bed, rather pretty. Different view of the park.

'Celine's room. Poor thing. Always in the shadow of her sister. I can't think what will become of her. She takes up this and that and then drops it. Poetry one minute, watercolour lessons the next, then pottery. I told her she must keep her art school messes in an outhouse which, to give her credit, she did. Can't get a man for love nor money. The men swarm around her sister but she never gets a look-in. Says she's above all that. Hunh!'

Bang the window open. Bang the window shut. 'Imran's taking any job he can get, not qualified as an electrician but he's picked up enough to pay his way without leaving the area.'

Another room. Small. No window. Used to be a powdering closet? Or was that a different century?

'Imran's parents want him to marry a cousin, but he's set on a girl who's working at the doctor's surgery in the next town.'

A right-hand turn and another room which had been adapted as a bathroom. Mrs Maggs tested taps, but there was no water yet. 'Next week, they say. Should all have been finished ten days ago. We have water and electricity in the kitchen area but nowhere else. Imran rides a motorbike, keeps it in the barn here. He's got a driver's licence.'

Bea understood that Mrs Maggs was giving out a great deal of information on which she could act or not, as she thought fit. Mrs Maggs was saying that the present situation had to be looked at not only in terms of what the older generation might like, but also what the future looked like for the youngsters.

On the ground floor, all the floorboards had been replaced, which made for a less perilous tour of the property. Dust sheets covered everything in sight.

Mrs Maggs burbled on. 'Old Sir Florian let everything go to pot. Worn down by that harpy of a wife of his. You wouldn't believe it if you hadn't heard her at it, but I did, and I was sorry for him. Next came his son, Julian the First as you might say. Poor lad. He gave everyone hope that the Hall would survive and continue to employ local people until he was eased out and that Frederick took over, egged on by his dear mama. We was all amazed Frederick's wife stuck him for so long, but there, she did get away without too many bruises and he never laid a finger on his daughters that I know of. His son Bertram took after his father, but without even as much brains as Frederick had. It's good riddance to bad rubbish for that lot.'

Mrs Maggs swept them through to the picture gallery, still talking.

Someone had been busy here. The floorboards shone with polish, the portraits had been dusted, and some blinds had been installed to filter the light in without causing damage.

'Lady Paula has taken responsibility for the gallery. She's done a good job, hasn't she? She's going to tackle the entrance hall next.'

Mrs Maggs led Bea through the hidden doorway into the passage that ran between the gallery and the rooms that fronted the house.

'So what with the old lot going, and times changing . . . who knows what will happen next? And now we have to decide what we're going to do in the future. You'll join me for a cuppa? I think Lennie's lot will have left by now.'

She opened the door into the kitchen, and stood aside to let Bea through.

Imran – Third Man – was already there, helping a middle-aged woman setting various dishes out on the table. There was a quiche, a Victoria sponge, some cheesecake, a plate of tiny sausage rolls and a selection of cheeses. The older woman ducked her head at Bea and departed.

In the corner, Bruno happily worked on a large bone.

Bea realized she'd been ambushed. She remembered the phone call Mrs Maggs had suddenly decided to make before they went on their tour of the Hall. That phone call had been to organize this meal, hadn't it? And all of Mrs Maggs's apparently aimless chatter had been designed to draw Bea into the troubled affairs of the Hall.

Bea told herself she could walk away, saying that this was none of her business. Or she could don an apron and get her hands dirty.

'Earl Grey or breakfast tea?' asked Mrs Maggs.

NINE

Thursday late lunch

Bea subsided into a seat. 'Breakfast tea, please.'
Curiosity ruled OK. Mrs Maggs plus Imran meant that they'd formed some sort of alliance, which was interesting. Bea started the ball rolling. 'You've been checking up on me? You know I run an employment agency?'

'There is that. Lady Paula told us you've also got a flair for sorting out difficult situations.'

Lady Paula – not 'Polly'. Yes, that's the way it's going to go. Polly has to lose her nickname and become Paula.

Bea eyed the food. 'Bribery and corruption. Who's responsible for this wonderful spread?'

'Kate from the village. I thought you might like to see what's available locally. She bakes pies every week for sale in the local shop. She has all her permits and certificates and whatnot. She's been trying out a whole range, thinking she might supply the farm shop when it reopens. Unfortunately Mona doesn't think they're good enough.'

Imran didn't speak, but helped Bea to a slice of quiche, which was delicious. Next came some cheesecake, followed by a chunk of Victoria sponge cake which had Bea rolling her eyes in enjoyment. 'Kate works by herself?'

This time it was Imran who replied. 'She's got a couple who want to work with her. There's her daughter, for instance, who works in an office in town. Hates it. Loves to cook, but there's no work for her locally. She's got a boyfriend, a local farmer, who wants to switch a field to veg, if he didn't have to waste money sending it up to town every day.'

Bea nodded. Imran had done his research, hadn't he?

Mrs Maggs took up the tale. 'There's my niece, too. Dab hand with pastry. Married a man that used to work in the amusement park till he got laid off. They're struggling to pay the rent, which I've been helping out with, but I don't know how much longer I can keep it up. Kylie's just about done with breastfeeding, so she'll be available for full-time work again soon. She's working at the pub now waitressing and that, but she could do with a steady job. As could he. And the kids are growing up with nothing to look forward to.'

Bea nodded. She'd registered the heavy-handed hint all right. She polished off a couple of tiny sausage rolls, which were tantalizingly good. She eyed the cheeses. 'Local produce, Imran?'

'Of course. Try a mouthful of each.'

Bea sampled and sighed with pleasure. She realized what this was all about, of course. Mona wanted to simplify her life by getting everything for the farm shop from a website, but the whole point of a farm shop was that goods were sourced locally and to the highest standards. Food ordered from a website couldn't compete.

Imran had been researching what could be done locally.

Bea accepted a second mug of tea strong enough to stand a spoon in, and tried to concentrate on business. She eyed the cheese. Could she manage another morsel? Yes, she could. If bribery and corruption were on the menu then she might as well enjoy it.

Bea said, 'I understand what you're trying to tell me. Before we go into details, let's look at the overall situation. As I understand it, Sir Julian has all the right ideas to relaunch the Hall and park, which will supply employment for many. He's short of capital because Frederick's emptied the bank account, so he's having to borrow to get essential work done.

'Closing down the Hall and all its activities was the right thing to do because the premises were not safe. Necessary rewiring and plumbing were well under way. Problems had arisen, but Julian, working all hours a day, had been dealing with them and the future was looking good.

'Let's set aside the discovery of the priest hole for the moment. That may well help with publicity for the Hall in the future, but it's irrelevant to the overall plan. Also irrelevant is Lady Paula's being whisked away to deal with her father.

'So let's go back a week. There was slow but carefully thought-out progress in all directions. The local community watched and waited, many of them feeling sore because they were out of work. But, on the whole, giving Julian a somewhat grudging vote of approval.

'Then everything changed. Sir Julian was shot at while out riding,

Dora was murdered, Sir Julian met with an accident that could have killed him, and Craig surfaced. These developments threaten the timetable for reopening the Hall . . . which is why you two decided to take matters into your own hands and invited me to sample your wares.'

Two nods. That was exactly what they had done.

Bea said, 'As I see it, there's three problems here: one is how to get the Hall ready in time for Easter; next is how to solve the murder and, last of all, how to deal with Craig.'

Imran said, 'Sir Julian didn't murder Dora. Why would he? They're saying in the village that she was trying to blackmail him, meeting him at night and all that. Well, I don't know who it was she was seen talking to the night she died, but it wasn't him. For a start, he wouldn't have met her in the stables like that. Why would he? If he'd met her and they'd argued and he'd pushed her and she'd fallen and hit her head . . . Yes, that I could just about believe. But he'd admit it, wouldn't he?

'Another thing: Bernie, the taxi driver, he told us in the pub what happened when Craig came up here, demanding to move in. Bernie told us that Sir Julian said he'd walk away from the Hall if it turned out that Craig is the real heir – and I believe him. I wouldn't work for Craig, either. Craig's got no feeling for the Hall, has he? He doesn't understand what it means to the people hereabout. What's more, he and his followers made my life hell as a child, and don't tell me he's changed, because that sort doesn't.'

Mrs Maggs said, 'I agree. I've watched Sir Julian and listened to what he says. Imran's right. Sir Julian judges as how things are right and wrong, and he cuts his coat according to his cloth. If Craig could prove he was the heir, Sir Julian would go back to London and his well-paid job and forget all about us.'

'We-e-ll,' said Imran. 'He's a soft touch. He might think it his duty to work for Craig if Craig turned out to be the real heir.'

'It wouldn't answer,' said Mrs Maggs. 'Craig would drag us all down into the gutter, and we'd all be worse off and the Hall would have to be sold anyway. Craig's a lazy, foul-mouthed, spiteful brat that I've known since he was a toddler snatching other kids' toys and that's what he's still trying to do – snatch other people's toys. Mark my words, there'll be tears before nightfall if he takes over.'

Bea said, 'You've both thought it all through, you've decided you need outside help, and you've decided I'm it. Well, I have my own business to run and my own family to care for, but I'll see what I can do.

'First: the Hall. I think that Sir Julian will kill himself if he's allowed to go on trying to manage everything. The paperwork! The permits, the meetings, the planning, the publicity! These things are time-consuming but necessary and he could do them all if there were more hours in the day. But there aren't, and he needs help. He and Lady Paula need someone to manage the day-to-day business of the estate, to keep their diaries straight and take care of this and that. Now, I'm arranging for someone I know to apply for the job. Hopefully she'll arrive tomorrow, driving her own mobile home so you don't need to find accommodation for her. Oh . . . just a minute.'

Her phone had buzzed. Another message from Piers. A short one. She listened to it and had to laugh.

Piers said, 'Bea, I'm held up here. The solicitor told me not to shift as his client will be released in a few hours. Apparently the police can't hold him without some further evidence that they hope will drop into their laps, so he'll be back and wanting to resume his sittings, probably while he instructs counsel to sue everybody in sight. It's amusing, in a way. Are you all right?'

Then, without waiting for a reply, 'I'll ring later.'

Bea switched off her phone and bent her mind to the problem before her, saying, 'Mrs Maggs, let's look at what's holding progress up. Those electricians are behindhand—'

'Don't talk to me about those lazy, thieving—'

Imran said, 'Lennie's cut the workforce so he doesn't have to share the bonus with so many people. Sir Julian's on to it, I know. He'll sort them out when he gets back from hospital. That Lance, the builder, now. He's first class and his men know what they're doing. Forget the brother. All talk, no substance that one. Sir Julian could switch to them, but the contracts would be the devil to sort out.'

'That's where my girl will come in,' said Bea. 'She cut her baby teeth on confusing contracts. Now, Mrs Maggs, you have to get all these rooms ready for Easter and there's no way you and Lady Paula can do it all by yourself. Can you get your niece and her friends up to help you?'

'Yes, but they'll need paying.'

Bea was silent. Julian was walking a tightrope, financially. He'd borrowed as much as he could to get the infrastructure working. Any more and the interest rates would cripple him. But if he didn't find some more money, he wouldn't open on time. Oh, if only Frederick hadn't emptied the bank accounts . . .!

She said, 'I'll speak to Sir Julian about that. Now, Imran; you know that you're wasted as a day labourer. You want to stick around these parts, so you're aiming to do what? Take over the farm shop or the restaurant?'

Imran produced a laptop, opened it, and turned it round so that Bea could see what information it contained. He scrolled up and up. He'd contacted all the farms around, asking who'd be prepared to provide what, at what price, and how often. There were names of local cooks and their menus. There was one file for possible advertising, and others for suggested delivery dates and costings. He'd done a good job.

Mrs Maggs said, 'He's been thinking what he could do with the farm shop for ages. He's been travelling around, doing deliveries for this farm and that, getting to know what's going on.'

Imran nodded. 'I could make the farm shop a must-see for tourists and local people alike.'

Bea said, 'I'll ask Sir Julian what he wants doing about it. Now, the main problem. How to keep Sir Julian alive.'

Neither of them wanted to think about that.

Mrs Maggs said, 'Oh, surely, it's not as bad as . . .?'

Bea said, 'Who killed Jack? Perhaps even more important: where's Mickey?'

Mrs Maggs and Imran consulted one another without words. Eventually Mrs Maggs said, 'Mickey came in here this morning first thing, said Jack had died overnight. He asked me to phone the people at the rescue centre to come and get his body. He said they'd arrange everything but he was due some holiday and he was off. I said he should stick around, but he got his knapsack and pumped up the tyres on his old bike and off he went.'

Imran said, 'Mrs Maggs told me about it when I arrived. She was upset, and so was I. Jack was quite something. So I went out to the stables, and the animal rescue centre people were there, and the van came and took the horse. I asked them why the horse had died, and they said it wasn't my problem. I couldn't argue with them. I mean, Jack was their horse, not his.'

Mrs Maggs said, 'We didn't think Sir Julian would have let Jack be taken off like that, without a vet seeing him and all. If only he hadn't fallen off his horse and hurt himself!'

Imran said, 'Then Lennie arrived, and the others. They wanted to start work so I went up with them. Then we found the priest hole and everything got out of hand. When's Sir Julian due back?'

Bea got out her phone and tried his number. It went to voicemail again. 'He's still at the hospital. He told Polly to stay down south.'

'And the police want to talk to him again.' Mrs Maggs was gloomy.

Bea straightened her shoulders. She thought of her comfortable life in town. It had been hard work building up the agency over the years, but lucrative. There was also the huge sums of money which Piers earned by his paintings. She thought of her agency and the staff there, which seemed to be managing very well without her. Yes, she was now in a place in which she could help others to solve crimes and catch criminals. And that is what she should do.

She said, 'Imran, what is your rate for a day's work? I am only a poor townie who doesn't know anything about the countryside. I need someone who can show me around and tell me what's what. I need help dealing with local people who may well talk to you, but not to me.'

Imran grinned. 'I'm an off-comer, too, even though I was born here. Do we fetch Sir Julian from the hospital today? Your car or his? Mm. Lady Paula took his good car and the one he's left himself with is on its last legs. We'll take yours.'

Bea had to agree that was only sensible. 'As I'm sure you've understood, he needs someone to guard his back. He wouldn't think of hiring anyone to do so of his own accord, but I'm hoping my office friend will help out . . . if only I can get Sir Julian to employ her. You see, it was no accident that Jack threw him. A teasel head had been put under his saddle to send the horse crazy.'

Mrs Maggs's mouth dropped open.

Imran shuddered. 'Who would do that? Mickey?'

Mrs Maggs shook her head. 'Mickey's not exactly all there, but he'd never hurt an animal.'

That chimed with what Bea thought. But, if not Mickey, then who? Someone who didn't care about animals? An image of Craig slid into her mind and stuck there. Would Craig be likely to do such a thing? Mm. Er, no. He wasn't exactly a country-dweller, was he? On the other hand, he had been brought up here, so . . .

Mickey must have his suspicions, but how to extract information from him when he'd gone AWOL?

Bea's smartphone rang. It was Julian. 'Morning, Bea. Hope you had a better night than I did. They woke me every hour to make sure I hadn't died on them. Doctor's rounds are due shortly, and then they'll tell me if I need an op or not. Hopefully not. I'm hoping to be released, in which case, can you collect me? How's things your end? What did the vet say about Jack? And I hope Bruno's not being too much of a nuisance.'

'Bruno's fine,' said Bea, mentally running through a list of what Julian ought to be told about and decided that most of it was not appropriate as of that very moment. And definitely not to mention Jack. 'And yes, there's the most astonishing thing. The electricians have uncovered a priest hole behind the bed in which Lady Fleur used to sleep!'

'What? A priest's . . .? Are you sure?'

'It's between her room and the next, but the way in is behind her bed. It's a triangular space, widening out towards the outside wall. Tall enough to stand up in, but not very wide. No window, but some ventilation. There's nothing in it except a prie-dieu, a rush mattress, and a wooden chest which is falling apart. The electricians thought there might be buried treasure—'

'Buried . . .? No way! I wish I could . . . But I'm stuck here until . . . Did my grandfather say something about the family being fined because they were Catholics in the reign of Elizabeth I? I remember! It's in the leaflet about the history of the Hall. Polly said it was very badly written and she was going to have a go at rewriting it herself, but we hadn't got round to it yet. Yes, I'm sure there was a rumour about buried treasure, but almost every building as old as this has the same, doesn't it? If it isn't buried treasure, it's ghosts.'

'It's good news. It will attract tourists.'

'We'll have to report it and then . . . restricted access . . . the tourists will be all over it. That will have to be handled with care or we'll have queues at the door wanting to take selfies in it. Who do we notify first? I'll ask Lance; he'll know. This is going to need careful handling.'

'I had the lot photographed and the room closed up again. I'll send you the pictures in a minute. I swore the electricians to silence but whether they'll keep quiet about it or not—'

'Lennie and co.? No, they'll sit on it till they get down to the pub. What's the time? I doubt if they'll let me out of here till . . . And Polly! I must tell her straight away. What an amazing thing!'

Bea tried to lighten up. 'I'm sorry there's no buried treasure. The electricians thought there must be at least a gold coin each. One of the men keeps going on about it but Lennie can only talk about it getting in the way of claiming a bonus you've promised them.'

'Ah. Yes. Lennie. My uncle Frederick gave him a contract to rewire the kitchen quarters, he quoted a decent price for the rest and his references were good, but he hasn't delivered. With hindsight, it would have been better to cut my losses and start over again with another firm. I've been meaning to have a word with him . . .'

His voice faded.

Bea said, 'You're being properly looked after? They've cleared you of concussion?'

'Yes, yes. I'm fine.' Clearly he wasn't fine, but wasn't going to admit it. 'What's the time? I can't think straight. Send me those pictures, will you?'

Bea recognized the tone of someone fighting a bad headache, and knew it was no good telling him to take it easy. She sent him the pictures and waited for him to comment. No comment. He clicked off, and so did she.

Mrs Maggs and Imran had both been following her conversation with Julian.

Mrs Maggs said, 'You didn't tell him about Jack.'

Bea grimaced. 'Would you have done?'

Imran said, 'He loved that horse, and he loves Bruno. If anything were to happen to that dog . . .'

'Yes,' said Bea. 'So we'd better see if we can get some answers for him while keeping an eye on Bruno, too. Imran, would you like to drive me to the rescue centre straight away? I want a look at their paperwork for Jack. They must have some from the people who took the carcass away. For a start, we need to know what killed Jack. And I'd like to find Mickey as well. Any idea where he could have gone? The rescue centre got him the job here, didn't they? So would he have gone back to them now?'

Mrs Maggs said, 'He's local, been around for years, taking a job here and there. Those who have the knack with horses, they tend to drift from one stables to another.'

Bea said, 'Mickey must have seen what happened to Jack. When I got there, I found he'd been shut in and I had a struggle to open the doors. When I did get them open, he hid from me. He lives in that end box, doesn't he? At the opposite end to the one in which Dora died? The security lights in the yard are working now, and are triggered by any movement. Were they working when Dora was killed?'

A frown from Mrs Maggs. 'I'm usually off by the time they're supposed to come on.'

Another frown, from Imran. 'We had a job getting them to work. They worked one day and the next, they didn't. No, I don't think they were working the night Dora was killed.'

Bea said, 'They were working last night. I went out for a bite of supper. I was out for some time and when I got back, they came on. Now if Mickey had spotted the lights come on, he'd have gone out to see what was happening, wouldn't he? And he'd have recognized the people who'd arrived, who presumably were there to deal with Jack.

'So either Mickey got shut in because he saw them, or to make sure he didn't see them. I don't think he killed Jack but he probably saw – or guessed – who did. This morning early he found Jack dead, asked Mrs Maggs to contact the rescue centre, jumped on his bike and fled. I suggest, Imran, that we go to the rescue centre and make a nuisance of ourselves.'

Mrs Maggs patted Bea's hand. 'You've got a head on you, haven't you? I'll wrap up some of the cake and the cheeses for you to take with you, in case you fancy a bite later on.'

From the paddock at the back of the barn, the rescue centre had seemed only a hop, skip and a jump away, but by car it was a different matter. Imran directed Bea to return to the main road, turn right and then take the first right again. The centre of operations seemed to be in a run-down cottage, beyond which lay the shanty town of stables and huts, coops and styes, which Bea had spotted from the barn. A field beyond that was divided into two: pasture for goats on one side and, on the other, for a number of llamas. Squeaks and squawks greeted their arrival. Enquiring heads appeared over fences.

Bea had brought Bruno in the car with them, but he seemed happy enough to stay and look out of the half-open window while they got out of the car and stretched.

A minibus packed with children was drawing away as they arrived.

A sign informed them that the centre was open on weekdays for visits, bookable in advance. Schools, perhaps? Families wanting to introduce children to the animals?

A scarecrow of a woman in a battered old jacket over worn denims came out of the cottage to shout at them. 'We're closed!'

Imran said, in a low voice, 'That's Jessie, the boss lady. Double-barrelled name. Has a shotgun licence. Does most of the work looking after the animals. Her partner looks as if she's been through the wash too many times, but don't be fooled; she's the brains, keeps the books straight. There's also a couple of lads who hang around doing nothing much.'

Jessie strode towards them. 'Didn't you hear me? We're closed for the day.'

Bea said, 'So sorry to trouble you. I'm Bea Abbot, here on behalf of Sir Julian. You may have heard—'

'It's not our fault if he fell off Jack. We warned him the horse had been badly treated and might—'

'Sir Julian's in hospital. They may be operating on his ankle today.'

A shrug. 'He knew what the horse was like. He can't blame us for—'

'Sabotage? For putting a teasel under the horse's saddle?'

Jessie gaped. 'What! Who would . . .? I mean, that's criminal! No, nobody would—'

'Somebody did.'

A pale blonde with a tired face came out of the cottage and hesitated, not sure whether or not to join them. This would be the partner who did the paperwork? About forty, perhaps. Behind her appeared the head of a gawky, bony lad with pale blue eyes. Her son? Was this one of the lads who hung around and didn't do much?

Jessie said, 'Are you trying to say that Mickey . . .? No, he'd never—'

'No, I don't think he'd harm the horse. But he may know who did. Do you know where he is? I need to speak with him.'

Jessie took a step back. 'He's very upset, finding Jack dead. He did the right thing, getting someone to report it, and then he took off for a few days. I said it was very inconvenient, but he—'

'What did the vet say that Jack died of?'

A flushed face. 'That's no business of yours.'

'You entrusted the horse into Sir Julian's care, and he would like to know.'

'Well, I suppose it was colic. Mickey would have walked the horse up and down for some hours, but it can be fatal.'

That was a lie, wasn't it? No one was walking the horse up and down when I got back from the village. He was dead by that time.

Jessie said, 'It's always upsetting when an animal dies. The best thing to do is to get shot of it and get back to normal.'

Bea tried again. 'Sir Julian would like to see the vet's certificate.'

'Tough. The horse belonged to us, not to him. He has no right to see anything.'

A brawny young man came round the side of the cottage. Worn leather jacket, aggressive demeanour. Dark of hair and eye. He said, 'What's this? Someone making trouble?'

Bea thought that if there was any trouble, this lad would be the one starting it. She sharpened her tone. He might respond to the voice of authority. Or not, as the case might be.

She said, 'The rescue centre asked Sir Julian if he could house and provide pasture for three of your horses and he agreed. Something has happened to one of them and he would like to see the vet's certificate as to the cause of death.'

Some emotion passed over the lad's face. Was he laughing? Surely not. He shrugged. 'Nothing to do with me.'

'And,' said Jessie, 'we're closed for the day.'

Bea said, 'Is it possible that you didn't bother to get a vet in when the horse developed colic? That you just let him die? There must be a law against that.'

Bea didn't know if there were such a law or not, but it sounded about right.

Jessie said, 'There was no reason for a vet to be called. It was our horse, he died of natural causes and we dealt with it.'

'On the other hand,' said Bea, thinking of the pack of meat left for Bruno to eat, 'the cause of death might not be colic. Was he poisoned?'

Jessie gaped. 'What? Ridiculous! You'd better leave.' And that did sound like affronted innocence.

Imran touched Bea's arm. 'We'd better go.'

TEN

Thursday afternoon

Bea stared at the little group. Jessie, the country type, who probably liked animals better than human beings; the pale woman who kept the books and the lanky youth with the same colouring; the dark-haired young man who had the brash demeanour of someone who enjoyed picking fights. Where did he fit into the picture?

Bea and Imran got back into the car, and drove off.

She said, 'I'm beginning to wonder if they called a vet in at all. Do you know who they'd have employed to remove the body?'

'Officially, there's rules and regulations. Unofficially . . .' He shrugged. 'Look, horses can be buried on their owner's land, but I can't see Jessie and co. digging a pit big enough for Jack. There's a firm which deals with such things . . .'

He set to work on his smartphone. 'Ah. Here it is. It's a good ten miles away in the nearest town. Do we have time to get there and back before we collect Sir Julian from the hospital?'

Bea drew into a layby and parked. 'Let's phone them, see if they'll tell us what we need to know before we start chasing rainbows.'

He tried the number. 'Engaged. I'll try again in a minute.'

Bea said, 'What do you think of the centre?'

'Run on a shoestring. If they get enough people coming to pet the animals, it just about gets by. If they've a hard winter, they feel the pinch. Vet bills are probably an expense they could do without.'

'Those two lads must cost them something?'

'No, not really. The fair-haired lad – his name is Lars – is the son of Lena, that's the woman who does the books. Lars is taking a gap year before uni. The other's a local lad, been in and out of trouble for ever. Did you notice the likeness? He's one of Frederick's. His mother was a decent sort; got married and moved away some years back. She'd had enough of young Fred, as have all her family. He's putting in some voluntary work at the centre instead of doing time in jail.'

'Is he one of Craig's followers?'

'Nah. Chalk and cheese. Young Fred thinks he's tough because he's come off best from one or two fights in the pub. He'll probably end up as a club bouncer somewhere.'

'I get you. Now, do we believe what Jessie told us? She says Jack developed colic and Mickey walked him up and down for hours but the horse still died. I don't believe it. Mickey had been shut into his box and Jack was dead by the time I got back from the village. That horse was an asset to the centre because, with Julian riding him every day, they could be sure of using the paddock and stabling, and I don't suppose he insisted on the rent being paid promptly. Jack's death is bad news for the centre. I don't think those who look after animals usually kill them but I do think they are hiding something.'

Imran tried the number again. Still engaged.

Bea said, 'Why didn't they call a vet?'

'Well, the owner would usually want to call a vet to find out why the horse had died, but Jack wasn't to everyone's taste and if the owner isn't bothered . . .?'

'But surely there must have been some paperwork? For one thing, the removal company would need paying to dispose of the body, wouldn't they? Who paid for that, eh? Imran, I don't like this situation, not one bit. Julian loved his horse and his dog. Jack's dead, and last night I found a suspicious-looking package of raw meat on the doorstep. Left out for Bruno. Was it poisoned? I don't know. But just in case, I put it in the freezer and informed the police of what I'd done. I'm right in thinking the dog's in danger, too, aren't I?'

Imran groaned. 'I hope not.'

Bea hit the steering wheel. 'The village must be rife with gossip. What do they say about the situation? Now, Craig said there was a witness who saw Julian with Dora on the night she was killed. Who was that witness, do you know?'

'It's just rumours. No names.'

'Who do you think it was?'

'I know who I'd like it to be, and that's Lance's younger brother. He was born years after his parents had stopped hoping for another child, and they spoiled him rotten. He's a nothing who thinks he's the tops.'

This would be the lad Bea had called 'Skinny'. He'd tried to bully Julian about outstanding bills for the builders and had not been helpful when Julian had admitted his mistake over the plans for the Tithe Barn. Also, he'd taken Craig's side when that young man had attempted to invade the Hall. Could Skinny be upping his game by claiming to have seen Julian with Dora, in his anxiety to see Julian ousted?

Imran tried the phone again, and this time got through to someone. He handed the phone over to Bea, saying, 'We're through.'

Bea said, 'Good afternoon. My name is Bea Abbot, and I'm currently staying with Sir Julian Marston-Lang at the Hall. He's been exercising a horse called Jack from the animal rescue centre until yesterday when it threw him. I believe the horse died in the night. Sir Julian's anxious to know what happened. You dealt with the matter and were asked to remove the body?'

A tinny girl's voice said, 'Yes, I believe so. Who did you say you are?'

'Bea Abbot. A friend of Sir Julian's. Now Sir Julian had become attached to the horse. Presumably the vet who attended the horse must have—'

'I don't think there was . . . Hold on a moment?' Muffled voices in the background as the girl consulted someone else? She came back to the phone. 'Yes, we got a call, and dealt with it straight away.'

Bea said, 'Would it be all right if Sir Julian asked a vet to have a look at the horse before it's . . . er . . . dealt with?'

'Sure. Maybe. Or . . . I'll have to ask the boss. I think you'd have to get permission from the owners. Perhaps you can ring back sometime? The boss is out now, on another collection.'

The phone went dead. How annoying.

Bea handed Imran back his phone and started the car, saying, 'Dead end. We need to find out who's been billed for the disposal of the horse. I have an uneasy feeling about the people at the animal centre. But, why would they cover anything up? What do you know about them?'

'Well, Jessie ran it for years with someone else, a much older woman. There was some kind of bust-up and the other woman went off in a huff and Jessie couldn't manage by herself and was going to give up. Then somebody said that this businesswoman they knew was looking for a job outdoors. That's Lena. She's been running the office side of things ever since and locals say it's an improvement.'

'And Lena's son – on his gap year, you said?'

'Lars, yes. A bit odd. Doesn't look you in the eye. Never heard him speak.'

'Odd in a worrying way?'

Bea's smartphone rang. She had it on hands-free, so kept driving. It was Julian, sounding as if he were on strong painkillers. 'Hi, there, Bea. How you doing? The doctors say I've not broken anything. Just pulled a muscle. They've released me from durance vile and I'm on my way home. Polly says she's coming back, too. Where are you?'

'Imran and I were on our way to collect you.'

'No need. As soon as I knew I was being let go, I phoned Lance to tell him about the priest hole and suggest another meeting soonest. He came round to the hospital straight away to collect me. Are you far away? We're just turning off the road to the Hall.'

'So are we. I think I can see Lance's car ahead. Are you all right?'

'In patches. Limping a bit but nothing that won't mend. Lance says that when he was a child, his grandfather and his friends used to go digging for treasure in the grounds of the Hall. Apparently *his* father had told him a tale about buried treasure, which sounds most unlikely to me, but there you are. Perhaps this discovery will cast some light on the matter. Are you sure there's no gold coins in the chest?'

He was making a joke, wasn't he? Though finding buried treasure would be an enormous help to his finances.

'It didn't look like it,' said Bea, laughing. 'Though the papers there might tell us something.'

'Either way, it's good news for the Hall. Ah, we've arrived. It's good to be home.'

Bea followed Lance's car round the Hall and into the yard at the back, and parked. And there was not just Julian, but a whole crowd of people come out to greet him.

Julian was laughing, flourishing a pair of crutches, saying how glad he was to be home. Two of Lance's workmen were helping and/or hindering him. Out of the back door of the Hall came the electricians led by Lennie, with Whiny in tow. Behind them, Mrs Maggs waved a welcome.

Bruno, in the back of Bea's car, made so much noise at seeing his master that Bea covered her ears while Imran let the dog out.

Bruno immediately leaped at his master, and had to be fended off and caressed.

The noise level was quite something.

Imran laughed. 'It's good to see him back again. He's only been away for a day, but the place isn't the same without him.'

Bea noted that though Julian would never have thought of himself as being loved, yet his reappearance had sparked off a surge of emotion. Perhaps 'emotion' was too strong a word for his effect on everyone? But everyone was talking, laughing, wanting to know what the doctor had said, telling him about the priest hole and mentioning – of course – the treasure that was bound to be hidden there.

Julian balanced on his crutches, acknowledging their welcome with a smile. One leg of his jeans was slit to the knee. One shoe was on with a hospital boot on the other foot.

Bristles – sorry, Lance – that solid expert on the restoration of old buildings, was standing over Julian as if he'd produced a rabbit from a hat. He was also grinning.

Julian looked flushed, and happy as he said 'thanks' to this person and that. 'It's good to be back! I'm all right, just a bit bruised, and I'm dying to see what you've found. It's upstairs, isn't it? I'm not supposed to put this foot to the ground but if you'll show me . . .'

Lance produced the ancient bath chair and Julian was swept into it, expostulating that he could manage perfectly on his own.

Bruno practically climbed on to the chair with his master, and was made much of by him. And everyone, builders, workmen, electricians, Mrs Maggs and all, followed the chair into the kitchen and along the corridor to the Hall, all talking at once.

'What do we do about the stairs?'

'No problem.'

A giant of a man, whom Bea hadn't seen before and whom she mentally labelled the Incredible Hulk, loomed over Julian. This must be Teddy, who was a martyr to his teeth? Teddy picked up the back of the chair, two of Lance's merry men lifted the front, and they carried Julian up the stairs, still protesting that he could manage by himself.

Bea noted the bright faces of all concerned. They were enjoying this. Bea had to think about why they wanted to help Julian out. No, it wasn't only that they'd looked into the future and decided that Julian was their best bet for keeping the place going, but it seemed that they also liked and respected him. And of course, there was the lure of treasure to be found.

Self-interest ruled OK.

The chest was pulled away from the door to Lady Fleur's bedroom, and the spotlight was produced and connected. Imran was here, there and everywhere. Bruno sat beside his master's chair, tongue hanging out, observing all that went on. Suggestions were offered, everyone talked over everyone else.

Bea considered the one quiet person in all this gathering. This was Lance, who had taken Julian to the hospital and collected him from there this morning.

He caught Bea looking at him, and grinned, acknowledging her as someone on Julian's side. Of course, self-interest ruled here, as it did with everyone else.

The Incredible Hulk pushed the bed aside as if it were a feather, and Imran pulled the loose panelling away to reveal the priest hole.

Lennie switched on the lamp, holding it up inside the priest hole and everyone crowded round to see.

Whiny muttered something about gold coins again. 'Just one or two, just to see me through . . .'

Everyone was bright-eyed and interested. Breathing accelerated. Even Bea could feel the pressure.

Julian got to his feet, balancing himself with difficulty, and craned forward to see what was there.

Bruno growled and then barked, sharply. Intruders!

'Sir Julian Marston?'

A strange voice, sharp and authoritarian. Two men pushed through the crowd. Plain clothes. The foremost man held up a badge and recited his name. Detective Sergeant—

'Not now!' Whiny almost shrieked.

'You've led us a dance,' said the detective sergeant. 'All over the hospitals, we've been, looking for you. We'd like you to come down to the station to—'

'Not now!' Whiny was almost dancing with impatience.

'—answer a few more questions.'

Julian said, 'Not again! I've told you all I know.'

Whiny said, 'This is harassment, that's what it is. Getting in the way of us going about our business.'

The detective sergeant was a podgy sort of man, who looked as

if he'd roll if you dropped him on the floor. His sidekick was thin,
almost cadaverous. 'If you please, Sir Julian. You'd have saved us
time if you'd signed into hospital under your own name.'

'My name? Oh, I used the name "Lang" at the hospital. It's easier.
I'm sorry if you've been inconvenienced, but really I have nothing
more to say.'

'Are you refusing to come with us?'

Julian grimaced. 'If I do, then you'll have me for resisting arrest?'
He sighed, and turned to Bea. 'Can you take over here? Ring my
solicitor, take care of Bruno and tell Polly what's happened. Lance,
can you see to getting everything here covered up again?' He tried
to put his bad foot to the ground, and winced. 'Where are my
crutches?'

'Downstairs.' The Incredible Hulk, aka Teddy with the bad teeth,
pushed the chair forward, Julian was helped back into it, trundled
out of the room and along the gallery. Everyone followed, this time
in silence.

Downstairs, he was reunited with his crutches, told Bruno to look
after Bea and Polly, and made his slow way to an unmarked police
car.

Bea, like everyone else, stood there, watching as he was driven
away.

She wondered how the police had known he'd been released from
hospital. Her eye wandered over the crowd as they watched Julian's
departure . . . and spotted someone she hadn't noticed earlier.

Skinny, Lance's much younger brother. He was grinning while
everyone else looked dour. Bea's mind leaped at the truth. Skinny
had heard that Lance was going to collect Julian from hospital, and
he'd phoned the police. Skinny had definitely thrown in his lot with
Craig.

Bea watched as Skinny eeled his way out of the crowd and started
for the kitchen door. Was he wanting a look into the priest hole
when no one else was around?

She started for the door and found Lance just behind her. And
Imran.

Lance said, 'The first one into that hole has got to be Julian.
We'd best close it up again for now.'

They ran along the corridor and up the stairs, only to see Skinny
disappearing into Lady Fleur's room.

Lance pushed Bea aside and reached out a long arm to grab his brother by his T-shirt and pull him away from the gaping maw of the priest hole. 'Not yet, Brother!'

'Surely we can just have a quick look?'

Lance lifted his brother almost off his feet.

Skinny yelped. 'You let go of me!'

Lance shook him. 'Show some respect, man!'

Imran removed the light on the end of the cable, and fitted the panelling back into place. 'I'll get Teddy to put everything back.'

Bea said, 'Julian needs his solicitor! I did know his name once, but I can't think . . .! And I don't have his number!'

'Where's his laptop?' said Lance, setting his brother down on his feet.

Bea fled back down the stairs, through the corridor and out to the stable yard. The workmen hadn't gone back to their toil but were standing around, chatting. Difficult times, yes. And should they knock off now, because it was only fifteen minutes till the end of the working day, and . . .

Bruno was waiting by the door to Julian's quarters. The door wasn't locked, so Bea went straight in, only to hear the phone ringing. It stopped as she entered, so she went to the low table Julian had been using as a desk to find an address book, a folder, anything to enable her to get on to the solicitor. What was his name? Why couldn't she think! She clutched at an elusive memory. He was a man with a poker up his spine and a deadpan expression. He approved of Julian.

Ah. Got it. Routledge. Efficient, very. She found his office number, got through, and managed by great good fortune to find him at his desk and not out on business. A quick word of explanation and Mr Routledge was galvanized into action and on his way to rescue Julian.

Feeling as if it had been a long, long day and it wasn't over yet, Bea sank into Julian's big chair and ignored the flashing light on the landline.

Lance appeared, to ask if Bea had connected with the solicitor. She nodded. He sank into a chair opposite and commented that he'd sent his men home as their minds were not on the job, but he'd get them to work longer on the morrow. And, Teddy had shoved everything back upstairs.

'Good for Teddy. I'm exhausted.'

'Yes.' He sat forward on his chair, frowning. He said, 'Julian trusts you. He said you were pure gold and had saved his life several times. How much do you know about what's happening here?'

'Some. Julian brought me up to date about what's going on at the Hall, and told me how he discovered Dora's body. I believed him absolutely when he said he didn't know anything about her death.'

Lance grunted. 'What do you make of Craig?'

She closed her eyes. She was tired. 'A lightweight. Self-centred. He tried to have his wicked way with Celine last night. I was stupid; I should have insisted she report him, but she wouldn't hear of it.'

'Why ever not? It's about time someone squashed him underfoot.'

Bea shrugged. 'She's ashamed and shocked. I've seen it before. The victim can't cope.'

Lance grimaced. 'To think that he claims to be the heir! It would be a disaster for the Hall. He wouldn't have killed his mother though, would he?'

Bea shrugged. 'I wouldn't have thought so, but I don't know him well enough to judge.'

'I can't think who else it could be. My little brother is a bit of a fool, gets ideas into his head about backing the favourite but his judgement is not sound. And he wouldn't, couldn't . . .' He let that trail away.

She said, 'Of course not,' while inwardly reserving judgement.

He took a deep breath. 'I need to work out what we're to do next. That priest hole! There'll be specialists crawling all over it . . . we need to get some better lighting . . . which reminds me, the electricians are way behind, aren't they? Julian was saying we must have a chat about that . . .'

Bea suspected that Lance could produce a seasoned team of electricians and plumbers to check what had been done and complete the job within days. But Bea couldn't possibly comment. That was a problem that only Julian could solve.

'I'm sure he'll deal with it soonest,' said Bea, sliding down in her chair and putting her feet up on a nearby stool.

Lance raised a hand to his head. His voice was heavy, tired. 'What a day! Swings and roundabouts.'

'Yes. Who do you think killed Dora?'

A shrug. 'She wasn't exactly popular. Most people think she's little loss to the community.'

'So nobody's really concerned about it? Except the police.'

He sighed. 'Maybe it was a stray visitor, stopping by for a quick one. It all went wrong, they fought and she died. He dumped her body and left.'

Bea shook her head. She didn't think it had been like that, but she could understand why local people would like the idea.

They were both quiet for a while. Bea thought she might just keep her eyes closed for a few more minutes before she had to spring into action.

Bruno suddenly ran to the door, barking. A car drew up outside. Bruno pawed at the handle of the door and was out into the yard before either Bea or Lance had managed to get out of their chairs.

A sharp voice rose into the air as the engine of the car died. 'Come on, come on! Help me out of here! You there! Can't you see I need a hand?'

'Who?'

Bea's mind went into overdrive and came up with an unacceptable answer.

ELEVEN

Thursday early evening

Polly staggered in. She was cradling a sleeping baby and looked to be at the end of her tether.

Her father's voice filled the stable yard. An ex-teacher of many years of experience, he knew how to make himself heard. 'You, there! Yes, you! Help me get out of here!'

Bruno leaped around Polly, welcoming her back. She stumbled to the nearest chair, gasping, 'Oh, Bea. Thank God you're here. My father's in the car. I couldn't stop him. Down, Bruno! Where's Julian?'

'At the police station. Further questioning.'

Polly's composure broke. Tears came. 'No, no! Surely they can't think . . .! What are we to do? Oh, Bruno, down! Oh, my poor love! My father got into the car, I told him we can't cope now but he won't listen, and I couldn't leave him on the street!'

'Listen! Julian's solicitor has been informed of the latest police palaver and is on to it. He's good. Julian will be back in no time. As for your father, we'll cope somehow.' Bea tried to convince herself that they could. She took the sleeping child from Polly and laid him in his cradle. There were tear tracks on his cheeks, but at least he was asleep for the moment.

Polly was in pieces. Bruno was distressed. He tried to climb into her lap to lick her face.

Bea told Bruno to control himself and shot a look which said 'over to you' at Lance.

Lance got to his feet slowly, shaking his head. 'I've heard about Mr Colston. Domestic tyrant, isn't he?'

Polly hiccuped and coughed, trying to control her tears. 'He thinks we should have him living with us at the Hall, and that we'd look after him better than the Home, and I've told him and told him that there's no water and no electricity yet and we don't have servants, and he just won't listen!'

'Just like my old dad,' said Lance.

'I must go down to the police station and rescue Julian. Only, I can't, can I? There's the baby and my father! I had to bring him because they wouldn't take him back into the Home, and I thought Julian might find somewhere in the village and . . . What am I going to do?'

Lance patted her shoulder. 'Let's get him in here, that's the first thing.'

'He's got a pile of his things in the car, but I couldn't get everything in, and I had to leave two cases back at the Home, his books and stuff, and what do the police want Julian for? And the boy cried almost all the way back, and my father said I was a bad mother not letting him have a bottle, but I've always had enough till today.

'I should have stopped and fed him, but when I said I'd do that, my father went bananas! But in the end I did stop, and he went on and on at me and . . . I think all this is making my milk dry up and . . . This is just not like me to give way like this. Julian would expect me to manage, somehow.'

'You're all right,' said Lance. 'You're a star, you really are, Lady Paula.'

Bea put the kettle on.

Bruno wuffed, and in stalked Mr Colston, his aristocratic nose leading the way. He was a tall, thin drink of water with the habit of command, and was supported on either side by large Teddy-with-the-bad-teeth and one of Lance's builders.

'A decent chair! At last!' Mr Colston sank with a groan into Julian's big chair, and was deferentially handed an ivory-handled stick.

'We'll bring your things in next,' said Teddy, whistling through what remained of his teeth. 'No worries!'

Mr Colston wasn't into saying 'thank you'. Instead it was, 'Aargh, my back! My knees! That car seat was at the wrong angle. And my daughter is such a poor driver. Sit up straight, girl! What are you crouching like that for! And where's my son-in-law? It's the least he could do, to be here to receive me.'

'He's at the police station,' said Polly, reaching for a box of tissues to blow her nose.

Mr Colston roared, 'What have I always said? Don't let that meek exterior fool you. I've known him since he was a child! Butter wouldn't melt till you get to know him. He's a criminal, that's what, and . . .!'

Lance's eyebrows rose to his hairline and he vanished.

Bea said, 'Please! Moderate your tone, or you'll wake the baby.'

'What? Who are you? How dare you! Do you know who I am?'

'I'm an invited guest here. Now, there's only two bedrooms. Are you prepared to sleep on the settee?'

His face purpled. 'What! What are you saying? What? Out of the question. I shall sleep in the Hall, of course.'

Lance toted in two hefty suitcases of ancient vintage and dumped them on the floor. He was followed by Big Teddy, making light of a load of bags.

Polly struggled to sit upright. 'I told you, Daddy. There are no beds made up in the Hall. No lighting, no water. We'd better get you down to the village and see if there's someone who can take you in. Then tomorrow we'll find you a good place to stay where you'll be properly looked after.'

'What nonsense! Where should I stay but with my only daughter? This guest of yours can find somewhere else to stay.'

'No,' said Polly in a small but determined voice.

Bea made a pot of tea, knowing already that if she didn't find a bone china cup and saucer, Mr Colston would reject whatever she gave him. Oh dear, there were only mugs in the kitchen. She told herself that yes, she could sleep on the settee if necessary, but she didn't like to think of Mr Colston getting his own way.

'You ridiculous child!' Mr Colston heaved himself to his feet by the simple expedient of catching hold of Teddy's arm and pulling. 'Take me over to the Hall, there's a good lad. Find me a good room with a view.'

'Tea first?' said Bea, putting mugs and milk on a tray. She noticed the light was still winking on the landline. She must attend to that, in a minute.

'I do not drink tea out of mugs!' declared Mr Colston. 'There'll be someone at the Hall who knows how to make a decent cup, no doubt.'

Teddy hovered over Mr Colston. Teddy had been aware since childhood that he was not the brightest card in the pack, and that his best chance of getting through life unscathed was to obey orders from someone in authority. He said, 'Mrs Maggs might still be there. She's the housekeeper, and she makes a fine cuppa.'

'No doubt she can sort me out a decent bed to sleep in. You may bring those two bags across with me.' Mr Colston accepted Teddy's services as his right and made his way slowly, regally, out of the barn and across to the Hall.

Lance put his head round the door. 'I've got to brief the men about what's happening tomorrow. Phone me if you need me, right?' He disappeared again.

Silence seemed to thunder around the room. Bea rolled her head on her shoulders to release tension. Mr Colston's voice died away as he disappeared into the house opposite.

Bea poured tea for Polly and herself. The baby stirred but didn't wake. Worn out with crying, poor lamb.

Polly said, 'Father will pick the best room and get Teddy to set him up with bedding and candles or an oil lamp. Then he'll demand a three-course dinner with wine. I'm holding it together. Really, I am. But . . . Why have the police taken Julian in again? I can't believe this is happening.'

Bea found the biscuit tin and put it at Polly's right hand. 'I've been doing some poking around. Someone – maybe more than one person – is doing their best to incriminate Julian. Any ideas?'

Don't tell her about Jack or the parcel left for Bruno.

'His old family, I suppose. Every single one of them. Lady Fleur and her son, and his son and all those dreadful women . . . Oh, take no notice. I'm post-whatsit and I'll be all right in the morning.'

She's worried about her milk drying up. What day of the week is it? Where can I get some baby formula for her?

Bea said, 'Your milk will come back when you've had a good rest. But if not, for tonight, have you any baby formula?'

'Someone gave me some. Where did I put it? Do you know how to make it? I don't. Bea, I'm falling apart.'

'Not you. Have a little nap while you can,' said Bea, hurrying to the kitchen to open drawers and cupboards all crammed with this and that cast-offs from the Hall. In the third cupboard she found a packet of formula, a brand-new bottle and a heated warmer, which she plugged in straight away. She made up a bottle and put it to warm. She could hear the baby stirring, and yes, Polly had fallen asleep.

A tentative mew from the cradle, and Bea made haste to extricate the baby from his nest to wash and change him. Nappies? Ah. Next to his cradle? Good.

Baby was fussing, not happy, getting ready to scream the place down. Bea settled herself in a chair with him in her arms and thrust

the bottle into his mouth. He rejected it. Of course. She tried again.
He gave her *such* a look! And opened his mouth to yell. She plugged
the gap and he glugged, spluttered, coughed and opened his mouth
to yell again.

'Right!' said Bea. 'Third time lucky.' She plugged the wide-open
mouth before he could waken Polly from her sleep. He rejected it
again. A prayer for help might do the trick. *Please! Let him take
the bottle!*

She tried again. 'Take it, baby,' she said, holding him in the
long-forgotten, newly recalled hold of women feeding a baby. Her
own son was now grown up, married, and the father of two children
whom she rarely saw. She sighed. *Ah well. You never forget how to
feed them, do you?*

Baby glugged. He wasn't fooled, but he was famished and this
stuff – whatever it was – would be a stopgap. And this woman –
whoever she was – would do for the time being.

'What's your name?' murmured Bea. 'They always call you "the
boy". What do you want to be called?'

The baby shot her a look which she interpreted as, 'Don't
interrupt.'

She burped him and changed sides. He settled down again. He
was going to take the whole bottle if it killed him. He was slowing
down, though. His eyes closed, his hands clutched the bottle . . .
and fell away. She could feel his heart beating.

Such a tiny creature, carrying so much baggage, his heritage, his
father's blue eyes and wisps of fair hair, his mother's pretty mouth.
The future . . . which could be snuffed out so quickly, with a pillow
placed over his face and . . . Bea told herself not to be fanciful.

She burped him again. Satisfactory. She walked around, letting
him look out of the windows. Bruno kept pace with her, looking
up at the baby. Baby looked down at Bruno and expressed satisfaction. Bea sat the boy in his bouncing chair-thing – what was its
name? Bea was out of date with what babies' equipment was called
nowadays. Bruno settled at his side. Baby played with his hands,
blew bubbles, expressed contentment with life. Bea thanked the
Lord that the baby had taken the bottle.

During all this she'd been vaguely aware of movement in the
yard. Cars left as workers knocked off for the day. Imran's moped
fired up and departed. Bea hoped Mrs Maggs had got herself a lift
with someone and was not still at the Hall, pandering to the selfish

whims of Mr Colston, who had not reappeared. Perhaps he'd fallen
down the stairs and knocked himself out. Goodie!

Although – sigh – if he had done so, she supposed she'd have
to clear up the mess. The landline light was still winking. She
reached for it, only to hear another car draw up outside. Bruno
stirred and wuffed. Baby made an enquiry. The door was opened
by Bernie, the taxi driver, ushering Julian in on his crutches.
Presumably the solicitor had managed to extract Julian without too
much trouble?

Bruno leaped at Julian and had to be fended off, Polly woke up
with a start and the baby cooed a welcome.

Julian looked weary and in need of painkillers, but somehow
managed to get one arm around Polly before he collapsed in his
big chair, taking her with him. He was smiling.

Bea dumped the baby in their arms and stood back to appreciate
the picture of the family reunited. Family plus dog, of course. Bruno
was trying to climb on to the chair as well.

Julian kept saying, 'I'm all right, really. I kept saying "no
comment" until Mr Routledge arrived, and by then I was feeling so
tired that I sort of went to sleep. They didn't want me to die on
them then and there, so after an injection of common sense from
the solicitor, they let me go.'

He was still in shock, still in pain, and still in trouble, but he
was smiling. So was Polly, and so was the baby. And Bruno. And
so was Bernie, who said the fare was on him, but accepted a note
from Bea anyway.

Bea said, 'Food. I'll get something on the table.'

Polly tried to struggle to her feet, but was told to lie still, and
did so.

Julian said, 'How's Jack?'

Bea would have preferred to leave the subject till morning, but
perhaps it was best to get it over with.

'Your accident was caused by someone putting a teasel head
under your saddle. That's why Jack went mad and tried to throw
you off. It wasn't Mickey's fault. He honestly didn't know.'

Julian gaped. 'A teasel? Would a teasel drive Jack crazy? Yes, I
suppose it would. Oh, poor Jack.'

Bea braced herself. 'I walked around the yard in the evening.
Bruno disturbed an intruder who'd left a packet of meat on your
doorstep. Fortunately he waited for me to give him permission to

eat it, so I picked it up, double-wrapped it, labelled it and put it in the freezer. Mrs Maggs gave Bruno a bone and I fed him as well.'

Julian went white.

Bruno whined, understanding his master was distressed.

Polly said, 'But Jack's all right now?'

'No. He died in the night. The rescue centre had the body removed early today. Since it was their horse and not yours, I couldn't get a vet's diagnosis. The rescue centre say it was colic. Mickey has disappeared.'

Julian's eyes closed and his face went blank. Jack had meant a lot to him.

Polly was distressed for him. She said, 'Oh, you loved that horse.'

Julian brushed a hand across his eyes. 'If you have animals, you have to recognize their lifespan is shorter than yours. I'll buy another when funds permit. Bruno had better wear a muzzle when he goes out for his run.'

Bea made mushroom omelettes, brewed tea, buttered bread, found a tray to carry it through to the main room. She found the family on the verge of sleep again, with Polly burrowing into Julian's side while her spare arm circled the baby. Baby was intent on Bruno, who lay at their side.

The adults ate. Baby played with his hands and exercised his legs.

For afters Bea found some bananas and sliced them up over yoghurt in individual dishes. Some redcurrant jelly added a touch of colour, and a swirl of cream helped the dessert go down. Another pot of tea, an administration of painkillers and everyone felt better.

Julian set aside his empty cup. 'I was on the point of inspecting what seems to be a priest hole when I was so rudely interrupted. I was thinking about it all the while I was at the police station. It reminded me of people whose faith sustained them through persecution. We need to find out if anyone ever made use of it. Perhaps the parish records can cast light on it? The history of the house is going to have to be rewritten.'

'Another little job for me,' said Polly, looking rather daunted.

'Or,' said Bea, 'for someone to help you with the paperwork. The "archangel" that I told you about should arrive here sometime this evening or tomorrow morning for an interview. I'd hoped she'd be here by now, but she must have been delayed en route. And, before you say you can't afford her, Julian, you can't afford not to.

She's expensive, yes, but she'll save you money left, right and centre. No, don't argue. You can't carry on like this, either of you. It's not sensible. Your faithful retainers are worried for you. The locals, ditto. They want you alive, Julian, and with very few exceptions they don't want Craig—'

'Because he'll run the place into the ground?'

'Exactly. Now, I think you should ask Imran to chauffeur you around for a while, because you can't drive till that ankle's mended. Imran will also act as bodyguard. Mrs Maggs will repel boarders as far as she can. Which reminds me—'

Polly gasped. 'My father! Where is he?'

'Over in the Hall with Big Teddy to run his errands for him. I'll check on him in a minute but I suspect he's fine. I'll borrow a torch, if you have one. Now, you both need an early night. Julian, can you get up the stairs or will you have to make do with the Portaloo in the courtyard and sleep on the couch?'

'I'll manage. Don't worry about me.'

Typical male, pretending he's not in pain.

'My father . . . .!' Polly began.

Bea said, 'I'll take Bruno out, give him a run and then check in the house to see that he's all right.'

The evening was cool. Bruno ran about the paddock at the back of the barn. There was no sign of the two elderly horses which had been grazing there before. Mickey's place was dark, and the stables had the air of having been abandoned. Presumably the rescue centre had collected the two remaining horses now that Mickey had disappeared?

Bea checked her watch. What time did the security lights come on? Not yet, apparently.

Bruno reported back for duty and Bea let them into the kitchen quarters at the back of the Hall, and sniffed the air. It wasn't dark enough yet to have to put the lights on, but she checked that the switch there worked. Which it did.

Everything in the kitchen had been left clean and tidy, and someone had laid a place out for breakfast on a tray on the big table. Was that meant for Mr Colston?

Bea's lips twitched. In a way, she had to admire the man. He knew exactly how to make himself comfortable, didn't he? The downstairs rooms were quiet and dark. She climbed the stairs in the dusk with Bruno at her side, knowing she'd see a light under one of the bedroom doors. Yes, there it was, and the big chest of drawers that had been manoeuvred in front of that door earlier had been returned to its place along the gallery.

She might have known he'd choose Lady Fleur's room. Had he bullied Mrs Maggs into making the bed up for him and providing him with a snack for supper? The next thing he'd want would be a television set, and a power point for an electric shaver. And running hot water, of course.

She told Bruno to stay where he was, tapped on the door, and was told to enter.

Mr Colston was seated in a high-backed chair by the curtainless window, reading a book by the light of a Victorian oil lamp. He had a rug over his knees, and a tray with the remains of his supper stood on a table at his elbow. The huge bed had been moved away from its original position towards the window, and yes, it had been properly made up though it still lacked its curtains.

'Yes?' He spoke as to a servant. And yes, from the other side of the bed rose the smiling face of that ungainly giant, Teddy-with-the-bad-teeth.

'Nearly done,' said Teddy. 'I've put all the floorboards back and nailed them down. I told Mum I'd be back for the snooker, 'cos she needs me to adjust the set. Got a thing for snooker, Mum has. All right now, Mr Colston? Don't forget the potty's under the bed. Now I'll be back nice and early in the morning and bring you up some brekkies and a newspaper like you said. You know how to turn off the lamp when you're ready for bed? And there's a torch on the bedside table if you need it in the night.'

'Thank you, yes. That will be all.' It was an acknowledgement more than a thanks, but it was what Mr Colston considered appropriate. Given their respective backgrounds, Teddy probably thought it appropriate, too.

Teddy heaved a bag of tools up on to his shoulder and departed.

'Just checking,' said Bea to Mr Colston. 'Your daughter was concerned for you. I'm Bea Abbot, by the way. A friend of theirs from London.'

'Thank you. I am well enough. No doubt the room can be made comfortable tomorrow, and someone will have to see about emptying the chamber pot if the water still isn't turned on by morning. Have the police arrested my son-in-law yet? Nobody thinks to tell me anything.'

She tried to understand him, this horrible, lonely old man. The key was lonely, of course. His wife had died young, and the daughter he'd expected to look after him for life had married a man without a name or background. What's more, said man had once been a schoolboy taught by Mr Colston.

Ironically it had been Mr Colston himself who'd caused Julian's DNA to be sent off, only to be hoist with his own petard when Julian proved to be a Marston-Lang and the heir to a substantial property.

As teacher, his career had stalled; the headmastership he'd hoped for had evaporated, and he'd been dumped in a retirement home with nothing to look forward to.

She said, 'Julian was asked some questions and released. He's back here, but worn out.'

Mr Colston grumbled. 'He shouldn't have left me to make my own arrangements here. The facilities are not what I'm used to, though it is a relief to be out of that rest home. Hardly anyone there can sustain a conversation. They're all gaga or dying or drugged to the eyeballs. I was constantly being left alone in a roomful of noddies.'

He wants to play the 'lonely' card? If he'd treated his daughter better, or acknowledged Julian's worth . . . but he didn't. And hasn't. And there's a whole lot of venom stored in that clever head of his. He could still do Julian a lot of damage.

She said, 'Mr Colston, you should perhaps consider that if your son-in-law were to be found guilty of murder—'

'He's guilty of many things. The man's whole life is a charade. Brought up as he was, how can he possibly understand what it means to inherit a place like this? But he's not a murderer. Not my son-in-law.'

Bea persevered. 'No. Quite. But if he was, he'd not be able to provide you with a place to live. Nor would he be able to help you if young Craig pushes him out.'

'Eh? What? Some pretender? Polly told me about him. A no-hoper.'

'Maybe. But if he succeeded in taking over here, then Polly and Julian would go back to London to rebuild their lives, and you'd have to find yourself another residential home, and put up with life there.'

Contrary as always, Mr Colston said, 'Nonsense. Julian's the best hope they have for this place. He may not be my idea of a fit husband for my daughter but he's a demon for paperwork.'

'And you've already worked out that if he stays on here, you'll have a standing in the community as his father-in-law? Do you see yourself staying on here at the Hall, or perhaps taking a house in the village with a resident housekeeper? You'd become something of a local celebrity, invited here and there as a matter of course. Involvement in local affairs would inevitably follow. Parish affairs would welcome your educated point of view, charities would ask you to be a patron. And you'd only be as lonely as you wished to be.'

She could see his brain working on what she'd said. He'd already considered the possibilities of the situation, hadn't he? He just didn't want to admit that Julian was his passport to a better future.

He managed to look stricken. 'I'm an old man, of no use in the world.'

A clever old man, who knows how to press emotional buttons. Two could play at that game.

'I see you chairing committees, watching as your grandchild learns to ride a pony in the park, and taking him out for treats. How quickly you'd become part of the social scene in support of your daughter and her husband!'

'Humph. The lad's not interested in socializing.'

'No, but he can do it when he has to. And Polly loves him.'

'She loves him more than her old father.'

'Probably. That's the way it goes, isn't it? I don't see my son and his family nearly as much as I would like but there are other ways of filling my life.'

'Julian had his way with her when she was still at school. That's why she had to marry him.'

And that's a lie! You dirty-minded old so-and-so!

Bea wanted to hit him. But no. Softly, softly. She made her voice sympathetic. 'Now you know that's not true. Polly told me they waited till she was in her second year at university and she'd had a chance to look at what else was on offer. I understand that your own future has not turned out as you hoped, but—'

'He cost me my headship!'

No, he hadn't. Mr Colston had simply not been considered up to date enough for the post, but it wouldn't help to say that. Some people will always bite off their nose to spite their face.

It was getting dark outside. She must go. One last thing. 'Did
Big Teddy show you the priest hole behind the bed? That's going
to bring the tourists flocking, isn't it?'

An angry twitch of the shoulder. 'What nonsense! Priest hole,
indeed! A cupboard that's been shut up for ages and forgotten. I
can't be bothered with all that.'

'I'd have thought you'd have wanted to see what the papers were
in that chest. They might have valuable information about Tudor
times.'

He huffed, looked away from her. Picked up his book.

She was being dismissed.

Oh well, she'd done her best. She left the room, collected Bruno
and switched on her torch to light her down the stairs. A fall here
wouldn't do her any good. She wondered what the old man would
decide to do. He could go either way: refuse to acknowledge Julian
and condemn his declining years to bitter loneliness, or accept a
comfortable way of life courtesy of that same man.

TWELVE

D usk had closed in on the house and grounds when Bea and Bruno walked out into the yard.
Night noises had taken over the busyness of the day. Birds whizzed past, twittering. Bruno snorted and snuffled. Had he found another dicey packet? No. There was illumination in Julian's end of the barn, but nowhere else. The timer wasn't programmed to switch on the night-time lights as yet.

Bea shivered, pulling her jacket around herself.

Bruno disappeared in the direction of the stables, and Bea followed him. She remembered that she ought to have muzzled him before letting him out. Oh dear.

But he checked various corners of the yard without indicating excitement. Bea wondered if Mickey had resurfaced. He hadn't many possessions, but surely he'd gathered some bits and pieces while he'd stayed here?

At the far end, she leaned on the gate which led to the paddock beyond. She had a fancy that the Hall itself was a living thing, crouched at her back. It had been there for centuries and it seemed to be telling her that it would survive this and that the future would be good. The house was not owned by anyone but cared for by this generation and that, one succeeding another. Some looked after the place better than others.

Julian would be one of the good ones, but there were those who wanted him gone. Where to start looking for them? Polly had said everything bad came from Lady Fleur and her descendants. Bea had a lot of time for that point of view.

Consider Celine's behaviour, for instance. She'd suffered an attempted rape but not wanted to report it. Why? Perhaps she was aware that the attempted rape had given her a hold on Craig if he managed by some means to get control of the Hall.

Would Celine really dare to blackmail Craig? How would he

react if she did? Bea rather thought he'd lash out . . . and then Celine would run for the hills.

Bea moved on to consider Mona, who had blithely assumed she could run the farm shop with one hand tied behind her back, while paying court to an elderly but wealthy man who had a chauffeur-driven car and property all over the world.

Bea didn't think Mona – like Celine – had the slightest idea of what it meant to hold down a job these days. Their lazy, youthful years had instilled the belief that there would always be money for those who lived at the Hall.

Were they actually facing reality yet? It didn't seem like it.

Suppose Celine and Mona joined forces to support Craig? No, their interests were too diverse.

But considering what had been happening, there were a number of queries shooting into the mind. Who killed Dora? Who was the man seen with her the night of her death? Why was she in the stables?

Next: who sabotaged Jack's saddle? Was that the same person? Um, possibly not. And did the person who put the teasel under the saddle also kill the horse? Um, possibly.

And was the person who killed Jack also responsible for leaving poisoned meat out for Bruno? If it *was* poisoned, of course. She couldn't be sure about that.

Craig's appearance on the scene had triggered off the present situation. Why had his mother been given a lump sum of money and a cottage for life? Who had his father been? Could he possibly be the real heir to the Hall?

Now another question. Was Lance's younger brother, the one Bea had called 'Skinny', involved with Craig? And if so, why? For money? For kudos? To spite his elder brother? For sheer devilment?

Different ideas spun round in Bea's head. If A had met up with B and they decided to work together to get rid of Julian, then which was responsible for this and which for that? Or did both act together all the time?

Could a man kill his mother? Bea didn't want to think so, she really didn't.

A gnat sang around her head, and she realized darkness had descended. She whistled Bruno back to her side, and set off back to the barn. As she did so, the security lights came on. She watched

Bruno carefully in case he scented any more interesting parcels of meat, but he didn't. Thank goodness.

Normality seemed to have returned to the family's living quarters. 'Normality' is, of course, relative.

As Bea let herself and Bruno in, Polly was engaged in pulling cushions off the settee. 'We've lost his dummy! I don't like him having one, but just occasionally when he's overtired, I've used it. I'm sure I put it in his bag when we left but I can't find it anywhere!'

Julian was standing, propped up against the table, with the baby in his arms. 'Bea, can you take him? Let him put one of your fingers in his mouth and he'll be perfectly happy till we can find—'

Polly upended the cradle, sorting through the coverings. 'I bought a pack of them, though I don't think they're at all helpful in the long run, but—'

Julian handed the baby over to Bea. 'I had this idea, right in the middle of trying to convince the police I was not the guilty party who'd done for Dora and . . . Where's my laptop? Is it too late to ring Lance? Yes, I suppose it is. And, by the way, it *is* a real priest hole up there, isn't it? I can't wait to have a look in the morning.'

The baby was mewling, kicking and lashing out. Bea held him with difficulty.

She said, 'Yes, it is a real priest hole. And your laptop's on the table by the window.'

Julian dived, hopped and stumbled for his laptop. 'We were in a room down at the station without a view, no window. It was on the chilly side too, and I was thinking about how to get some cheap electricity—'

Polly raised her hands in despair. 'I think I must have dropped it when we visited my father.'

The baby was bright red from frustration. No milk, no dummy, no Mummy. He opened his mouth to express his displeasure. Bea put her little finger into his mouth; he looked wide-eyed at her. What was this? It didn't taste like . . . he sucked on. He liked it. He gurgled his appreciation.

What a strange sensation it was. Bea was thrown back through the years, to breast-feeding her son, who was now grown up and no longer needed her.

The baby's eyes were wide open. He'd registered that he'd seen her before and she'd been a bit of all right then. His colour faded to normal. Bea rocked from one foot to the other, remembering well how to soothe a fractious, tired child.

Polly sat back on her heels. 'Oh, Bea. You are wonderful with him. He doesn't take to everybody.'

Julian had regained his laptop and dived back into his chair. Pushing his glasses up his nose, he said, 'It's been a problem. We need solar panels but British Heritage say we can't alter the look of the place from the yard in any way. I thought we might try laying out the meadow at the back here with solar panels, but it would be a bit of an eyesore and we'd not be able to use it for grazing livestock.

'And then I got it! We can't alter the look of the barn from the yard, but we could cover the whole length of the roof on the meadow side with panels. The roof's sound enough, I think. I'll contact Lance in the morning, see what he says. But even if we have to strengthen some of the beams, which look pretty sound to me . . . it would be such a help. Limitless electricity, more or less for free, except for the original cost, of course.'

'That's brilliant,' said Polly.

'Yes, it is,' said Bea. 'By the way, what's the baby's name?'

They both laughed. Polly said, 'We argue about it all the time. Julian goes from "Twit-face" to "Arbuthnot". My suggestion of one of his family's names has not been well received.'

Julian said, 'Gradgrind. Percival. Honourable Hereward the Wake.'

They all laughed.

Bea said, 'What's your father's name?'

Silence. They stopped smiling.

Polly got to her feet. 'You can't be serious. I'll take the baby now.'

Bea handed him over.

Julian said, 'We used to make fun of him at school. We called him "Cold Face", because he was.'

Bea said, 'You're not children any longer. He's a lonely old man who doesn't belong anywhere. He's taken a misstep in life, and he knows it.'

Polly said, 'He's Philip Sydney. My mother called him Sydney.'

Julian contributed. 'At school they called him PS, meaning postscript.'

Polly shook her head. 'You have to admit he was a good housemaster.'

Julian shrugged. 'Yes, he was. Someone suggested he'd be "Pip" for short, but it didn't catch on.'

They both stared into space. Julian raised his eyebrows, and said, 'Philip Marston-Lang?'

Polly nodded. And there it was. The boy was going to be called 'Philip' or 'Pip' for short.

Julian pushed his laptop away. 'I've just punctured another pipe dream. We can't afford to buy enough solar panels and I can't afford to borrow any more money.' He let his head loll back on the chair. 'It's been a long day.'

Polly changed Pip, collected a bottle from the kitchen and began to feed him. Bea and Julian watched, willing the baby not to object to the bottle. He pulled a face at first, closing his mouth against the teat, but finally allowed it to slip into his mouth and soon settled down.

Polly had tears on her cheeks. 'It feels like the end of an era. Anyone can feed him now. He won't rely on me for everything. I tell myself it's just as well. We've got so much on . . .' She looked at her tired husband with concern, and then at Bea for help.

Bea thought, What now? It's been a long day for me, too. Then she had an idea. 'Julian, you said you'd handed over the search for the money Frederick had stolen from the Hall to the accountants you used to work for, but that they haven't been able to find the password. Why don't you have a go yourself? You've studied this family, you understand the way they think. You might be able to imagine what sort of password Frederick might use.'

Julian shook his head. 'They've tried talking to him about it. They even hinted it would mean a shorter sentence if he made restitution of what he's stolen. He just laughs. He says the money's his pension and he's looking forward to a comfortable retirement when he gets out of jail. Strangely, he doesn't think he's going to get a long sentence.'

Julian tried getting to his feet and fell back into his chair.

Bea helped him up, handed him his stick. 'Off to bed. If you can make it.'

'Of course I can make it. Don't fuss.' His tone was peevish, a small boy tried beyond endurance. 'If only everyone will leave me to get on with things. But the police said they'd need to talk to me again and . . . I've a horrible feeling they'll be back tomorrow and the day after . . . The only good thing that happened today is that

I had a chance to chat about this and that to our solicitor, Mr Routledge. He's a good man.'

Bea and Polly watched Julian drag himself to the stairs, consider how to mount them, turn round and manoeuvre himself backwards, step by step. He nearly fell halfway, but finally made it to the top and disappeared.

Polly burped Pip. The boy was fine, but Polly was showing signs of wear and tear, too.

Bea said, 'Off you go, too. Comfort one another. You're a great partnership, and young Pip's going to be just fine.'

Polly took the baby up the stairs with her. Bea did a little perfunctory tidying. The landline was no longer winking so Julian must have dealt with any messages that had been left for him.

She got out her own phone. Sure enough, some messages had been left there.

The first was from her efficient manager asking how to locate a particular file on the computer, and the second was to say she'd found it. Good.

There were two missed calls from Piers and one from the almost 'archangel' Rosemary.

Piers first. She rang his number and oh, it was great to hear his voice again. He was still in . . . wherever it was; his client was still either being questioned by the police or closeted with his lawyers, and Piers was still not able to leave.

'I'm informed that it would be a vote of no confidence in my client if I were to desert him now, and that this would be held against me. As he's connected by marriage to the leader of the armed forces, I'm choosing to stay put for the time being.'

Much amused, Bea asked, 'And is he guilty of whatever it is they're questioning him about?'

'Of course not!' said Piers, very loudly.

Was his phone tapped? Was someone monitoring his calls?

Bea said, 'Oh dear! Poor man. To be accused of wrongdoing when you are innocent must be so frustrating.'

'Indeed.' Piers sighed. 'It is hard to stand by and watch. So how are you getting on with your family?'

Should she tell him all, or keep a still tongue in her head? She usually liked to talk over any problems she encountered with Piers, who had a wide experience of eccentric people and a clarity of vision which was part of his ability to portray a character accurately.

But in this instance, given that he'd hinted that his call was being hacked, it might not be best to air this particular family's dirty linen in public.

Besides which, she found she had somehow begun to make a list of what questions to ask which person in the morning. So she made an amusing tale of how the family were talking about names for their son and heir and what would Piers have suggested instead. Trivia. Always useful to be able to burble on about nothing much.

He said he'd ring her again on the morrow and she said she'd remember to keep her phone switched on.

One last message. Rosemary, the almost archangel, had rung to say she'd been held up finishing her last case, but would hopefully be at the Hall on the following day.

Good. Very good.

Bea switched off her phone and made her weary way up the stairs to bed.

Friday morning

Bea overslept again. A cold morning with frost on the paddock. She pulled on a warm sweater in her favourite greeny-blue and a skirt to match. And her boots, of course.

She made her slow way downstairs to find Julian in his big chair, playing with baby Philip – Pip for short, and Polly preparing breakfast. Both adults were fully dressed, while Pip was wearing a nappy and a delighted smile.

A knock on the door and there was Imran. 'Reporting for duty.'

Julian blinked. 'What duty?'

Bea stepped in. 'I'm employing him as a bodyguard for you. He will drive you. He will fetch and carry for you. He will be your ears and your eyes. And Polly can stop worrying whenever you are out of her sight.'

Julian said, 'What!'

Polly giggled. 'You tell him, Bea! Imran, I absolutely approve. And, have you had breakfast?'

'Yes, Lady Paula. I thought the master would want to see the builder first and then look at the priest hole, while Mrs Abbot goes into the village – she knows the way – to pay a visit to the two sisters.'

Bea suppressed a grin. So Imran was going to play puppet master, was he? On consideration, that seemed like a good idea. She said, 'I'll grab a coffee and some toast and be on my way.'

Julian said, 'But . . .!' And let Pip relax on to his chest, spread-eagled.

Polly kissed her husband, and removed the baby to change and dress him in something suitable for a cold spring day. 'Shall I ring Lance, dear? Or will you do so?'

'Yes, I was going to . . . What's going on?'

Bea said, 'Plenty. Your job is to get on with the Hall. It's an enormous job and you need help with it. Rosemary Sweeting – who looks fifteen but is nearly thirty – will arrive sometime today for an interview with a view to being appointed your PA. She's a pretty little blonde who's made of steel and eats paperwork.'

'Yes, but I can't afford—'

'Which is why you yourself need to get on the track of the money Frederick stole. You do that and I'll get on with solving the murder. But before you do anything else, Imran needs a quiet half-hour with you on the subject of the farm shop.'

Julian caught on. 'But Mona said . . . What's she been up to that I don't know about?'

Imran spoke to the ceiling. 'She's having talks with a big conglomerate who will guarantee to keep the farm shop supplied with first-class produce, sourced from countries all over the world.'

Julian sat up straight. 'But not local? The whole point of a farm shop is that the produce is local.'

Imran didn't take his eyes off the ceiling. 'She plans to manage everything by using the internet, whether she's living here or up in town. It will be very efficient. On the other hand, I have a proposal to run the shop using local produce and . . .' He let his eyes drop to meet Julian's. 'Will you let me show you?'

Julian stared at him, and relaxed. 'Give me ten minutes. I have to make a couple of phone calls. After that, we can talk.'

Imran beamed. 'Right. I'm just going to check on your car. I think you may be running short of petrol.' He did an about-turn and left.

Julian looked as if he'd bitten a lemon. 'Don't tell me, Bea. Imran's been working out how to source material locally. He already knows who can supply what food and what are the costs. He wants to be appointed to run the farm shop. Right?'

Polly was indignant. 'Mona should have told us what she planned. It's against everything that we want to do, to keep the economy going around here.'

Julian closed his eyes and lay back in his chair. 'What else have I missed, and who can I trust to tell me the truth without fear or favour?'

He knew, really. He just had to adjust to the idea. He murmured, 'I'm an idiot. I wanted to be the one who brought prosperity to all. I wanted to be liked. I've been weak, haven't I? Letting some people carry on in their own sweet way when I should have kicked them out and got in the professionals, however unpopular it made me. I've allowed Lennie and Mona to build castles in the air and now I've got to knock them down.'

Polly said, 'Yes, dear. Quite right. And the sooner the better.' She bent to kiss him. 'And I love you because you do the right thing, however unpopular it may make you in the short run.'

Julian snarled, 'That's one too many home truths before breakfast! And what are we going to do about your father?'

Polly gave an unhappy little laugh. 'I don't know how to manage him.'

Bea said, 'He's established himself in Lady Fleur's room with Big Teddy as his slave, but he knows, really, that that can't last. I've painted a pretty picture for him of what his life could be like if he became an elder statesman living in the village, looked after by a full-time housekeeper, and with everyone showing him the respect he deserves. He needs an occupation. Maybe you can get him involved in local affairs?'

Julian managed a small – very small – grin. 'From the best bedroom in the Hall, to a cottage in the village? I'll see what's not only vacant but also in a reasonable state of repair. There's Dora's cottage for one. She had it for life but now it reverts back to the estate. I think someone said she had a tenant in it, though I think her lease forbade that. Another problem.'

Polly giggled. 'He won't want a cottage. He'll want the biggest house in the place. He'll get himself elected to the parish council, and demand to read the lesson in church on Sundays.'

Julian got out his phone. 'Mrs Maggs will know what house might be available for him, and I must speak to Lennie, see what we can work out. Then I'll check with Lance because he wants to come round this morning to look at the priest hole.'

Polly said, 'I have to check on progress at the Hall, what rooms we can get into and what we can't. I want to tackle the entrance hall next. We can't rehang curtains and put down carpets till the electricians and the plumbers have finished kicking up dust. I'm afraid we're terribly behind. Then I'll take Pip to see Jack. Oh! Oh dear.'

She'd remembered that Jack was no more. She said to Bea, 'Julian gave Pip a ride on Jack's back last week, can you believe? How can we find out how Jack died? And how Mickey's coping?'

Bea said, 'I might have an idea about that.'

Bea drove to the village to have a chat with Celine and Mona.

Their house looked ever so slightly unkempt this morning, with an empty can of beer and the packaging from a pizza in the strip of garden which divided house from pavement.

It was a chilly morning. Bea was glad she'd thought to wear her jacket.

Bea rang the bell and waited. She could hear raised voices inside. Radio? Television? People on the phone?

The door opened. Unlike Celine, Mona had spent money on herself. A silk kimono, gold sandals on tanned, shaved legs, hairdo delightfully, deliberately mussed, immaculate make-up. Lips that looked as if they'd been lightly bruised. A perfume that hadn't come out of a market stall.

Mona was one very expensive package. Who was paying the bill?

Mona stared at Bea. 'Yes? Who are . . .Wait a minute.' Click fingers. 'Got it. Julian's sugar mummy.'

Bea said, 'Yes, I suppose . . . Sort of. May I come in?'

'You've heard, then?'

'What have I heard?' Bea stepped inside.

Mona closed the door on the outside world. 'Bertram, our brother, died on the operating table yesterday. He was such a sweet-tempered boy. Never amounted to much but I'll miss him.'

Bea was shocked. 'What happened?'

'He hadn't been well. They found something nasty, something to do with his accident. They said an immediate operation might save his life. It didn't. Gerda – that's his wife – shot up there last night, wanting to see his body. Whether they'll let her, Lord alone knows. She doesn't know what to do with herself. Never did know what to do with herself, if you ask me.'

Bea said, 'I'm sorry to hear that. Poor woman. I heard she was
devoted to Bertram. No children?'

'He'd sown his seed in other places and Grandfather had had to
pay out for two – no, three – abortions, but it never took on his
wife. And now she's no chance of having a child. Heaven knows
what she'll do with herself. I don't want to sound unsympathetic,
you understand, but she's a dead weight in the house here, never
lifts a finger.'

'Has she no family? Does she have a job?'

'She helps out at the rescue centre, but it's not a proper job. At
least Celine has been facing facts and is trying to make something
of herself and I'm all set to go. But Gerda! I understand why Bertram
lost patience with her sometimes. Now you know, you can tell
Julian. No doubt he'll want to pay for a fine funeral for our brother.
Bertram was a Marston-Lang, after all.'

Bea wondered, but didn't say, if Julian would want to pay for
the funeral of a man who'd tried several times to kill him. But she
said, 'I'll tell him.'

Mona gave Bea the once-over. 'So if you didn't know, and didn't
come to condole with us on losing our brother, then what are you
here for?'

'To ask if you knew the name of the firm which disposed of the
horse Julian used to ride.'

'What?' Mona seemed genuinely surprised.

*Did she not know about it? Was she innocent of involvement in
the horse's death?*

THIRTEEN

Friday morning

Mona said, 'No. Sorry. I know nothing about that. I did hear someone say . . . But no, I'd nothing to do with it. I wouldn't.'

Bea believed her. 'Who did you hear talking about it?'

'Well, Gerda said . . . but she's so stupid that . . . she heard it at the rescue centre, I suppose. She's always down there, dripping tears over the latest puppies or whatever. The horse died? Really? What about the dog?'

So Mona knew Julian's father had lost both his horse and his dog?

'The horse died. There was a suspicious package left out for the dog but it wasn't given to him and he's all right, so far. Julian is distressed about the horse but he won't be intimidated. You understand that even if Bruno were killed, too, Julian wouldn't stop trying to save the Hall.'

Mona crossed her arms and held on tightly. 'Yes, I understand that. He may be a jumped-up nobody but yes, he's got guts. I admire him, in a way.'

The door to the sitting room opened and Celine thrust her head out. *'Will* you be quiet! I'm working!' She banged the door shut again.

Mona met Bea's eye and giggled. 'Tread softly. The Muse is at work.'

Bea began to like Mona.

Mona said, 'Want a coffee? I'm gagging for one.' She led the way into the kitchen, leaving a trail of expensive perfume behind her.

The kitchen looked as if everyone in the house had eaten takeaway food at different times but nobody had bothered to clear up. There wasn't a clear space anywhere.

Mona put the kettle on. 'My friend Marcus will be down in a minute. He was great last night, when Celine rang. He got his chauffeur to drive us back here and he stayed the night, which I

must admit I wasn't too sure he would. We've only got three
bedrooms here so his chauffeur found a room at the pub. But we
didn't get in till midnight, he's got a video meeting at noon and he
needs proper coffee to start the day with. Do you think there is any?
Celine usually sees to the housekeeping but now the Muse has taken
hold of her . . .'

Bea chucked off her jacket, seized an apron and set about the
dishes, saying, 'Try the cupboards. I'll wash the dishes and you can
dry. Did Celine tell you I was here when Craig tried it on? I offered
to stay with her, but—'

'She always runs to me when she's in trouble. She should have
brought her knee into play and done him an injury. Nasty little
weasel. Tried it on with me once, years ago. I bloodied his nose
for him and all. Never thought he'd try it on with Celine, poor kid.
She's terminally insecure and would have no idea how to cope with
his sort.'

Mona opened and shut cupboards, saying, 'Celine should have
been born a hundred years ago or more, when her family would
have married her off to a much older man who'd teach her how to
enjoy sex, and leave her a widow at an early age.'

Bea began to like Mona very much indeed. 'You're the elder
sister who always has to pick up the pieces?' She spotted a cafetière
on the top of the freezer. It had been used and left with the grounds
in it.

Mona found a bag of coffee. 'Ta-da! Look what I've found! Even
older sisters need a spot of assistance now and then. Marcus came
up trumps last night. I hadn't seen that side of him before. He even
let her cry on his shoulder. He's made a mint, you know. Owns
property all over, private jet and all that. Now he's hankering after
a stately home, which is why he finds my company so
fascinating.'

Bea thought Marcus might well be interested in acquiring a stately
home, but what he primarily wanted from Mona had nothing to do
with bricks and mortar.

Mona said, 'Now, I'm not stupid. Marcus has been married before
and I'm not expecting this to last. That's why I have to get something going for myself.'

Bea handed Mona a tea towel. 'You dry while I make the coffee.
You don't have any income of your own? Didn't your grandfather
leave you anything?'

'My grandmother set up a trust fund for us but my father managed to divert the money into the Hall's accounts somehow, and sent it abroad. He said he'd a friend who'd shown him a clever trick, some sort of alphabet code – or do I mean a cipher? – to hide his password. And the password had to be something important to him, something only he would know. I doubt we'll ever see a penny of it.'

Bea said, 'Frederick must have left a clue. Suppose he dies in jail? Has he made a will?'

'No, he hasn't. I tried the family solicitor, thinking my father might have left some instructions with him, but he hasn't. Nor had Bertram; not that he'd anything much to leave. Nor Grandmother; she's furious with my father, anyway, for upsetting all her arrangements. She's lucky; she's got her family's money to fall back on, unlike us.'

A current of air swept through the kitchen as if a door had been opened on to the outside world.

A man came into the kitchen. He was not tall but he carried his own force field around with him. A silver fox, oh yes! No product of Eton, he'd worked his way up the ladder and now had others doing his bidding. He was wearing designer smart casual wear and the expression of one who'd detected a bad smell in the toilet.

Bea understood several things: Mona was a frail little pussycat compared to this man. He had money and influence and he was accustomed to getting his own way in everything. At the moment he desired Mona, and had acquired her. Now he wanted the Hall, too?

Was he a murderer? *He was capable of it, yes. He might not have been responsible for getting someone to kill Jack and attempt to kill Bruno, but he wouldn't have lifted a finger to stop anyone who did so.*

Had he killed Dora? *No, he wouldn't have bothered. Why should he? She didn't threaten him in any way. Unless he'd been in the pub, she'd led him on and then failed to deliver? Um, no. Wishful thinking, that. This man would never have given Dora the time of day.*

Where did he stand on the Julian-versus-Craig business? *He was waiting to see who won, and then he'd decide what to do.*

His aim? *To acquire the status of a man who owned a country estate. He wouldn't want the bother of running it, but he could leave all that to Mona, couldn't he?*

Would he marry Mona? *Yes, if it was necessary to ensure he had the right to move into the Hall.*

Would he stick to her? *Yes, until he found a bigger property to give him even more status.*

Bea watched as the man embraced Mona with one arm. She pressed herself against him, elongating her body, clinging to him. A powerful wave of sexual tension ran through her and heightened the colour in her face. And then through his.

Bea realized that this was how Mona's mother, Lady Fleur, had managed to get her own way at the Hall. Sex rules OK.

He said, 'Where's my coffee?'

Mona put her arms around him and rested her head on his shoulder. 'Mrs Abbot's making you some.'

He gave Bea the attention you'd give to a waitress in a café. 'Do you make decent coffee?'

Bea fought off an urge to curtsey. 'I'm Bea Abbot, a friend of Sir Julian and Lady Paula's. I'll do my best.'

He lost interest in her when she agreed to do something for him. He disentangled himself from Mona and walked out of the kitchen, concentrating on his smartphone.

Mona called after him, 'Celine's working. Use the dining room opposite.'

Bea lifted her eyebrows at Mona, who had the grace to apologize. 'Sorry. He's used to servants, who . . . And proper coffee. I can't make it how he likes it, and he says . . . but when I'm back at the Hall then, of course, things will be different.'

Bea wondered how Marcus would get on with Julian, and concluded that they'd understand one another pretty well. Who would win out in a fight between them? Um. Difficult to say.

So would Marcus disappear if Julian decided not to let Mona run the farm shop?

Thinking this through, Bea went on automatic pilot to make some proper coffee. It wasn't going to be perfect without a supply of really fresh coffee grounds, but it would have to do.

Mona put the coffee, sugar and milk plus a bone china mug on to a tray and took it off to the dining room.

Did she really expect Bea to clean up for her?

Probably.

Bea decided to call it a day so resumed her jacket. There was no one in the hall, but a murmur of voices came from rooms on either side. Mona being lovey-dovey. Celine talking to herself as she wrote? Bea called out, 'See you around,' and took herself off.

She got into her car and made some phone calls. First to Julian. The call went to voicemail. Irritating. Bea left a message for him to ring her back, urgently.

Next to Paula, back at the Hall. 'Everything all right? Do you want anything from the village? Give me a list.' She jotted down Polly's requirements.

She tried Julian again. Voicemail. She hesitated. Was what she had to tell Julian important, or not worth bothering with? She left another message.

The next call was to her own agency. 'All well? Everything settled down again?'

The voice at the other end clacked on about this and that. A few niggles had arisen, but nothing important. Good.

Lastly, she rang Imran. 'Is all well?'

Noises off. Imran said to someone, 'Hold on a mo. I'll take this outside.'

More noises off. Then Imran said, 'Mrs Abbot? Sir Julian has had a little talk with Lennie, who's now got a deadline to work to, and is doing his nut. Lance and Sir Julian are in Lady Fleur's room, looking into the priest hole, taking measurements and photos and debating as to which national organization has to be informed about it first.'

Bea asked, 'Where's Paula's father, Mr Colston? I thought he'd moved into that room.'

'He did, and he was huffing and puffing about the intrusion and there being no water laid on in the bathroom nearby and Sir Julian turned to Teddy – who's a bit lacking but very willing, if you know what I mean – and said to him to show Mr C downstairs where his breakfast would be served up by Mrs Maggs. You could see Mr C had been expecting his breakfast to be brought up to him, but as it was clear that wasn't going to happen, off he went, as meek as anything, with Teddy offering to carry him down the stairs and Mr C telling him not to be a fool!'

'Brilliant,' said Bea. 'Now, Imran. I need to reach Sir Julian urgently. He's turned his phone off. Would you tell him I need to speak with him, now?'

Imran knew when the word 'urgent' meant 'immediate action required'.

Muffled voices followed and Bea switched off her own phone just in time for Julian to call her.

'Yes, Bea? There's a problem?' He did not like being interrupted, but was exercising patience.

She said, 'I had a chat with Mona. Had you heard about Bertram? They rushed him into the operating theatre yesterday but he died. So please, be careful.'

'What? Really? Oh, poor man. He didn't have much luck in life, did he? Thanks for telling me. I'm just in the middle of—'

'No, listen! This is important. Lady Fleur had set up a trust fund for the three children: Mona, Celine and Bertram. Their father Frederick managed to get control of it and diverted the money into the Hall's accounts which, together with the trust fund money, he sent abroad.'

'Yes, I know. My old firm traced it to the Cayman Islands, but can't get it from there without his password. He didn't tell Mona what it was, did he?'

'No, but he did tell her that a friend had taught him a cute trick, an alphabet code or cipher in which to hide the password. And the password is a word important to him.'

Silence. 'Repeat that.'

Bea did. 'Alphabet code or cipher. An important word. Does all that mean something to you?'

'It rings a bell. I've seen something, somewhere . . . but where? Now what method would Frederick have used to encode a password? A smartphone, maybe? No, phones can be hacked. It's back to pen and paper.' He repeated the words, 'Pen and paper. Now that reminds me of that drawerful of loose papers we found and put aside to be dealt with later. There's bills, fliers, receipts, scribbled sums, business cards . . . and yes, I think there may have been something that looked like a crossword. Or did I imagine it?'

'Do you know how many letters the password has to be?'

'Numerals, not letters. It's eight numerals, like an account number. He took a word and turned it into numbers. We have to find the numbers before we can get hold of the money. I'll check when I'm finished here.'

'Good. I need to speak to Imran again. Can you ask him to ring me?'

Julian clicked off, and Imran came through.

Bea said, 'Listen, Imran, while Lance is with Sir Julian I don't think there'll be any more trouble, but the moment he's alone—'

'There'll be another attempt? You want me to stick with Sir Julian, regardless of Lennie wanting extra hands today?'

'I know Lennie needs help, but it's important to guard Sir Julian. You know that Bertram Marston-Lang injured himself during his last attempt on Julian's life? His condition deteriorated; they operated yesterday and he didn't make it. I fear there's going to be repercussions.'

Imran sounded startled. 'What? Bertram's dead? How about that! I mean, he was dead stupid and not popular, but . . . really dead? Well, I don't suppose anyone's going to shed tears for him. Not even his sisters. They never got on. That wife of his won't. Why she put up with him, I don't know.'

'Because . . .?'

'It's common knowledge he used to hit her. You could see the bruises, but she always said she'd walked into a door or fallen downstairs. She had a miscarriage early on and then couldn't have any more, and that didn't help. He used to beat his dogs till the old man took them away from him, and then she had a toy dog that didn't last long either. No one at the rescue centre would lend him a horse to ride. So he went mad on the gym, monopolizing the equipment, and then driving that motorbike of his through the village at all hours of the night. Nearly killed old Mr P, who used to work up at Maggs's farm. And the girls, the ones that are still in the village, they all carry a rape alarm when he's around.'

'Got it. Now, is Bruno with you?'

'No, Sir Julian told him to stay with Lady Paula and the boy.' Noise, voices, thuds. Imran said, 'Must go. We're on the move and so is Lennie.'

Presumably he meant that Sir Julian and Lance had finished in the priest hole and Lennie was on the rampage about not having enough labour to finish the job?

Bea made another phone call, this time to her husband, Piers, who answered his phone in the same guarded tone as before. He sounded fit and breezy but was clearly being overheard. 'Good to hear from you, my love. All well with you? What's the weather like? It's wonderful here, just like in the tourist brochures. I'm

having a splendidly lazy time, being waited on hand and foot. You've
never seen anything like the luxury I'm living in.'

Bea accommodated her words to the situation. 'I'm glad you're
enjoying yourself. I've got your next client wanting to know when
you can start on his picture. Can I give him a date?'

'No, no. I'm enjoying myself far too much to think of work. I'll
let him know when my holiday's over.'

So he was still being held there while the local politics worked
out who was for the chop and who might survive to play another
day?

Annoying, very. But at least Piers didn't sound as if he personally
were in danger.

Bea stashed her phone, retrieved her car and took the road to the
nearest town, where she had more chance of getting the items Polly
needed than in the village shop. Also, she wanted to check out a
theory she'd been trying out in her mind for a while.

The knacker's yard. Where was it? Her smartphone informed her
that it was not far away.

She drove slowly into the town. It had an ancient centre with a
new estate of identical houses tacked on to it. The old part of the
town was still, thankfully, occupied by individual shops, and the
supermarkets were tucked out of sight down side roads. That way
the residents got the best of both worlds. The police station to which
Julian had been taken must be somewhere here. Yes, there was a
sign to it. And the hospital where he'd been kept overnight? Yes,
another sign pointed to that, too.

The business she wanted was down by the railway station, a little
way out of town. Enclosed by a high wall, it had high gates to deter
the curious. And a certain air of being separate from the rest of the
town. Rather like a prison.

Bea parked and managed to talk her way through a door in the
outer gates, and into a reception room – very clean, very neat, very
up-to-date equipment – occupied by a heavyweight youngish woman
in jogging clothes and a massive charm bracelet. Her demeanour
advised that she was definitely the Person In Charge. She'd probably
been with the company since she left school.

Ah, yes. There was a sign on her desk, announcing that this was
a Ms Boardman, no first name given.

Bea presented an agency card. 'My friend, Sir Julian Marston-
Lang, suffered injuries in a fall from a horse known to be lively,

supplied by the animal rescue centre. He could easily have been killed, and has been seriously incapacitated. He understands the rescue centre is a charity, but they must have insurance and so they should at least cover his medical bills. If necessary, he'll have to sue them. Mine is a fact-finding mission to discover who should be involved. I understand you disposed of the animal the day after the incident.'

Ms Boardman did not react, save to narrow her eyes. 'He's making an insurance claim against the rescue centre? That's nothing to do with us.' Her eyes were very sharp. Bea would wager the woman 'ran a tight ship'.

Bea was soothing. 'I'm told there's a query about the horse's death. I need to ensure the proper procedures were followed. If all is in order here, I will advise Sir Julian not to include you in his claim. All I need is to see the vet's authority for you to put the animal down and a copy of the order from the rescue centre to remove the dead body. That done, you're in the clear.'

'Of course we're in the clear. We was asked to collect a dead horse by the rescue centre, which we did. All done by phone.'

'They left you the vet's paperwork, then?'

The muscles around Ms Boardman's mouth hardened, and her eyes narrowed. There was a long pause. A bluebottle buzzed at the window. With marked reluctance, the woman turned to her computer and brought up a file. And sighed. 'The boss dealt with it. The bill is to go to the rescue centre. All in order.'

'And the vet's paperwork? You must see that I need that.'

'There was no need for a vet. Animals die, we deal with the remains. That's what we do. Horses, now. It's usually colic. Swollen belly. Something he'd eaten, no doubt. Some of these grooms, they don't know a poisonous weed from a salad leaf.'

'So you think Sir Julian should be suing the groom? Then I think I must get a statement from the vet to the effect that the horse died of colic. A post-mortem may be necessary.'

A huge sigh. Ms Boardman lumbered to her feet, opened a door behind her, and disappeared.

Bea waited. Five minutes. The fly buzzed at the window. Bea opened the window and let the fly out. A phone on the desk rang. A message was taken; would someone please ring the following number.

At long last Ms Boardman returned, looking sour. She said, 'They didn't leave no paperwork. Phone call from the rescue centre. A horse had died, please collect. Bill to them. So that's what we did.'

'So no vet was involved? Are you prepared to give me a statement that the horse died of colic? If not, we'll need to arrange a post-mortem.'

The woman flumped into her chair, and said, 'The boss says it had all the marks of a professional job. We've seen it before. Animal goes loco, way out of control. Nothing to do but end its misery. This time there was no paperwork because there was no vet. The rescue centre have used our services before, and no doubt will again. You'll have to ask them what happened.'

'A professional job? How was it done, and how did your boss know?'

'Retractable bolt gun, used by vets to kill. Supposed to be held only by vets but old ones do occasionally drift into other hands.'

'Retractable . . . what? How does that work?'

The woman stared at Bea. 'You don't know the first thing about horses, do you? You put the gun to its forehead and bang, he's dead. Bolt retracts back into the gun. Small hole, nothing much to see. The boss has been at the game all his life, like his dad before him. He found the horse, dead. He looked for the cause. He saw the hole from the bolt. He got the tackle, hauled the body out, loaded it up and brought it back here. We sent the bill in.'

'Your staff use such guns all the time?'

'Under careful supervision. We don't do outside jobs.'

'You think a vet killed the horse? Which vet do you use?'

The woman scrabbled in a desk drawer and gave Bea a card. 'I don't think it was them. They're careful about paperwork.'

'You're thinking that someone at the rescue centre killed the horse because he'd thrown Sir Julian and they didn't want any repercussions?'

'The boss thought it must be Mickey, the groom who looked after the rescue centre's horses.'

'Would Mickey be able to get hold of one of these guns? And did he know how to use it? I've met him, and I doubt if he had the guts to do it.'

'If the horse had gone crazy, the rescue centre shoulda called a vet.'

'Yes, they should. I'll check. Have you disposed of the body already, or would it be possible to have a post-mortem done?'

'For a horse?' Distaste and incredulity.

'To save a man's life. That accident . . . Sir Julian was meant to die.'

The woman dropped her eyes to her hands. 'Nothing to do with us.'

She fiddled with the catch on her charm bracelet. Several of the charms were of dogs. No horses. Maybe she didn't even like horses.

Bea said, 'If you would let me have a statement about what you discovered—'

'I'd rather not.'

'Then Sir Julian includes you in his insurance claim.'

Stalemate. The woman considered her options, drew her computer towards her, typed a couple of paras, read it over, and printed a page off. She signed and dated the statement in teeny-weeny writing and handed it over to Bea, who read it over and nodded. It was as much as she could have hoped for: there'd been no paperwork, nothing from a vet, just a phone call from the rescue centre. Cause of death not mentioned. Carcass already disposed of; bill sent to the rescue centre.

Ms Boardman said, 'See yourself out.'

Which Bea did. Now, what should she do next?

FOURTEEN

B ea sat in her car and considered her options. Time was marching. Rosemary Sweeting would be arriving soon for an interview with Julian, and Imran would be on guard. Double insurance. Bea was not needed there.

Besides which, she was ravenously hungry and needed to check on the vet while she was in town. And buy the things Polly needed.

Was there a cosy-looking tea room around? On the High Street, perhaps? She drove around. Ah, there was a good-looking coffee shop which was not a chain, displaying eats in the window which looked as if they were home-made. The café looked busy, which was always a good sign.

The thought of a slice of a good quiche made Bea's mouth water and she went in. She sat at a table for one and ordered. Yes, the quiche was as good as it looked. The coffee wasn't bad, either.

The lunchtime rush was pretty well over by the time she'd eaten. The lad who was clearing away the used crockery suffered from acne but was otherwise clean and tidy. He bore a name tag which identified him as Jan. He looked local so, knowing how gossip travels around a neighbourhood, Bea risked a question.

'I wonder if you could help me. I'm new around here but I need to find a vet. Can you recommend one?'

His eyes were sharp. 'You have a pet? Small animals, is it? Try Better Vet's, just off the High Street. They're old fashioned but do farm stock as well as small animals. Otherwise, there's the new place down by the river; small animals, treat your cat for cancer but you have to pay through the nose, like.'

Should she risk another question? Yes. 'I'm a guest at the Hall, or rather, in the Tithe Barn at the back. My friend needs a vet. He used to ride a horse named Jack, on loan from the rescue centre. He also has an Alsatian named Bruno.'

His busy hands paused and he gave her a sidelong look. '*Used* to ride . . .?'

'Something caused Jack to go mad and he threw Sir Julian. The horse then met an untimely end. I found a hunk of meat, which I suspect was poisoned, left out for Sir Julian's dog, Bruno. Any idea which vet might have an opinion on the subject?'

He said, 'I'll get you another coffee,' and disappeared.

Why was he getting her another coffee? Because he had something to tell her about these troubling events?

Bea looked at her watch. Should she depart, or should she wait?

A pretty blonde with slightly over-the-top make-up and tattooed eyebrows brought Bea another coffee and set to work cleaning the next table. Her name tag identified her as 'Ivy'. She said, 'Jan says you were asking . . .?'

Bea repeated her story, during which time other customers came and Jan attended to them. Bea noted that he was keeping an eye on Ivy and maybe also listening to what Bea was saying?

The girl said, 'You gotta unnerstand. My dad and my brother both worked in the amusement park and I had a job in the restaurant. Me mum used to run the launderette but now no one's got any work, she's had to close that down, too. We heard about the horse throwing Sir Julian. A bit of a laugh, really, seeing as how he's supposed to be such a good rider.'

Bea listened to what the girl was saying – and what she was *not* saying. She was the voice of the village. The local people didn't care that Frederick had cleared out the bank accounts, or that Julian had had to sell his flat, downsize and borrow money to kickstart the repairs at the Hall. They didn't care that Health and Safety would have closed down everything if Julian hadn't done so. All they knew was that in the old days there were jobs, and now there weren't any.

This one-sided opinion would have generated a certain bias against Julian, leading to . . . what? Barely contained resentment? There would have been amusement that Julian had fallen off his horse, and gossip. Jokes, each one coarser than the last.

Two more customers arrived in the café and one left. Jan attended to them with a smile and an efficient manner which indicated he was in charge that day. Ivy, on the other hand, continued to lurk. She even started cleaning the table on the other side of Bea. She still had something to say?

She did. 'You said something about the horse. What happened to him?'

'Killed by a gun with a retractable bolt. Thursday night, Friday morning. Taken away by the knackers, who were told to send the bill to the rescue centre. No vet seems to have been involved. Also, I found some dicey meat, possibly poisoned, which was left for the dog.'

The girl polished the table, hard. 'The dog's all right though, isn't he?'

'So far. If he's killed, though . . . Sir Julian really cares for his animals.'

The girl started on another table. 'They say the farm shop's reopening soon. I asked Sir Julian about a job there last week, when he was riding through the village with his dog. It would be much more convenient, save me making the trek here every day. Sir Julian cut me off short. Dead rude, he was. Said he'd be appointing a new manager soon and rode off without so much as asking my name. My boyfriend said I should have had him for inappropriate touching.'

Ivy tossed her pretty head and looked sideways at Bea to see what effect her words might have had.

Bea was so furious she didn't know how to contain herself. The girl had lied through her teeth. Julian would never have touched her inappropriately. For two pins, Bea would have shaken the fake eyelashes off the girl or given her a good spanking!

But, no. Bea knew she couldn't make a scene. That wouldn't help anybody.

In a low voice, she said, 'I'm sure you are accustomed to men finding you attractive and you were annoyed that he didn't seem to do so. You say he touched you inappropriately? I wonder how he did that when he was riding on his horse? Did you think he was like Frederick and Bertram, and could be tempted by a pretty girl smiling at him? Well, he's not like them. He's a thoroughly decent man who loves his wife dearly.'

Heightened colour. A chin in the air. But Ivy still didn't walk away. Perhaps there was some way to get through to her still? Her co-worker, Jan, was shooting glances in her direction. Customers needed serving and Ivy was not doing her job properly.

Bea realized she would only have a moment to connect to the girl before Jan whisked her away. She said, 'Look, I do understand the anger in the community at losing so many jobs. I do see that in that atmosphere, crude jokes can start to circulate in the pub. Perhaps some wit linked Julian's name with Dora's? This might have caused laughter and some speculation as to what would have happened if she had tried it on with him. From there it would have been only a small step to someone saying he thought he'd actually seen Julian arguing with her. And so it becomes an amusing anecdote which people begin to believe is true. Is that how it worked?'

A shrug. 'I know what my friend saw.'

'Your friend says she saw Sir Julian out with Dora on the night she died?'

'That's what she said.'

'Does this friend of yours have a name?'

A shrug. 'Ask me no questions and I'll tell you no lies.'

Bea made her voice soft. 'Don't you see how dangerous such a rumour can be? I understand that you all thought it was a good joke at first, making up stories about an off-comer to the district who had put so many people out of work.

'But, weren't you the least bit worried when the police picked up the rumour that Julian had been seen arguing with Dora the night she died, and started to take it seriously? Didn't you understand that if Julian were found guilty of murder, the Hall would have to be sold and you and everyone else would be out of a job for good? Where's your common sense?'

'How dare you!' Tears spurted. Ivy half walked and half ran to the door to the kitchens, then disappeared.

Bea was shaking. She put both hands flat on the table, and told herself to breathe deeply, in and out. In and out. Her blood pressure must have gone through the roof.

The boy Jan followed Ivy to the kitchen. Noisy sobs were to be heard as the door opened and shut. Several people looked around, waiting to be served. Jan reappeared, sent a glance at Bea which she couldn't interpret, and attended to the impatient customers. He was good at his job. Deft, quick and with a pleasant manner.

Bea told herself to get moving. And found she couldn't.

Jan appeared at her side, frowning. He gestured to her unwanted cup of coffee. 'Have you finished?'

'Thank you, yes.' Did he understand what the girl Ivy had been up to? Yes, there was knowledge in his eyes, but no condemnation. Rather, he seemed unsure of himself. He picked up the coffee cup. 'I overheard what you were saying. Ivy's a bit . . . Well, she takes things hard. When we were made redundant at the Hall, lots of us had to go elsewhere for jobs. I was at school with Ivy, see, and I've got an old banger, so I give her a lift every day. It's only temporary, I told her. Sir Julian's the sort that'll pull things round. But she . . . well, I think you got it right. She tried it on, he told her to behave herself, and she took it badly. And so she sort of made up that . . . well, she did see someone, but . . .'

'Ivy saw someone? Or her friend did? Ah, Ivy made the friend up?'

He fidgeted. 'Dunno. Either. One day she said she'd seen him with Dora and the next, she said as someone else told her that . . . I think she, or her friend, saw someone but wasn't close enough to know who it was.'

'Would Ivy have been out and about that night, near the stables? Unlikely, isn't it?'

'It's where we all go for a bit of peace and quiet, like. Mickey don't mind, and you can take refuge in one of the boxes if it rains. Mind you, now they've got the security lights going, it won't be so popular. But Ivy and her boyfriend did use to go up there all the time, she on the back of his bike. She thought it was dead romantic, what with talk of the ghosts and buried treasure. People believe what they want to believe.'

'Not you?'

'I got my own transport and my own girl. We're cool. I'm taking a year off, going to uni in the autumn.'

'What about Craig? Do you think it was he that Ivy saw with Dora?'

'Could have been him with his dyed hair and all. He thinks it makes him look like a Marston-Lang. Says he's an internationally famous interior designer. As if!' He glanced at the door to the kitchen, from whence came the sound of someone crying noisily.

'Don't you worry none about Ivy. I'll talk some sense into her. She's an OK waitress, you know, if someone keeps an eye on her. Just not very bright.'

'Thank you, Jan. I take the hint, and I appreciate your point of view. Now I'd better get moving.'

Bea shopped for the bits and pieces which Polly wanted. Then, returning to her car, she wondered what to do next. Well, while she was in town, she might as well have a word with the two vets, to see if one of them could cast light on the goings-on at the rescue centre.

The Better Vet had decent premises, light and airy, with parking at the back. It looked well patronized and prosperous.

The reception desk was occupied by not one but two clean-looking women who looked as if they enjoyed life and the odd pastry. Two people were sitting in the waiting room: one cradled a cat in a basket and the other had a dog on a leash. The cat didn't want to know about anything, but the dog wanted to know all about the cat. The cat was called in first, which left the dog looking for someone else to play with.

Bea spoke to the receptionist nearer the door. 'I wonder if someone can help me. I'm enquiring about the rescue centre and—'

'Come to settle their account, have you?' Her companion laughed.

Bea blinked.

The first receptionist said, 'Now, now. Don't you take any notice of her. It's like an old joke around here, the rescue centre and its overdue account. We've had to stop taking their calls.'

Bea didn't know what to make of this. 'I'm Bea Abbot, a friend of Sir Julian and Lady Paula's, and I'm staying in the old Tithe Barn with them while the Hall gets sorted out. There's a query about the horse from the rescue centre which Julian was riding. The horse died and I'm trying to find out why, and which vet attended the death. Also, a suspicious packet was left for his dog. Am I to understand that you haven't been called out to the rescue centre recently?'

The first receptionist said, 'A horse and a dog. History repeating itself, innit? No, we wouldn't be going there, no matter what.'

'Tell you what,' said the second receptionist, 'old Mr Potter might know something, right? He's officially retired but he was their vet for years and someone said he still went out there now and then. I could ask him to ring you, if you like. He enjoys a good gossip.'

Bea handed over a card. 'Yes. Thank you.'

Bea sat in her car and worried. Time was marching on. Had Rosemary arrived yet? Was there any point in ringing her to see how she'd got on with Julian? No, of course not. Either Rosemary was there or she was not.

Bea asked herself about trying the other vet.

No, that wouldn't be any use. The one she'd just visited was the one which dealt with farm and small animals. The other wasn't equipped to deal with the large animals – the horses, the llamas, the goats and sheep and goodness knows what else which were housed at the rescue centre.

Bea told herself that she was wasting time, hanging around in town asking questions about vets, when she should be . . . doing what? Standing in front of Julian so that he wasn't attacked by some madman? Running to the police with the theory that the sighting of Julian with Dora was a consequence of the resentment local people felt at the loss of their jobs? And possibly a certain annoyance by that pretty young lass, Ivy, with her belief that she could get herself a job by wiggling her bottom?

Yes, the police needed to be disillusioned. But perhaps not now.

By the pricking of my thumbs,
Something wicked this way comes.

A rhyme kept whispering at the back of her mind. She pulled on her seatbelt and started the engine. She must get back to the Hall as quickly as she could, to warn Julian. She didn't know why she had an impulse to warn him, but it was very strong.

Her phone pinged. Bother. She drew in to the side of the road, parked and cut the engine to take the call.

It was Piers, her beloved husband, ringing just when she wanted to be off and away. He'd landed himself in a difficult situation, and although normally he'd be perfectly capable of extricating himself from anything from a full-scale riot to an earthquake, he did seem to need to keep the contact with her going.

He sounded just fine. 'Yes, here I am relaxing by the pool. We're supposed to be going to the races this afternoon. I'm glad I brought my sunscreen. And tonight there's some sort of banquet we're supposed to attend.'

Bea ventured a query. 'How's the portrait getting on?'

'Slowly. Days to go yet. I'll bet you wish you were here, too. The weather is something fantastic. A cold wet spring in London doesn't appeal.'

He knows I'm not in London. What's he on about?

She said, 'If you're going to be some time away, do I need to phone anyone, cancel your appointments?'

'Mm. It's a possibility. I'll let you know, shall I?'

He clicked off. Bea stared at her phone. That was a coded hint, wasn't it? He was being kept in luxury but couldn't leave, and it might be time to scream for help to some of his London pals.

This was most upsetting. Most.

Bea blew her nose and ran a comb over her hair. Piers had put her on red alert, and there was nothing she could do but wait. Oh, and a spot of prayer might be helpful.

She sent up a few arrow prayers. She didn't know exactly what to pray for except, *Dear Lord, help! You know what's needed more than I!*

Look, if you want me to do this or that, please make it clear to me, because I don't know what I'm doing any more. Oh, and please look after Bruno. You don't mind my praying for a dog, do you? Because of course human beings are more important, but you know without my having to remind you about what's going on here. Which is more than I do . . .

She started the car and waited for a gap in the traffic so that she could pull out, and at that very moment her phone rang again. This time it was a warm, older man's voice.

This was getting annoying. She parked again, killed the engine and took the call.

'Someone said you wanted a word? Oh, Tom Potter speaking. I gather you've been enquiring about the old days at the rescue centre. I've been their vet for many more years than I care to remember, but Anno Domini, you know, getting on, knees not what they used to be, so I don't practise nowadays. Now, who are you exactly, and where do you fit in?'

Bea explained again.

Mr Potter said, 'Well, well. That brings it all back, doesn't it? I remember it well. A dog and a horse. So long ago and yet it seems like yesterday. Yes, I looked after all the animals at the Hall in those days. Old Sir Florian owned some crackers of horses, and young Julian took after him. Excellent seat, he had. My son that's a vet now, too, was friends with him, young Julian.'

His voice cracked. He was no youngster, that was for sure.

Bea said, 'You were called in when this Julian's father's horse and dog were killed?'

'Shotgun for the horse. Messy. Bad. Young Julian was beside himself. And then, two days later, his dog was shot, too. Frederick had done both, of course. He denied it, but we all knew it was him. I had the horse taken away and I helped Julian bury the dog in the meadow behind the stables. Julian was gutted. Then Frederick came by and he was laughing and . . . Well, you can imagine.'

'There was a row?'

'To end all rows. Young Julian accused Frederick of killing the animals. He denied it but you could see he was lying. Sir Florian and Lady Fleur came out. She was backing her son up as she always did, telling Julian not to be so childish. Sir Florian looked as sick as a dog but didn't say anything, as usual. That's when young Julian said he'd had enough and decided to leave.'

'Just like that? Overnight?'

'He'd been sorely tried. Lady Fleur was like a . . . what was she like? Like a snake, hypnotizing you and then going for the jugular. That's mixing my metaphors, but you know what I mean? Whatever she wanted, she got. Perhaps young Julian thought his leaving might bring his father round. In fact, we all thought that Sir Florian would bring his son back, but he didn't. He withdrew into himself and got rid of his horses, all of them. I don't think he ever rode again.

'Then Frederick was a bit rough with his dogs and I had to put them down. The same thing happened with his son, Bertram. Sir Florian said there were to be no more dogs at the Hall after that. No, wait. I tell a lie. There was one other dog. A chihuahua, which one of the women had. Swedish or Norwegian, wasn't she? She'd been an au pair somewhere local, I think. Carried the dog every-where. Bertram trod on it, or threw it across the room. Broken bones, anyway. I had to put it out of its misery.'

'It was Bertram did that, not his father, Frederick?'

'The son, Bertram. I always said he'd come to a bad end. He used to hit his wife. I've seen the bruises myself. She always made excuses. Gerda, that was her name. Sounds like something out of a fairy-tale, doesn't it? I see her sometimes down at the rescue centre, petting the smaller, sweet-tempered animals. She's afraid of the llamas and the goats, and well, anything that could answer back. Poor creature.'

Bea had come across women like that before. In her experience, women like Gerda didn't fight. They cried. She was born to be a victim.

Bea said, 'Had you heard that Bertram died yesterday? He had to have an operation and he died in theatre. Gerda is said to be inconsolable.'

'Well, well. He's no loss, but I'm sorry for her.'

'So do you still look after the animals at the rescue centre?'

'I'm officially retired now, and there are some days when I just can't seem to get going, but I like to go along there, keep my hand in, have a chat. They're very good to an old fellow, and if I can't remember the names of all the llamas, they don't fret about it. On my good days, if it's just a question of antibiotics or stitching a small wound, I'll do it, they give me a cuppa and we call it quits. We both know they can't afford to pay the going rate.'

'You know that the rescue centre let the present Sir Julian have one of their horses to ride? Had you heard he'd been killed, too? I'm trying to find out how he died. Were you called out for him?'

'Really? Are you sure? First I've heard of it. Well, that's a shock. Who . . .? How was he killed, do you know? A fine animal. Can't remember his name. He'd been mistreated earlier but responded well to this Sir Julian's handling.'

'A teasel head was put under the saddle. The horse went spare. Sir Julian jumped off but suffered an injury. The horse was all right after that. Nervous, but OK. He died that night and his carcass was removed early next morning on the orders of the rescue centre people. As far as I can make out, no vet was involved.'

'Ah. Colic, you think?'

'Or a bolt from a gun.'

Silence. Bea could hear the man breathing. Was he going to switch off?

No. But he wasn't going to volunteer information, either.

She said, 'You visit the rescue centre often? You take your bag of medication and surgical implements with you. And sometimes, things go astray? Like an old gun, used for putting larger animals out of their misery?'

'I must go.' Hurriedly. 'Duty calls and all that.' He ended the call.

He hadn't missed his gun? Or had missed it but hadn't known where he'd left it? How old is he now? Perhaps too old to be as careful about his equipment as he ought to be?

Bea drove back to the Hall, trying to put all the different bits of information that she'd gleaned into their appropriate boxes. Nothing quite fitted.

Turning into the yard at the back of the Hall, she saw the usual clutter of workmen's cars. She also spotted a large, expensive mobile home.

So Rosemary Sweeting had arrived. Good. After a traumatic house fire, Rosemary Sweeting had taken to the travellers' life, moving from job to job around the country as the whim took her. How long had she been here? If she'd decided the job was not for her, she'd have left within the hour, but hopefully she'd have learned enough to give it a go. Surely she'd have got on well with Julian and Polly?

Bea got out and stretched. Bruno rose from his post with a companionable 'wuff' and a glance back at the end of the barn to inform her where Julian might be found.

The door was open. Bea went in to find Julian lying in his chair, head down, with his bad foot holding down a clutter of paper on the table. And no one else in sight. Was he asleep or in despair?

FIFTEEN

Bea dropped her jacket and handbag just inside the door. Julian lifted his head and grinned at her. 'Bea, I love you dearly. I was just giving thanks. And more thanks. I want to shout it from the rooftop. Thank you, Lord. And thank you, Bea.' She guessed at the truth. 'You've broken the code?'

'I'm hoping so. Remember we'd dumped a whole lot of paperwork from Frederick's time in a drawer till we could sort it out? I thought I remembered seeing something that looked like a crossword only not. So I went through the pile and found a couple of receipted bills where he'd been trying out how to turn a word into letters. It's a good old system which has been updated dozens of times, but in essence you write down the numerals from one to nine across the page . . . here!'

He picked out a much-scribbled-on bill and pointed out where someone had done just that.

'Then underneath you write the letters of the alphabet from A to Z. When you get to number nine which is "I", you go back to the beginning and put "J" under number one. And so on. Then you choose your important word. I chose "Marston" and "Florian" and tried both. "Marston" comes out as 4191265 and "Florian" as 6369915. It's not so easy to turn them back, because you will have three possible answers for each letter.'

Bea's brain couldn't cope. 'I'm full of admiration.'

'It's a bit rough and ready, but I think it's right. It feels right. I've let my colleague at the old firm know what I've done, and he's going to try it on the bank in the Cayman Islands. We should know by tomorrow morning if I've guessed right, but if I have, our money troubles are over.'

'Indeed,' said Bea. 'But where is everyone?' She tried to keep the panic out of her voice but could hear it rising. Julian had been left all alone? With a killer on the loose?

He wasn't worried. 'The electricians are revolting because I've reminded them that under the contract they should finish this weekend or forfeit their bonus. They pretended to have forgotten that and are now fighting one another as to who was responsible . . . and doing no more work. Lance has his plumbers tidying up this and that. They're on schedule and should be finished today or tomorrow.

'Lance is working out what's needed if Lennie walks off the job – which he may do. Mrs Maggs is trying to woo my esteemed father-in-law into looking at a suitable house for rent in the village and he's refusing to shift. Imran has been hovering, but he's now gone off with Lance to work out how many solar panels they can fit on the roof here . . . that is, if I can access the money from the Cayman Islands to pay for it.'

Bea smiled, because he was smiling, too. 'And . . . Rosemary?'

'Polly has taken Pip and Rosemary for a tour of the Hall to show her the extent of the problems there. Oh yes, and the meeting in the parish hall has been scheduled a little earlier than planned. I'm dreading it. That's when I'm supposed to tell everyone everything's perfect and there will be jobs tomorrow. Oh, and various historical associations are lining up to visit the priest hole and advise me on any documents which we may find there.

'As if that isn't enough, my cousin Mona has invited herself to tea, bringing her billionaire lover who, I understand on the grapevine, is looking for a Stately Home to buy for weekends. I've turned the phone to take messages because Bertram's widow keeps ringing to say that she's holding me responsible for his death, and . . . I've probably forgotten a great many other important things and I can see you have news of your own to impart. I'm all ears.'

'Good,' said Bea, smiling. 'You're feeling better.'

He glared at her. 'Which is more than I can say for Rosemary Sweeting. Is she human, I ask myself? Or – and I think you should have warned me – is she human or has she suffered some trauma which has turned her into a robot?'

'Yes,' said Bea, not smiling at all. 'I expect she'll tell you about it when she's learned to trust you. In the meantime, I'd suggest you make use of her incredible talents for as long as it takes.'

He looked hard at Bea. 'She has the situation here down to a T already: income, debts, problems, new ventures. She's done the maths and has decided to take me on for as long as is convenient to her. There's to be no nonsense about where she's to stay because she'll live in her mobile home.

'Oh, and she said she doesn't expect to be asked to babysit as she's allergic to children until they've reached the age of reason. She's running off a contract for her services as soon as she comes back from the Hall, where Polly is giving her the low-down. Or high spots. Not sure which. I get the feeling Rosemary thinks people who own stately homes ought to be taken out and shot at dawn, unless of course they are doing it for the benefit of humanity.'

Bea said, 'You hit it off? Good. Will she train Polly into becoming Lady Paula, do you think?'

He grinned. 'The jury's out on that. Now, what have you been up to? You look as if you've got indigestion.'

Bea sighed. 'Too much information, not fully assimilated. Here's a quick round-up of the highlights. Craig attempted to rape Celine; I was there, he left, she refuses to charge him. She thinks she now has a hold on him. I doubt it, myself, but maybe he'll be more careful in future because I was there and can bear witness against him.

'Then I met this man Marcus, whom Mona has in tow. He likes sex and Mona can supply it. You're right, and he has his eye on the Hall to give him a leg up in society. Mona thinks taking over the farm shop would be a doddle by doing everything on the internet. She also thinks she's going to be able to move back into the Hall again soon.'

He grimaced. 'I had a quick word with Imran about the farm shop. He makes out a good case. We'll speak more tomorrow. What other shocks do you have for me?'

'The vet who attended to your father's horse and dog is now retired but still visits the rescue centre. From him and others I learned that your horse Jack was killed with a retractable bolt from a gun.'

He bowed his head. 'Poor Jack. Who did it?'

'Not sure. Those particular guns are commonly used by vets to finish off dying animals. Now, everyone's talking about your father's horse and dog having been killed by Frederick with a shotgun. It worries me that such a gun could be hanging around here and could be used again.'

'Guns are not my thing.'

'Julian, in a place like this, there wouldn't only be one shotgun. The family would have accumulated other weapons as well over the years: rifles with bayonets fixed, handed down after the First

World War; handguns from the Second World War and all sorts of
guns for use in the days when men and women went hunting and
shooting. We're not talking one or two. We're talking a collection.
I'm concerned as to where those guns might be nowadays, and so
I'm asking, where's the family collection of guns?'

Julian said, 'Ah. Now, let me think. My grandfather asked me if
I shot, and I said I didn't. He told me I should learn. I refused. I
said I didn't like guns. Grandfather told me I was an idiot, which
was fair enough. We did argue a lot.'

He'd been fond of old Sir Florian, hadn't he?

'He said he'd show me where the guns were and if I still didn't
want anything to do with them, he'd sell them. He showed me a
locked cupboard built into a wreck of a room which had once been
the estate office. There'd been a water leak from above and the
ceiling had fallen in. A metal filing cabinet, the old-fashioned kind,
had fallen across the door to the gun cabinet, and various pieces of
junk had been thrown in on top.

'We cleared away enough junk to get to the cabinet, he tried to
use his keys but couldn't make them work. He said I'd better do
something about the ceiling and he'd get rid of the guns and we
left it at that. I'm sorry to say I put the ceiling of that room on my
to-do list and forgot all about it.'

'He may well have sold the guns,' said Bea, not believing it for
a minute.

A quick frown. 'No, I don't think he did. I found an inventory
and a receipted bill for the insurance when I took over. It was one
of the few things Frederick had kept up to date. And yes, I know I
ought to have checked on the guns, and I'm clearly going to be
very sorry that I didn't. We'd better have a look, now. Let me find
Grandfather's keys to the cabinet.'

He struggled to his feet, his balance awkward, and picked up one
of the pair of crutches which had fallen to the floor by his chair.
Balancing himself with care, he pulled a large book out from under
the settee and opened it to discover a set of keys in a hollowed-out
shell. 'Right. Let's go on a treasure hunt, shall we?'

He set off for the door into the yard, swinging his way out of
the door with a speed that surprised Bea, who'd been thinking of
him as an invalid. Bruno attached himself to his master's heels.

Across the yard, and next to the kitchen door, there was a second,
unobtrusive entrance, partially masked with ivy. A worn notice on

the wall stated that this was the estate office. Julian shook the handle on this door, which refused to open.

'When the ceiling fell in, Frederick moved the estate office over to where we're living now. He had a woman come in from the village twice a week to attend to business for him, but the job was clearly beyond her. I found bills misfiled, some items entered on the computer three times, others not entered at all. Rosemary is going to have a ball with the paperwork.'

He led the way into the kitchen which, for once, was deserted, though clearly people had been eating and drinking here. Where was Mrs Maggs?

There were sounds of workmen arguing and various bangs and crashes overhead. A woman's voice, raised in anger. Mrs Maggs, having a go at the electricians?

A woman laughed, not upstairs but along the corridor. Polly? Where were Polly and Pip? And Rosemary?

Julian swung into the passage that ran the length of the house and took a sharp turn right. They came cross a door that looked pretty solid but which was not quite shut. Julian heaved at it, and it gave a couple of inches. He tried again, and something fell over. Another push, and the door opened just enough for them to see inside.

Bruno huffed at Julian's heels and was told to stay and sit.

'Junk' was the best expression to use for the contents of the room: cardboard and wooden packing cases, planks of timber, rusting cans of paint, a pile of broken chairs, a slithery pile of old news-papers, a sagging desk minus one leg with drawers spilling out of it, a dented filing cabinet – no, two filing cabinets.

Some of the junk was heavily coated with the debris from the ceiling, and some was cleaner. Clearly if anything needed to be got rid of in recent times, people just opened the door and threw it in.

There was a fairly clear path through the rubble to a strong metal cabinet built into the opposite wall. If a piece of furniture had fallen across it when Julian saw it before, it had been shifted by now. The door of the gun cabinet had been jemmied open and left that way. There were no guns inside. None.

Julian was furious with himself. 'It wasn't nearly as bad as this when the old man showed me this room, and the cabinet was defi-nitely locked at that time. We tried to open it and failed. I asked who had keys and he said only Frederick and himself. Frederick left a bunch of keys behind when he fled; I gave those to Mrs Maggs to look after because she needs access to everything. Grandfather's keys I have here. It doesn't look as if anyone bothered to find the keys in order to clear out the cabinet.'

Bea pointed. 'Footprints in the dust.'

They peered at them. Julian said, 'The top ones are from a work-man's boots, rather broad. Underneath . . . those look like mine? And Grandfather's? Longer and narrower. Shoes, not boots.'

Bea said, 'We'd better not go any further into the room or we'll be destroying evidence.'

Julian said, 'Let's try to construct a timeline. Some months ago, Grandfather invited me to take over at the Hall. He showed me this room. At that point the ceiling was down, and one of those filing cabinets had fallen across its door. We shifted it with some difficulty but failed to open the cabinet door. It looked secure, untouched.'

'Why didn't it open?'

'The door was damaged when the filing cabinet fell across it and that must have upset the lock.'

Julian pointed to the ruined ceiling from which chunks of plaster had fallen. Newish cabling hung down in a loop, not connected to anything.

'That cabling wasn't here when Grandfather brought me in here. Lance and his team had no reason to come into this room but the electricians did. Lennie or one of his men fed in new cabling and left it to be connected up at a later date. When he started, Lennie told me he had a workforce of seven. He did, for a couple of weeks, and then two left and he didn't replace them, probably to cut costs. Now he's down to Teddy, his mate Whatshisname, and Imran when he's not working elsewhere. One or more of them has been in here.'

Bea took up the story. 'Teddy's feet are enormous. He didn't make these prints. And Imran doesn't wear boots; or rather, he does, but they're lighter than those worn by the other workmen, and in good nick. The last person into this room was clearly a workman. You can see his prints over everything else. Oldish boots, by the look of it, slightly worn down on the outside. Those prints overlay another set made by the same man . . . and in turn they overlay the earliest prints which are of two people with long, narrow feet . . . and those are shoes, not boots.'

'My grandfather and I could almost have worn the same shoes.

We did both have long, narrow feet. The dust shows we didn't return after our first foray—'

'But the workman did. The first time he came in was after you and your grandfather's visit. He fed in the new cabling and left. Dust settled over your footsteps and his. Much later, he comes back in and walks straight to the cabinet. Very recently. There's hardly any dust in his latest footprints, which means—'

'The guns only disappeared recently. Within a fortnight or less?'

'A neat job, done by someone who knew when he wouldn't be disturbed. He brought a crowbar with him, prised the door open and removed the guns, possibly taking several trips to do so. How many guns were stored there?'

'A dozen or so.' Julian clicked his fingers. 'Biscuit. The one who's always complaining.'

'The one who expected to find gold coins in the priest hole? His name isn't really "Biscuit", is it?'

'Brisket, I think.' He drew out his smartphone. 'The idiot! I can see him decide that "finders keepers", planning to take the guns to the nearest pawnbroker and hoping to get fifty quid for them. Or he'd try to pass them on to a man in the pub or anyone who'd give him a couple of twenties for his trouble. His contact would pass them along the chain and get five hundred or more, until they reached a gunsmith, who'd know they were worth thousands.'

He got out his smartphone. 'They were probably out of the country within hours. Now I have to inform the police, find the inventory and the insurance details. I could do without this. The police are not going to be pleased at my reporting the theft, the insurance people will go spare, and I've got cousin Mona plus boyfriend descending on us within the hour.'

And to the phone, 'Police, please. Yes, I need to report a theft . . .'

The hubbub outside the room intensified. Mrs Maggs's voice was raised in alarm. She was on the warpath about something. Bea left Julian to his phone calls and slipped out to deal with it. She came face to face with Polly, who was carrying Pip in a sling in front of her, and Rosemary Sweeting, both of whom were suppressing the giggles.

Behind them came Big Teddy, cowering under an onslaught as Mrs Maggs beat him around his legs with a feather duster.

Behind them came Lennie the Boss, red in the face and shouting to Teddy to 'Come back up here, instantly!'

Behind Lennie rose the lugubrious visage of the whiny one, whose name it appears was Biscuit or maybe Brisket. Whatever his name was, he was not a Happy Bunny.

Polly winked at Bea, saying, 'It's my father. He wants—!'

Mrs Maggs was in full flow. 'And what I keep telling him is "I wants never gets"!'

'Yes, but—' bleated Teddy.

Lennie the Boss shouted, 'Who pays your wages, eh? You get back here and—'

Where was Imran?

Rosemary Sweeting, who had dressed to fade into the background, did exactly that. It always amused Bea to see Rosemary giving an imitation of a downtrodden wage slave.

Polly looked harassed. Pip woke up, decided he was hungry, thirsty, needed changing, didn't like people shouting, and opened his mouth to express his disapproval of the world.

Julian, phone to ear, managed to ease himself out into the corridor, assessed the situation at a glance, and produced his Head Boy of the School persona. *'Quiet! If you please!'*

Pip blinked. Polly pretended she wasn't there, Rosemary looked at her watch, and Mrs Maggs poked Big Teddy at the back of his knee so that he stumbled forward and nearly ended up on the floor.

'Humph!' said Mrs Maggs, folding her arms at the world.

Big Lennie moderated his tone. 'You tell him, Sir Julian. You tell him. We've got to get the job done, haven't we?'

Polly said, in a small voice, 'I'm afraid my father has co-opted Teddy to make himself comfortable and he did move some of the furniture around. He doesn't quite understand . . .'

'No, of course he doesn't,' said Julian. And then, into the phone, 'No, not you, officer. We'll seal off this room and expect you within the hour, right?'

It wasn't a suggestion. It was an order.

Everyone present recognized His Master's Voice. Feet shuffled; shouts were reduced to mutters.

Julian addressed the meeting. 'The gun cabinet has been jemmied open and emptied. The police are on their way. This is now a crime scene.'

A frisson passed through the assembly. Some mouths dropped open.

Bea had her eye on Whiny, who took a step back. His fingers went to his mouth. Did he bite his nails?

Julian said, 'Teddy, I need you to stop anyone going into this room until the police get here. Could you do guard duty for me, do you think?'

Big Teddy nodded. 'Yeah, but what about the old man, eh? He wants this and that. What do I say to him?'

'My problem, not yours. My father-in-law, Mr Colston, is a guest in this house. He understands the difficult circumstances we are currently experiencing and I'll assure him we will do all we can to make his stay comfortable.'

That was telling them, wasn't it?

Julian went on, 'Mrs Maggs, thank you. If there are any more misunderstandings, let me know and I'll deal with them. Lennie, a word with you in a minute. Polly, my dear, have you finished showing Rosemary around? Excellent. It's quite a place, isn't it, Rosemary? Now, perhaps you'll join us in our quarters?'

Whiny said, 'What about me? I'm not feeling too good. I reckon it's that pie I ate last night. I thought it was a bit off. I think I'd better, sort of, take time off.'

Julian wasn't having that. 'You'll sit in the kitchen and not move till the police come. Mrs Maggs, you'll see to it he doesn't change his boots or leave, won't you?'

Mrs Maggs restored her jaw to its usual position as she worked out what Julian was implying. She mouthed the word, 'Boots? Him? Ah . . . guns?' And nodded. She said, 'His boots. Dust, yes.' She nodded again. 'Teddy, we'll put him in the downstairs toilet in case he wants to be sick. You can stand guard in the corridor, making sure he stays put and no one gets into the junk room, right?'

'Excellent!' said Julian.

Lennie started rehearsing excuses. 'But I need him. We don't have enough labour to finish in the time given. You can see it's impossible—'

Julian said firmly, 'As I said, we have to reconsider our arrangements.'

Polly hastily led the way out into the yard, anxious to deal with a hungry baby.

Bea fell into step beside Rosemary, saying, 'I know you like a challenge. On a scale of one to a hundred, is this a difficult enough proposition for you?'

Rosemary laughed. Misquoting the famous comedians, Laurel and Hardy, she said, 'Another fine mess you've landed me in. Not only murder, attempted rape, peculation, but also theft. Don't tell me the books are in perfect order because I wouldn't believe it. I can't wait to get started.'

Bea put her hand on Rosemary's sleeve. 'Add some missing guns to the list. Julian is the target. If they succeed in getting him, Paula and the boy will be next. Understood? Are you carrying?'

Eyes widened with innocence. 'What? Me?'

Bea grinned. Rosemary was wearing a loose navy jacket over designer jeans. Bea guessed that the jacket carried one or two bits of this and that. In the old days she'd have carried a knuckle-duster. Nowadays, what would it be? A taser, perhaps? Actually, Bea considered that Rosemary could probably do more damage with her bare hands than most men with a machine gun.

Bea said, 'Look out for Imran, who's supposed to be guarding Julian's back. He's trustworthy. Which reminds me. Where is he?'

As they crossed the yard and entered the living room there came an unusual sound, as if someone had dropped a stone into a pond. *Plock!* Had a stone hit the barn, perhaps?

Bea said, 'Rosemary! Was that a gunshot?'

SIXTEEN

Friday afternoon

R osemary evaporated. One minute she was there, and the next
she'd disappeared.

Bruno looked up at Julian for orders.

At the same time an enormous, expensive car drove slowly into
the yard, taking care not to get itself scratched by impact with
inferior vehicles.

Julian said, leading the way into his quarters, 'Bruno, stay with
me. I don't want you wandering off on your own.'

Bruno wasn't happy. He gave a short bark to announce visitors
but stayed at Julian's heels.

Bea hovered in the doorway to the barn. Her heartbeat had gone
into overtime. If it had been a gunshot . . . then who and why?
Julian was safely indoors with his family. They were safe there,
weren't they?

The chauffeur opened the door of the limousine to assist his
passengers out. He hadn't heard the shot, had he? But it *was* a shot,
wasn't it? Not a car backfire or . . . something in the distance, far
away?

'Hello, there! We're not too late, are we?' Mona evidently hadn't
heard anything untoward. Marcus followed her out of the car, a
superb cashmere jacket slung over his shoulders.

The chauffeur did look as if he'd know a gunshot if he heard it, but
his attitude at the moment was that he was hired to look after Marcus,
and not to investigate other people's mysterious happenings.

Bea didn't know what to do, so did nothing at all.

Marcus looked around the yard and was displeased. With raised
eyebrows, he said to Mona, 'I thought we were going to look over
the Hall.'

Mona pulled on his arm. 'Come and meet Julian first. Then I'll
take you round.' He followed her inside, both of them ignoring Bea
as of no consequence.

She entertained pleasant thoughts of torturing people with no manners. Really, Marcus's attitude was short-sighted, to say the least!

Julian had collapsed into his big chair by this time, laying his crutch aside. He said, 'Do forgive me, I need to sit down. My accident, you know. You are both very welcome to the Hall. And may I introduce my wife, Lady Paula . . .'

Lady 'Paula!' Yes! She's gradually moving from 'Polly' to 'Lady Paula'.

'. . . who is currently juggling a dozen matters at once. The youngster whose nappy she's changing is Pip, short for Philip. Then by the door is Mrs Abbot, a businesswoman and a great friend of the family. Do take a seat, if you can find one. I'm afraid the Hall is not habitable at the moment. My father-in-law is trying to see if he can live there without running water and electricity, but he's not enjoying the experience. Mona, if you really want to show Marcus around today, do remember to find a couple of hard hats first. Health and Safety, you know.'

Marcus didn't like the sound of that. 'But you yourself will be moving in again soon, no doubt.'

Bea took a seat by the door and prepared to enjoy the spectacle of Julian cutting Marcus off at the knees. Politely, of course.

Julian said, 'We're aiming to get the house ready to show visitors at Easter, but there's some doubt as to whether we'll be ready in time.'

Mona flushed with annoyance. 'But I want to be back in my own room by then, and Marcus—'

'Forgive me,' said Julian, feeling behind his back for some object, which turned out to be a child's soft toy. 'Ah, I wondered where that had gone. Mona, I've no idea when it will be possible for anyone to sleep in comfort in the Hall again. No mains water yet, no electricity, no curtains, even. We plan to dress the downstairs rooms and three of the bedrooms to show visitors at Easter, but it's going to be a close-run thing.

'As for us, Polly and I and the boy will have to stay here in the barn for the time being. With luck, we'll move into part of the servants' quarters on the top floor by Christmastime, but Polly insists on having a workable kitchen and downstairs playroom, and I think she's right. Carrying a baby up and down stairs is not a good idea.'

Julian beamed at his visitors, who did not beam back.

'If you do want to see around,' said Julian, 'please mind the gaps in the flooring. The electricians, you know. I think they enjoy leaving booby-traps around. The ground floor's not too bad, but upstairs . . .' He shook his head.

Mona was not going to let it go. 'I can't see myself living in that horrid house in the village much longer, but I suppose I can run the farm shop from London. After all, it's only a question of ordering food from all over the world through a website.'

Marcus turned his head to look at Julian. The two men locked eyes. They both knew what a farm shop was about and they understood one another. Oh yes, they certainly did.

Marcus said, in the very mildest of voices, 'But my dear, a farm shop is all about local produce.'

Julian said, 'Mona, you cannot be serious. You can't want to be on site every morning by six o'clock to check deliveries, not when London is beckoning. I must say it's gratifying to hear that the farms hereabouts are falling over themselves to supply us. Ditto all the women in the area who can bake a good cake. They've been sending samples up day by day for me to try out. I fear I'm putting on weight. Local produce, no carbon footprint. What could be better?'

Marcus smiled – a shark's smile. 'Mona, my dear. We really must talk about your moving up to London, where your talents will be appreciated.'

Mona pouted, smiled and frowned. Weighing up the pros and cons.

Julian said, 'Paula, my dear, shall I feed Pip while you sort out whatever it is you were supposed to be doing?'

Polly handed over Pip, who was newly changed and looking cross. Julian settled the baby and reached for the bottle which Polly handed to him. The teat popped into the open mouth and Pip's expression changed from grim to grin.

Julian said, 'There's nothing like home-grown, is there?'

Whether Julian was referring to the child or to the farm shop, Marcus caught the drift. He settled himself further into his chair, saying, 'Well, well. We'll see over the Hall another time. Not today. Busy, busy. Always on the go. By the way, Mona tells me her father invested her trust fund money abroad. I assume that trust fund is now your responsibility?'

Julian gave Marcus a 'don't be daft!' look and said, 'I fear not.'

Marcus said, 'But surely you are now responsible for these family issues? You are taking steps to recover the family fortunes?'

Julian batted that one off to the boundary. 'And you are interested because . . .?'

Marcus narrowed his eyes. 'Naturally, I care for my friends' interests.'

Mona shifted, uneasy and not entirely sure that she understood what was happening.

Julian said, 'My old firm is on to it. They have a new lead which they're following up. If by any chance something can be retrieved from the wreck, then solicitors will no doubt have a ball arguing about who on the trust fund allowed Frederick to, er, interfere with its terms, and how much money can be made available to be redistributed to the family. I wouldn't have anything to do with that.'

'But you are making progress in reclaiming those funds?'

'As you have pointed out, this is a private, family matter.'

'And I am taking an interest.'

Mona exclaimed, 'Marcus, this is very good of you, but I don't expect—'

'Why not?' said Marcus. 'If I can help a friend out . . .? A close friend.' His mouth twisted and he changed tack. 'You are right, and this is none of my business.' He gave Mona a measuring look. 'Of course, if it became my business at some point . . . No, no. Too soon. Mona, let's go, shall we?'

Julian said, 'You will be very welcome to visit the Hall when it's up and running.'

Marcus nodded. He'd learned that some progress was being made on Mona's money, he'd made it clear he was interested in her future in other ways and he'd extracted the invitation he'd come for. He said, 'Are you ready, Mona? I've a conference call booked and we'll have a bite to eat somewhere on the way back to London. A pleasure to meet you, too, Lady Paula.'

Even as he spoke, there came a sharp crack . . .

. . . and the big window overlooking the meadow burst into the room in a shower of glass.

Bea shot off her chair, landing on her backside.

Julian threw himself sideways onto the floor, shielding Pip in his arms.

Bea gaped.

The window no longer existed.

Bruno leaped through the gap caused by the disappearance of the glass and vanished.

Mona, hands to head, had her mouth wide open.

Bea wondered why she couldn't hear anything.

Shards of glass twinkled everywhere.

Bea had gone deaf. No, she hadn't. She could hear, faintly. Someone was screaming. Mona? Or Julian?

Julian was shouting at Polly.

Bea couldn't tell what he was saying.

Polly, white-faced, froze where she stood, halfway into the kitchenette.

Sir Marcus's chauffeur dived into the room, swept his master out of his chair and into the yard.

Bea tried to speak. Failed. Was anyone dead? She checked. No bodies.

Julian, with Pip clutched to him, shook fragments of glass off himself as he rose to his knees. 'Polly! For God's sake!' A thread of blood ran down his temple.

Pip, startled but seemingly unharmed, began to wail.

Julian tried again. 'Polly! Move!'

Bea cleared her throat. She wanted to say that Polly was in shock and couldn't move. No words came out.

Mona went on screaming. There was a glint of glass on her shoulder and more down her left side.

Polly tried to speak. 'J-J-ulian . . .'

Bea told herself to move. The snipers had a clear view into the room and might try again. She must get out into the yard and ring the police. She couldn't remember where she'd put her phone. She felt a trickle of blood run down her leg. How annoying! Those tights were brand new. She brushed at her leg and saw another trickle run down her sleeve. Where did that come from?

How very odd it looked! Such a bright red!

Marcus's fine cashmere jacket lay discarded beside Bea's feet. It would have to be thoroughly shaken out to get rid of the glass or it would damage his master. Bea wondered how long that would take. Perhaps it would be best to have it dry-cleaned before it was used again?

Bea told herself she couldn't stay crouched on the floor for ever, could she? She looked around for something, anything to help her to her feet. The chair she'd been sitting on? It was on its side on the floor. Now, how did that happen?

There'd been no more shots. That was good, wasn't it?

But everyone in the room was an easy target for the man with the gun. They should move.

Immediately.

Only, she didn't know how.

Julian crawled across the floor to reach Polly. There were crunching noises as he inched over the broken glass on the floor. Pip hiccuped and wailed.

Where was his bottle?

Polly stood like a statue, but a statue that had started to tremble. Julian was still clutching Pip to him.

Bea couldn't summon enough energy to shift herself off the floor. *We're sitting ducks! We have to move!*

Julian reached Polly, and tried to move her into the kitchen, out of range of the shooter.

Bea managed to pull herself upright. Shards of glass fell from her clothes. She grabbed Mona's arm, and tried to pull her towards the door to the yard. Mona resisted. Mona didn't want to know about anything except how to scream.

Bea tried to remember what to do in cases of hysteria. Couldn't. So she slapped Mona, first on one cheek and then on the other. That did it.

Mona took a deep breath and then slapped Bea back.

Bea's neck twinged.

Mona began to hyperventilate.

Great!

A car roared to a stop outside. Police? At last. Well, thank God for that! No one was badly hurt . . . were they?

With an effort Bea pulled Mona out into the yard.

Mona slid to the ground, weeping.

Bea leaned against the wall. She felt for her phone which was . . . somewhere else. Where was it? She needed to tell the police that someone had been shooting at them from the meadow. WHERE WAS HER PHONE?

The police had parked their car askew, blocking the exit from the yard. Out of the car emerged two police officers who had come to see about some guns which had gone missing. Their attitude was one of slight boredom. This was a routine job, wasn't it? Checking on missing property.

Seeing Bea with blood on her arm and leg, and Mona lying on the ground, they sharpened to attention. 'What's this, then?'

At the second try, Bea managed, 'We were shot at!' She indicated they look into the room. Chaos. Glass fragments carpeted every surface. 'They're out there, in the meadow, shooting at us. Sir Julian, his wife and baby. You need to get them out of there.'

The two police officers recoiled. They hadn't expected to deal with this, had they? They were accustomed to traffic offences, domestics, drug searches, teens behaving stupidly, but this . . .! It looked like the aftermath of a bomb!

The taller of the two dived into the room to help Julian bring his family out into the yard. Julian emerged, half carrying a shocked, wide-eyed Polly, plus Pip.

The other officer tried not to panic as he contacted the station. 'Assistance needed. We're at the Hall. There's been what looks like an explosion. Glass everywhere. Ambulance needed. Senior police. Oh yes, and Forensics.'

Julian had blood running down his head and from the back of one hand. Pip wailed. His bottle had been removed just as he'd got down to his feed; he did not appreciate loud noises and being thrown around this way and that, and he was going to let everyone know it. A trickle of blood ran down one of Pip's legs but it actually came from his father's hand and not from him. The baby himself seemed untouched. And hungry.

Julian leaned against the wall, breathing fast, still holding onto his wife and child. Recovering. Both Julian and Polly were beyond speech for the moment.

The taller of the two police officers said, 'Who did this?'

Bea calmed herself sufficiently to explain. 'I don't know. There was no warning. The shots came from the meadow at the back. There were at least two shots. A sighting one which hit the wall and then another which shattered the window. Someone was trying to kill us.'

Polly lost her rigidity and began to weep. She stuttered, 'I . . . I . . .' And couldn't get any further.

Julian made an effort to stand upright. Tiny shards of glass tinkled as they fell from his hair and clothing. He said, 'We're all out safely?'

Bea looked around. Yes, everyone had got out. Marcus was presently sitting in his limousine, taking a restorative gulp out of a flask which his chauffeur had produced. Mona was on the ground, moaning.

From across the yard, workmen began to leave the Hall by the kitchen door as their day's work was done. But the foremost one hesitated. What was this? Police? Why?

Julian tried to attract their attention. 'Is Mrs Maggs there?'

The enquiry was passed along from mouth to mouth and brought Mrs Maggs out of the crowd around the kitchen door. She thrust her way through the workmen, identified that Julian was supporting Polly and the baby, and that Julian was bleeding. She gave a little scream of concern. 'What's happened?'

Julian said, in a quiet voice, 'Mrs Maggs, could you find somewhere for Lady Paula to lie down? I mean, immediately! Our home . . . isn't.'

Mrs Maggs did a double take. She bustled across the yard, poked her head into the living room and gave a squeak of horror at the sight of the wreckage within. 'Land's sakes! Whatever did this? That's going to take more than a pass with the Hoover to clear up. Come this way, my dear. You can have a nice lie-down in my sitting room and a cuppa. I'll get someone to look after Pip and we'll have you all settled back in the Hall where you belong in two ticks of a whatever.'

Mrs Maggs took the unhappy baby off Julian, put her arm around Polly and cleared a path through the workmen, talking as she went. 'Now Mr Lance, stir your stumps. You'd better take over from the useless lump, Lennie. I want you to get someone to turn the water and electricity on for the en suite to the Lavender Room where the old lord used to sleep directly, and if Lennie objects, just send him to me and I'll sort him out. Understood?'

Bea looked for Lennie among the workmen and found him skulking at the back. Even as she watched, he slid from view back into the house . . . and out by the front door, no doubt. Abandoning ship.

Lance said, 'Understood.' He signalled to a couple of his workmen and went into a huddle with them even as the police officer bleated, 'Look, nobody is to leave the yard here till we say so!'

Taking no notice of this, Mrs Maggs ushered Polly and Pip into the Hall, still talking. 'How far along are you, my dear? And do you know if it's a boy or girl yet . . .?'

Bea looked at Julian for confirmation of what most people had by then come to guess. Julian wore a slightly proud, slightly shame-faced grin, copied by everyone else as the penny dropped. There was some counting on fingers. It was a bit close to Pip's birth, but there . . . Whyever not?

Someone clapped. A small cheer rose from the ranks.

Yes, that's what everyone needed. To have continuity in the big house. An heir and a spare.

Marcus handed the flask back to his chauffeur and attempted to take control of the situation. 'Where's Mona? Mona, where are you? Are you all right?' He couldn't see her from where he sat in his limo.

Mona heard his voice and began to struggle to her feet. At a nod from Marcus, his chauffeur swooped across the yard to pick Mona up and stow her into Marcus's limo.

The taller of the two police officers attempted to regain control of the situation. He raised his voice. 'Now, come on! We can't have anyone just walking off like—'

Marcus had had enough of being pushed around. 'See here, officer. We're all in danger here! Someone shot at us at least once and can do so again. We need to vacate this place immediately. And I have to get Mona to a doctor.'

The second officer said, 'I can't see no one shooting now. We've only got your word for it. And, well, there's the mess in that room, I see that, but we've sent for reinforcements and you've all got to stay put till they get here, right?'

And then there was a hush.

Two young men, one somewhat weedy with fair hair, and the other a dark-haired bully boy, stumbled into the yard from the direction of the stables. They moved awkwardly, their bent-over posture explained by the fact that their thumbs had been tied behind them and then . . . *oh, Rosemary, I love you!* . . . the zips of their jeans had been pulled down, so that the denim sagged around their knees despite their increasingly desperate efforts to keep them hoisted to decency level.

Bea recognized the pair as Young Fred, Frederick's son, and . . . what was his name? Something to do with the woman who helped out at the rescue centre?

Both were deeply unhappy, cursing their fate and one another. Being caught by the police after their shooting spree was one thing, but the shame of this exposure – being paraded with their pants threatening to slip down to their ankles – was quite another.

Behind them came Bruno, growling encouragement to the two

to keep going or else . . . and behind Bruno came Imran, carrying
a couple of guns. A shotgun and a rifle?

Beside Imran came Rosemary, looking as if she were out for a
stroll in the park with nothing on her mind but a choice between
cream tea or – if you really pressed her hard – perhaps a small glass
of white wine.

Someone in the crowd tittered.

Teddy-with-the-bad-teeth snorted with amusement, and then
threw back his head and let fly with a belly-laugh.

That set everyone else off. Laughter echoed and re-echoed from
the Hall to the barn and back again. Fingers were pointed, men
doubled over with enjoyment.

Rosemary wore a demure little smile.

Imran grinned hugely. He had a black eye and the sleeve of his
shirt was hanging off.

*He'd let Rosemary and Bruno have first go, and then joined in?
Good for Imran.*

Bea knew that this scene would be inscribed on the onlookers'
memories for ever. The two perpetrators would never be able to
hold up their heads in the neighbourhood again. Spectators would
tell their children about it.

Bruno, conscious of a job well done, went and sat beside his
master, looking pleased with himself. Julian bent over to fondle the
dog's ears. 'Good boy!'

The lanky, fair-haired one – what was his name? Lars? Something
like that? – tripped and lost his grip on his trousers, which descended
to his ankles. He dissolved into bitter tears of shame.

*Any minute now he'd cry for his mummy. I could feel sorry for
him if he hadn't just tried to kill Julian and Pip.*

'. . . and I didn't mean to hurt anyone. I was only trying to see
if the gun would . . .!'

His companion wished him dead and buried. 'You blithering
idiot! If you'd only kept your head, if you hadn't gone after that
slag Dora . . .!'

Did he mean that Lars had done for Dora? But . . . really?

Losing his temper completely, Bully Boy aimed a kick at his
companion's bare posterior and connected.

Lars bit the dust, sobbing. 'You said she'd do anything I wanted,
but she wouldn't, and it's all your fault.'

If Bully Boy had been egging Lars on to try Dora, and Lars had

taken things too far, then . . . which of them was actually responsible
for her death?

'Enough!' Julian's voice cut through the hubbub. Everyone quiet-
ened down, as the meaning of what they'd heard filtered through.
There was some shifting of feet, and a low murmur which grew to
a growl. And the growl wasn't only from Bruno, who sensed trouble
but stayed at his master's side.

Dora might have been this and that, but she'd been one of their
own, and if Lars had killed her then . . . the growl became menacing.

Julian cut through the noise. 'Would the officers kindly remove
those two men for their own safety? You've heard enough to charge
them with attempted murder, haven't you?'

'Yes, sir.' The police officers got Lars to his feet and attempted
to pull up his jeans to cover his manhood. Bully Boy attempted a
run for it but was easily caught and restrained.

Screech of brakes and sirens! Not one but two more police cars
arrived, parking behind the others. This created a problem; not only
had workmen left their vehicles parked in the yard, but added to
that were Julian and Polly's cars, Bea's and the motorized caravan
that Rosemary used as her headquarters. Oh, and yes, Marcus's
limousine.

Marcus did not like being boxed in. His chauffeur became almost
agitated. 'They're blocking our exit, sir!'

'Hello, hello. What's this here?' A tall police officer, a woman
with immaculate hair and make-up came to the fore, showing her
identity card. Authority personified. 'Explanations. Fast!'

Explanations duly came from two, out-of-their-depth officers.
Both spoke at once, accompanied by helpful comments from the
workmen and expostulation from Marcus.

Authority switched her eyes this way and that. 'They were
shooting at this building? You have witnesses? What's the damage?
Anyone hurt?'

SEVENTEEN

Friday evening

P rompt on cue, an ambulance wailed itself to a halt behind the
police cars, Marcus's limousine, the workmen's vans and the
transport belonging to the house. Two paramedics erupted
from their vehicles and wove their way round the other vehicles to
reach the yard. 'Where's the fire?'

'Here!' Marcus thrust a still-sobbing Mona into the paramedics'
arms. 'She needs attention, at once!'

The paramedics mopped her up and removed her to their
ambulance.

Bea noted there was a certain sense of 'Well, get her out of the
way, yes!' among the onlookers.

Madam Authority took three long strides to inspect the wrecked
room. Without going in or touching anything, she barked out,
'Forensics are on their way? Good. No one goes in or out, right?'

Her eyes swivelled to left and right, taking in the two perpetrators
trying in vain to resist the officers' efforts to get them to move
towards the police cars. 'Yes?' she said. 'Who did what to whom?'

Rosemary put her hand up, like the nicely brought-up schoolgirl
that she was not. 'Please?'

Authority switched her eyes back to Rosemary and hardened.
Some sort of message passed between them. Authority wasn't fooled
by Rosemary's meek exterior. Authority recognized . . . what?
Competence? A hired bodyguard?

Authority said, 'Who are you? Did you observe the shooting?'

With a pretty air of modesty, Rosemary handed the initiative over
to her companion. 'Imran can tell you all about it. He's a hero.'

Imran picked up his cue. 'I work here. I spotted these two in the
meadow at the back, which is odd because there's no animals there
right now. I went after them to ask what they were doing. That's when
I saw they were carrying guns. I didn't like the look of that. Before I
could get close, they took aim at the back of the barn here. Lars fired
and hit the wall of the barn. I was going to go for help when—'

'I came along,' said Rosemary, smiling shyly. 'Horrid things, guns. I heard the first shot and thought it was odd so I went to see what was going on, which was silly of me, I know, and I should have just called the police, but there . . . and I was just in time to see the dark-haired one let off his shotgun and shatter the window, and then suddenly this dog appeared and knocked the shooter over. And the other one aimed his gun at Imran . . .'

Imran took up the tale. 'Only Rosemary leaped on him and we all sort of fell over and over. And Bruno got Young Fred down and, before they could get away, Rosemary managed to trip them up, and we got them on the ground . . .'

Rosemary was a black belt in judo. She'd probably tossed them both around as if they were toy dolls.

'. . . and Rosemary had a bit of string on her and we tied them up and collected their guns with a bit of help from Bruno, who really wanted to do them an injury but managed to restrain himself in good time. And here,' said Imran, handing over the guns to the police officers, 'please take them away. I hope I haven't destroyed their fingerprints, but it was all a bit of a muddle.'

'Imran,' said Rosemary, hands to heart and eyes wide, 'was wonderful!'

'That bitch!' spat Young Fred. 'Don't let her fool you. She's carrying a gun herself. She's a tiger. She shot me!'

'Oh, no, I didn't!' said Rosemary, lip quivering. 'I hate guns!'

And she couldn't possibly have been responsible for the lamentable condition the two men were in, could she?

Oh yes, she could! She carries a taser and she knows how to use it, doesn't she!

'I don't see any signs of your having been shot,' said Authority.

'I don't understand,' said Julian, brushing another trickle of blood from his cheek. 'These two lads work at the rescue centre, don't they? I'm sure I've seen them there. How did they get hold of those guns? Are they the ones missing from the old estate office? And why on earth did they want to shoot at us?'

Bea was trying to put everything she'd heard and seen into sensible order but Imran got there first.

'The dark one, Young Fred, that's a by-blow of Frederick's, has never been any good. He was given every opportunity – oh, yes. Good schooling and all that, paid for by the family here. But he got in with a bad lot from the town and has been sent down for drugs and for this and that, not to mention the other. On probation at the moment, isn't he?

'And the other lad, Lars, poor creature, has never been worth anything. He came here with his mother to work at the rescue centre, but had no more sense than to team up with Mister Stupid here. Officers, I'm telling you, you'd better be on your guard, or the bully boy will kick you in the goolies and laugh, which is what he did to a lad that lives opposite me, that's never been down the pub since for fear of coming across him.'

Julian said heavily, 'Chief Inspector, family connection or no, this can't be overlooked. The damage to the building and its contents is probably repairable, but these two men intended to kill us and, if it hadn't been for Rosemary and Imran, they'd have gone on to make another attempt and perhaps succeeded.'

Authority nodded. 'We'll set up an incident room and take statements.'

Julian said, 'The Hall is uninhabitable at the moment. May I suggest you set up in the end stable where Mickey the groom had his quarters? There's electricity there, and water. There's space in the barn, too, that you can use. The workmen saw nothing because they were working inside the main building when the shooting started. Perhaps you can take their details so they can go home?'

Authority nodded. 'Make it so.' She switched eyes to her officers, and indicated they charge and remove the two unhappy malefactors immediately. Which they did, without, Bea saw, untying their captives' thumbs. Bea approved of their caution.

A phone started to ring inside the wrecked room.

Julian started. 'That's my phone!'

Authority said, 'Leave it. No one goes in until after Forensics have done their job.'

Ouch! Bea put her hand to her pocket. Except that there was no pocket in the mid-length shirt she was wearing. So, no phone. Where was it? She'd dropped it somewhere? Yes, in the pocket of the jacket she'd been wearing . . .? Or was it in her handbag? She'd left them . . . where? By the chair on which she'd been sitting when Fred fired at the window.

What was she going to do without her phone? Or Julian? People were going to try to contact them and the phones would lie there, doing nothing at all except aggravate everyone in earshot.

Meanwhile, some of the police cars were leaving. A certain

amount of backing and forwarding ensued, not to mention three- and five-point turns being necessary in order to get the right cars leaving. It was done with only one scraped bumper and a certain amount of profanity on the part of the police.

A second phone started up inside the barn. Forlornly. After a pause, the first rang again.

The ringing phones were getting on Bea's nerves, but she didn't know what to do about it.

Marcus tried once again to suggest he be free to take Mona and depart, but Madam Authority was not listening. She surveyed the crowd still left with an expressionless face. She sensed their unease, and considered the best way to deal with it was to remove Julian, who was clearly the one who made decisions. She said, 'Sir Julian, there may be glass in those cuts of yours, and you may need stitches. You're going straight to hospital and then to the station so that we can take your statement.'

Julian shook his head. 'I must see to my wife and child.'

Authority said, 'That was not a request. It was an order. I'll get the paramedics to attend to you and to . . . er . . . Imran, straight away.'

Julian stood his ground. 'I was feeding the baby. His bottle is still in there. We have no other way of feeding him. And the phones . . . I was expecting an urgent call . . .'

'Not till Forensics have been in.' She wheeled around as Marcus pawed her arm. He was not pleased at having been overlooked for so long and was also trying to make himself look taller than Authority . . . which he was not able to do. She must be six foot if she was an inch!

But Marcus tried it on. 'Don't you know who I am? I have a conference call booked for six and it's five past now. I saw nothing, heard nothing. Here's my card. Contact me in town whenever you wish, but for now, I must be on my way, and I'm taking Mona with me.'

Mona, with a couple of plasters artistically placed on one cheek and her arm, reappeared.

Marcus held out his arms and Mona went straight into them, burying her head in his shoulder. 'Oh, Marcus! Take me away!'

Authority wasn't impressed. 'Not so fast, Mr . . . Whatever. We'll deal with you straight after the workmen.' And to Imran, 'You and Sir Julian – to hospital. Now.'

A phone rang again inside the barn.

Julian started to say, 'My phone. It's inside. Can I just get—?'

'No. It's a crime scene. No one goes in or out.' She strode off to organize setting the world to rights, towing various of her officers and some of the workmen in her wake.

There was a general relaxation of tension. One of the officers produced some tape and began to string it over the door into the wrecked room.

Julian put out his hand to Bea. 'I'll see if I can phone from the hospital. I suppose it would be only sensible to be looked at by the medics.'

'The sooner you go, the sooner you'll be back. If the police don't bring you back, ring Mrs Maggs and she can pass the message on to me. And then I'll come and get you.'

He said, 'Bruno, find Polly and look after her.'

Bruno whined. He didn't want to leave his master.

Julian bent to caress the dog's ears. 'Go, now.'

Bruno made for the kitchen door. He'd find Polly and look after her, wouldn't he?

Julian took a step forward and winced. Falling of his horse and then out of his chair to protect Pip hadn't done him any favours. Blood was seeping from the cut in his forehead and from his wrist. His clothes would need dry-cleaning – or dumping. He said, 'If Polly were to miscarry . . .!'

'She won't,' said Bea. 'Mrs Maggs wouldn't allow it.'

Julian tried to smile. Almost made it. He took another step forward, and a rictus of pain settled on his face.

Imran recognized his cue. He stepped forward, saying, 'Come on, Sir Julian. Put your arm over my shoulders. That's it. The ambulance is just over there.'

Julian took two steps and stopped. 'I'd forgotten. Where's Big Teddy? I left him guarding the man who I believe stole the guns. I can see Teddy, lurking at the back there, but where's Brisket?'

The smaller group of workmen who were still there drew apart, thrusting Teddy to the fore.

Teddy looked around him, stupidity ruling OK. 'Brisket? Well, I put him in the kitchen toilet, like you said. Then I stood in the kitchen watching the door, and then I come out here, and I swear he didn't come out this way.'

Julian faltered. He said, 'He went back inside the building, of course, to hide somewhere till he could sneak out when our attention is elsewhere. If he's any sense, he'll be long gone by now. In the town, gone up to London, anywhere.'

Bea said, 'No, he wouldn't leave yet. I think I know where he'll have gone. He's been itching to get in there all this time and he wouldn't leave without seeing what he could find.'

Julian said, 'Of course! The priest hole! But my father-in-law's in that room! I have to get up there and rescue him.' He put his bad foot to the ground and winced.

Rosemary said, 'Sir Julian, please go and get the attention you need. Imran, you need to be looked at as well. Mrs Abbot and I will go and rescue Mr Brisket. Is his name really Brisket? A local name, perhaps?'

'Nobody leaves,' said the police officer who'd been left on guard duty.

Julian exchanged a quick glance with Bea. He said, 'No, of course not. To the hospital, then.' He put his free arm around the officer's shoulders. 'Now it's not far to the ambulance. If you can just help me along . . .'

With the police officer distracted, Bea slipped away with Rosemary following at her heels. They almost ran along the corridor and up the stairs.

All was quiet inside the Hall. It was a listening quiet.

Bea voiced her fear. 'Suppose he's taken the old man hostage?'

Rosemary grinned. She flexed her fingers. She said, equally softly, 'I must thank you for bringing me here. I haven't had so much fun for ages.'

Bea tapped on the door of Lady Fleur's room.

'Come!' Unhurried, unworried.

Bea opened the door but Rosemary went in before her, looking warily this way and that. Was Whiny lurking behind the door to strike them down as they entered? Bea followed Rosemary, also taking care.

Mr Colston had made himself at home. He was sitting by the window, at a large table which hadn't been there earlier. He was fully dressed, with a rug over his knees, studying some scraps of paper with the aid of a magnifying glass. The bed had been made up, but there were still no curtains over the window.

There was a tray with the remains of some lunch on it, plus a bottle of mineral water and a cut-glass tumbler on a silver tray.

He said, 'You've taken your time. I really don't understand why I should have to be concerned with the antics of the servants.'

He indicated the boarded-up priest hole. 'This absurd creature came looking for some money he said he was owed. Before I could summon assistance, he dived into the priest hole, muttering something about buried treasure and started throwing out the papers he found in the old chest there. Vandalism! I pointed out that the papers in themselves might be valuable. I told him to hand them out to me, carefully, so that I could see if they were worth anything. Which he did. And indeed, from a preliminary examination, I believe some of these might well be of interest to historians.

'When I informed him of this, he demanded I pay him for finding them, and went as far as threatening me, at which, I am sorry to say, I rather lost my cool, as the young people say nowadays. He swung at me, which was a mistake on his part. In my younger days I boxed for the university and was noted for my left hook. He fell back into the priest hole, and I boarded it up again till someone should remove him.'

He waved his hand at the wall, from which could be heard thumps and a hoarse voice crying, 'Let me out!'

Mr Colston turned back to the papers. 'Quite fascinating. There must be a booklet giving the history of this fine old place somewhere. It will need updating, in view of these finds. Perhaps you'll find a copy and bring it up with my supper? It occurs to me that rewriting the booklet is something I could occupy myself with in my retirement. Oh, and please remind the builder that I have no water in the bathroom as yet. Tell him it's a priority.'

Bea found herself saying, 'Yes, of course, Mr Colston.'

Rosemary let out poor old Whiny, alias Brisket, who complained that it was about time or he'd have suffocated in that hell-hole. As he was taken down the stairs and through a busy kitchen, he poured out a string of complaints and excuses.

'He had no right to lock me up, I should sue him, I was only looking for the buried treasure that everyone knows is hidden somewhere around here, and by right, some of that should come to me.'

And so on.

Rosemary faded from view as Bea took Brisket to the officer guarding the wrecked living quarters. She said, 'This is Brisket. He's an idiot. He stole the guns and wants to confess. Can you deal with him, please?'

Another police officer was produced and Brisket was duly removed, still explaining that it was all a terrible misunderstanding; he'd only realized the other day that the guns were still in the old office, and he was taking them out to show Sir Julian, and he'd never had anything to do with guns – why would he?

It wasn't his fault, he said. It was all down to those two, particularly that son of Satan from the Top Farm, Young Fred, who'd been trouble since he was five years old and pushed his old grandfather into the river when he'd nearly drowned . . . Yes, it was he, the bastard, and yes, Brisket knew what the word 'bastard' meant and that lad was that and a whole lot more . . .

'Yes, it was Young Fred who'd stolen the guns off me, saying he knew how to get rid of them and promise him a fifty, yes, a fifty. And had he paid up as much as a fiver? No, he hadn't. And if everyone had their due . . .'

As his voice faded away, Sir Marcus, his chauffeur and Mona emerged from the stables. They'd had their statements taken and were free to depart. Marcus informed the policeman on guard duty that he needed to fetch his jacket, which had been inadvertently left in the ruined room, but was told that no one was to go in for the time being. Marcus fumed, to no avail.

Someone's phone rang in the empty room. Whose phone? The police didn't care.

The chauffeur popped his charges back into the limousine and drove swiftly and silently away. Bea wondered where Mona would sleep that night. In the village or up in London in one of Marcus's properties?

Bea was worried about Polly, but before she could discover how her friend was doing, she was summoned into the barn to account for herself to a police officer.

She'd hardly thought through everything she'd learned so far, but that was all right because she was interviewed by a detective sergeant who had a limited interest in what Bea had to say and who only wanted the answers to a few questions. Had Bea seen who'd fired the guns? No. What were her injuries? She'd a nick on her leg and another on her arm, both of which had stopped bleeding, and that was all.

Bea had been prepared to tell the police that she thought she'd worked out what had been done to whom and by whom, but this detective wasn't interested. Bea thought she'd better speak to a senior officer on the morrow about it when she'd got her head in working order again.

Because it wasn't all over, was it? With a start, she remembered the pack of meat she'd found and put in the freezer. She'd reported that, but nobody had been round to ask her about it yet. Well, someone would probably get on to it in due course, by which time . . .

She gave up. It would get sorted in due course.

The last of the workmen gave their statements and were ferried away. Only Big Teddy remained, complaining that he hadn't been paid that week and his boss had disappeared, and if he didn't have any take-home pay then his mum would do him an injury and what was he to do then, eh?

The ambulance departed.

It began to rain and two Forensic teams arrived in large vans. Four officers descended, masked and suited like white moon visitors. And a sniffer dog! One lot went to work in the wrecked room and the others took the dog and went looking for evidence in the meadow from which the shots had been fired.

Bea staggered into the kitchen and found herself a seat. Someone dumped a large mug of sweetened tea and a biscuit in front of her. She cradled the mug, trying to warm her hands, and reflected on the inconveniences of fashionable gear.

Trousers in general came complete with pockets; skirts and dresses didn't. Most women carried around a handbag to contain the usual small items which were in constant use. Her jacket had pockets but they were a little too shallow to carry her smartphone in safely. So she'd dropped her phone back into her handbag after phoning various people and now it was out of reach. Also her laptop. Her husband might be trying to contact her and . . .

Really, she could scream, she really could.

Mrs Maggs took command. Bea sipped hot tea and tried to relax. She began to look about her. Also in the kitchen was a burly woman with beefy arms, chopping vegetables as if trying to kill a spider . . . wasn't that the woman called Kate, who'd supplied that wonderful lunch the other day and wanted to be one of the local cooks to supply the farm shop?

A second woman was clashing plates together, washing dishes. A middle-aged woman wearing a headscarf and a long tunic over trousers, walked up and down with Pip over her shoulder, singing to him. Was this Imran's mother? Pip had food stains around his mouth, was naked except for a clean tea towel around his loins, and was not a happy bunny. He was tired and hungry. He'd only been halfway through his bottle before it had been taken away from him. He began to wail; the hopeless wail of a child deprived of his mother and his mother's milk.

His wail penetrated walls. Women are hot-wired to respond to a baby's wail. Every woman in earshot shuddered.

Mrs Maggs informed Bea that Lady Polly was resting in her, Mrs Maggs's, private room, but Bea could see her if she wished. 'Lady Polly's asking for the baby but when we took him in to her she couldn't feed him. They both got so distressed that we had to bring the baby away.'

Lady Polly? Is that how she's going to be known? Mm. Not a bad solution for the problem of what to call her.

'She's touch and go,' said Mrs Maggs. 'I got Old Jenny up to look after her. Been a midwife I dunno how many years. Better than those snooty young doctors as have never lost a child and don't know what it does to you.'

Bea, town bred, was horrified. 'But Polly ought to go to hospital.'

'The jolting in that old ambulance on these roads would bring on a miscarriage for sure. I've made her some valerian tea so she might sleep, but she's fretting for the child and for Sir Julian. The next baby may settle overnight. If not, she'll have to go into the hospital tomorrow for a clean out and try again later. It's this way.'

Mrs Maggs showed Bea into a room next door, which seemed to have been constructed out of a series of smaller rooms knocked together. The end result was pleasing. There was a big window which must look out . . . on what? On the paddock? Today there was a blind lowered over it. A television, an elderly but comfortable settee and matching armchair, an old Welsh dresser with a mismatched set of blue and white plates on it and a workaday desk.

Polly was lying on the settee, eyes closed, covered by a light blanket. She'd let one arm drop so that she could touch Bruno's head as he lay on the floor close by. He whined a welcome to Bea but didn't shift from his post. Bruno wasn't happy about his mistress and Bea found that alarming, too.

An old crone – she must be at least ninety years old – sat in a rocking chair by the window, crocheting something blue. She nodded at Bea but didn't speak. This would be Old Jenny, who used to be a midwife?

Bea drew up a chair beside the settee and settled herself. This was a good time to pray and, goodness gracious, there was a lot to pray about at the moment. Her husband, far away. The office staff and their problems. And then, flooding in, the situation at the Hall. Julian, trying so hard against the odds. Little Pip, wailing for hunger and for his parents. Polly . . . oh, Polly!

Polly's eyes opened, and she looked at Bea, knowing who she was, and why she was there. She didn't try to sit up, but held up her free hand to Bea.

Bea stroked Polly's hand. And tried to smile.

Polly tried to reciprocate. 'You heard about Pip? I feel so terrible. Is Julian back?'

'Not yet. I don't know how many pieces of glass they had to remove from him, but it's best they do it now rather than later.'

Polly said, 'The next baby's all right so far. Jenny says it's better to lose the baby now when he's only just begun and have another go later, but I don't think like that. This baby is part of me.'

Bea nodded. Yes, logic might dictate that it was better to lose something that was not properly formed yet, but logic didn't stand a chance against the age-old needs of the mother.

Polly's eyes closed. She wept, without sound. She dozed. Her hand slipped from Bea's. Her breathing became deeper. Calmer.

After a while, Bea dabbed Polly's cheeks with a tissue, and eased herself away from the settee. She met the eyes of the old woman in the window; they nodded to one another, and Bea left.

So, where was Rosemary? And where, oh where, were the rest of the guns?

EIGHTEEN

Friday evening

Rosemary was nowhere to be found. Bea checked. She wasn't in the kitchen, where Pip's wails were becoming more piercing but also less frequent as he wore himself out. The woman in the headscarf – Imran's mother? – had handed him over to the woman who'd been chopping vegetables – Kate, the wonderful cook? – but she wasn't able to calm him, either.

Mrs Maggs was still in control. Just. She said to Bea, 'That poor wee baby. We've tried all sorts from a cup: juice and cow's milk. Even water. He won't take it. I went across and asked that dozy officer if I could fetch Pip's bottle and he said he had his orders and no one was to go in or out. I've sent for some formula and some nappies from the village. They should be here soon.'

Bea looked outside. Various police officers had collected themselves together and were returning to their vehicles. There was some shouting as different police vehicles fought their way around one another to leave the yard.

The Forensic teams worked on. The wrecked room was brightly lit up as the officers in their Moomin gear searched every inch of the place.

Now and then she could hear a smartphone ringing . . . unanswered. If it were her husband ringing for her to help him do this or that . . . If it were Julian ringing to ask for a lift back from the hospital . . .! No, they'd arranged he'd get the hospital to ring Mrs Maggs, hadn't they?

Bea's car was parked at the far end by the stables. She could drive away and leave them all to it – if she had her car keys. Which she hadn't. They were in her handbag in the wrecked room.

There was a slight disturbance of air, and Rosemary appeared out of the dusk and said, 'Trouble?'

Bea said, 'I was thinking about that gun cabinet. There'd have been more than two guns in it when Brisket forced it open, so where are the rest?'

Rosemary said, 'When I gave my statement to the police, I mentioned that there were probably some more guns somewhere. They did sit up and take notice and they're sending teams to search Brisket's place and also the rescue centre. How much longer do you think Forensics will be? They might at least let us have the baby's bottle.'

'Mrs Maggs tried that. No go. But ah, here comes the cavalry.'

A well-used van drew up in the yard, and Imran dragged various packages out of the back and shot them into the kitchen. He had a wonderful black eye and a bandage on his left arm which was minus its sleeve, but he looked pleased with himself.

His mother – the woman in the headscarf – said, 'You took your time.'

'I broke the speed limit.' He showed off his purchases to Mrs Maggs. 'Nappies and formula. All present and correct. And, your niece Kylie said she'll be along as soon as she's sorted out a babysitter, right? Her man's in the pub.'

'Good boy. You've been patched up nicely? Nothing broken? Good. Want something to eat?'

'Dad's by himself in the shop. He let me take the van to fetch Mama and deliver what you needed. I have to get back.' He removed himself and his mother. Bea and Rosemary helped Mrs Maggs unpack.

'Oh, no!' Mrs Maggs looked for once as if she were losing it. 'That idiot Imran. He's got the formula, but no bottle! Trust a man!'

That was indeed bad news.

Bea said, 'We'll be able to get his own bottle as soon as Forensics have finished. I understand why we can't get in till then.'

'Ah, but when . . .?'

A wail from a tired, hungry baby made them all shudder. Bea went back to watching the police activity outside.

The temperature dropped. The officer on guard slapped his arms around himself to keep warm. One lot of Forensic officers came round the end of the barn and went into a huddle with those who'd been working inside. Had they all finished for the night?

They moved to and fro, taking things to their vans, returning for more.

Bea drew in a sharp breath. They were taking two laptops. Hers, and Julian's? And several phones? What on earth for? Did they think Julian and Polly had been inciting these attacks on themselves?

Someone laid a calming hand on her shoulder. 'Routine,' said Rosemary. 'They have to check everything. You can buy another phone and another laptop tomorrow, and you'll get yours back eventually.'

Bea tried to accept this. 'Understood. But what about the baby's bottle?'

Lights went out in the living room. The two teams of Forensics piled into their vans, manoeuvred themselves out and disappeared.

At last. Bea and Rosemary closed in on the officer left on guard. 'We can fetch the baby's bottle now?'

'What? No one goes in or out.'

'Not till Forensics have finished. But they have, haven't they?'

'Them's my orders.'

Bea gritted her teeth. 'Please will you ring whoever's in charge? We don't care so much about the phones but we need the baby's bottle.'

The officer blinked a bit. Pip's wails could be heard even from where they were standing outside. He was old enough to have a family, himself. He nodded and broke the tape to go inside the wrecked room. Lights went on inside as he searched for it.

'Where would it be?'

'By the big chair. Julian was feeding the baby when everything happened.'

'Got it. Oh!' He appeared holding something which had once been a baby's bottle but which had come off worse when pierced with shards of glass. 'This it?'

It was unusable.

Rosemary said, 'Thank you for trying. We appreciate it.'

They returned to the kitchen to report failure.

Another van nosed its way into the yard and parked. More workmen. Sheets of plywood were on the roof. Two workmen got out, yawning, a little bored. They talked to the officer on sentry duty, and then all three moved around the barn . . . to assess what they had to do to board over the broken window?

Mrs Maggs joined them. 'We've tried everything we can think of, but the baby won't take it. I hope my niece can come soon. She still has her last baby's clothes that will do Pip for now. They get through so many outfits in a day at that age, don't they?'

The rain was coming down harder now. The two workmen came

back round the corner, carrying their tools, but without the plywood. Job done. They exchanged merry greetings with the sodden sentry and passed on to their van. Starting the engine, they had four goes at turning their van round before finally making it out.

Bea was given a mug of hot tea and told to sit somewhere out of the way till Mrs Maggs found her something to do. Oh, and she was to sleep in the Waterloo Room that night. Bea didn't know how she felt about that. Was that the bedroom with the canopy over the bed, or another of the four-poster lot? Did it matter?

Lance and his men stayed on to work out what Lennie had and had not done, and to start connecting this up with that. Different parts of the Hall lit up as Lance managed to get various parts of the electrical system checked out and switched on, but he had to call a halt eventually and left, saying he'd be back in the morning and if they wanted to use the downstairs lights they could, but to make sure they were all switched off at the mains before the last person went up to bed. And no one – but no one – should expect electrics in the old estate office, was that understood?

The rain sleeted down. Pip slept for a few minutes, then woke and wailed again.

Another police car drew up outside. An exchange of comments and the previous sentry was removed. The other car remained. Its driver proved to be another officer. This one poked his head round the kitchen door.

'Everything all right here? Just to let you know, I'll be making my rounds of the premises every hour in future. So don't be alarmed if you see my torch shining through windows to see what you're up to, ha-har.'

Bea said, 'Are we allowed to get our personal belongings from the room yet?'

'Certainly not. It's a crime scene, innit?'

'We understand,' said Mrs Maggs, faint but pursuing. 'We'll be serving up food soon. Would you like some?'

'No, no. I've eaten already. And I've brought my dog with me. She'll let me know if there's any intruders, so you can sleep safe tonight.' He shut the outer door firmly.

A policeman who knew what was what, and a dog? A second dog on the scene? They'd have to let Bruno out at the front of the house before he retired for the night.

Rosemary said she'd sleep in her mobile home, so not to bother about her. Bea envied Rosemary's ability to get away from everything for the night.

Bea and Rosemary were asked to help Mrs Maggs to make up beds in different rooms, which at least gave them something to occupy themselves with. Somewhat to Bea's relief, the Waterloo Room was at the far end of the building from the room in which Mr Colston worked on his fragments of parchment.

True to form, Mr Colston made his presence felt, requesting that Big Teddy should bring up some supper for him. Big Teddy went to tell Mrs Maggs what the old gentleman wanted. Teddy said he didn't mind staying on for a bit. His mum didn't like him being out late, but he wasn't going home with no wages and everything still up in the air, and anyway she'd told him to stay and make himself useful so that's what he'd better do.

Mrs Maggs told Teddy to tell Mr Colston that he could have it when it was ready and not before. Mr Colston was wise enough not to argue.

The turmoil in the kitchen began to sort itself out. Some women left.

Food was put on to cook.

The yard lights came on and went off as the police officer and his dog began their rounds.

Rosemary said, 'I'm going to start Julian on a course of self-defence tomorrow. How do you feel about it, for yourself?'

Bea said, 'I don't think I could concentrate at the moment.'

Rosemary said, 'You do the thinking. I'll see he's protected. It's not over yet, is it?'

'No. Some things are clear, but others are not. I'm worried about the guns. If the wrong person managed to get hold of one tonight, say, then they could still have a go at Julian tomorrow.'

Rosemary took Bruno off to make her rounds of the house, carrying a torch for those parts still unlit, and Bea drifted back to the kitchen in time to see a busty youngish female arrive and dump an awkward-looking bundle on the table.

'Sorry I'm late, Auntie. You asked for baby clothes, and I've put in one or two other things, too. Glad to be rid of them. Had to wait for his lordship to get back from the pub. I sent to tell him, but would he budge? Emily's taken to the bottle as easy as pie, thank the Lord and bless all his creatures, eh?'

Prompt on cue, Pip began to wail. A heart-rending wail. He was hungry and tired and in a strange place and his mum was no comfort to him at all.

Mrs Maggs's expression cleared and she began to grin. 'Well, Kylie. Could you manage another one for a bit?'

Bea blinked. What did Mrs Maggs mean? And then, she understood. And was horrified. Did Mrs Maggs really mean her niece should take over from Polly and breast-feed Pip? Of course in the old days, foster mothers were often brought in when milk failed an aristocratic breast, but nowadays . . . was Kylie clean and not incubating anything nasty? All right, she'd been breast-feeding her youngest till lately, but . . . things like that weren't done nowadays, were they?

Bea realized that Mrs Maggs was like Old Jenny, crocheting further links between her family and Julian. After this, Mrs Maggs could never be sacked. She'd live out her days at the Hall, and receive a nice pension when she eventually retired.

Oh yes, and here it came . . .

'Give him here,' said Kylie. 'Might as well. I've got more than enough milk, the Lord knows.'

Pip was introduced to Kylie and the milk flowed. He suckled and burped and suckled again. Pip was refreshed with a clean nappy and baby-gro from among the cast-offs which Kylie had brought for him. She'd also brought a selection of soft toys, among which was an almost pristine toy giraffe which Pip took to immediately. Fed and clean, he was taken through to where Polly was trying to rest and settled into her arms. Polly cried tears of thankfulness, and peace and quiet reigned at the Hall.

Kylie returned to her own home and family after having expressed some of her milk into a cleaned milk bottle which they hoped Pip would consent to accept if he needed feeding during the night.

Julian finally reappeared, courtesy of a police car, wearing several badges of honour on head and hand. He looked tired and moved with a wince and the help of his crutch, but was clear of eye and head. His first words were, 'Now don't fuss! I'm all right. Just a few stitches here and there. Where's Polly? Is she all right? And the boy?'

He was taken to see Polly, who wept when she saw him, and couldn't rest till she'd checked that he still had both his arms and legs.

She said, 'I may lose the baby . . .'

He said, 'We've been through worse, you and I. We'll survive.' Which was precisely the right thing to say.

Next he inspected Pip, who was soundly asleep and didn't object even when Mrs Maggs transferred him into a nest of blankets lining a drawer from a nearby dresser.

Bruno was thrilled to see his master again, signalling that he'd had a tiring day and wanted nothing more than to see his little family all settled firmly in one place.

Mrs Maggs took a huge plateful of her casserole for Julian to eat at Polly's side, and a big mug of chicken broth for Polly, who managed that before falling into a deep sleep.

Everyone else – including Bea and Rosemary, Big Teddy and Old Jenny – ate in the kitchen. Two of the village women – including Kate who cooked – stayed on to wash up and tidy. Bea did spare a thought as to how much Mrs Maggs had promised to pay all this labour and decided that however much it cost, it was worth it, and she, Bea, would personally be prepared to foot the bill if necessary.

When Polly was soundly asleep, Julian joined them in the kitchen for a large helping of apple pie and cream. Bea brought him up to date with the police officers' comings and goings, saying she hoped they'd all be reunited with laptops and smartphones on the morrow.

Big Teddy hung around, saying his mum had told him to stop on if Mr Colston needed him, and proved his worth by carrying Polly – still deeply asleep – up the stairs and into the Lavender Room and laying her on the four-poster bed. He then went back for Pip, making light of the child's weight in his drawer.

Mrs Maggs saw to it that the kitchen was clean and tidy, that everyone was supplied with torches and/or lamps, and that the electricity was turned off at the mains before summoning someone's husband to return her and her friends home. She said she'd bring fresh supplies for breakfast which she said they wouldn't want before eight, would they?

Julian made the journey upstairs under his own steam, with a little help from Teddy and Bea. The bedroom still lacked curtains, but the bed had been made up with fresh linen. An old oil lamp shed a golden glow over everything, and a couple of chests of drawers and a pair of steps had been put by the bed to ease the master's passage up on to the mattress.

Polly didn't stir when they came in, nor did Pip.

Looking around him at the big, bare bedroom, Julian said, 'I never thought I'd sleep in my grandfather's room. But then, I never thought I'd be shot at, or thrown off a horse.'

Bea said, 'I suppose we'll all have to sleep in our underwear and hope we can be reunited with the rest of our things tomorrow. Do you want help getting out of those clothes and into the shower? If there is such a thing as a shower here?'

Teddy beamed. 'Mr Lance says he'll be connecting the water and most of the electrics tomorrow. I'll bring you up a coupla cans of water for now, shall I? I'm doing the same for the old man down the other end. And potties to go under the bed for him and you, like. The old man's creating there's no commode, and I said I'd look for one in the barn for him, but I forgot. Mrs Maggs has gived me a torch to carry, and I'm to sleep on her settee in the house-keeper's room.'

Julian avoided Bea's eye. 'Thank you, Teddy. That would be wonderful.'

Bea wanted to giggle. Teddy went to fetch the water, and Bea helped Julian off with his ruined clothes.

He said, 'I was always supposed to be good at addition, but I can't make this sum come out right. Who's at the back of this? I mean, I suspect several people, but am I right? There's no proof. And do you realize I'm supposed to be meeting the parish council tomorrow night to fill them in on the future of the Hall?'

Bea said, 'Don't worry. I'm almost there. The great thing is to get through the night in one piece, and then get the police to act.'

Saturday morning.

They got through the night without incident.

Mrs Maggs arrived at eight with rolls and milk for the adults' breakfast, and with Kylie for Pip's. Kylie also brought a couple of baby bottles for use when she was not around.

The ex-midwife, Old Jenny, checked Polly over, said everything had settled down nicely, but she should rest as much as possible for the next few days. Jenny then took up a position in the kitchen, providing endless cups of tea for all and sundry and – in between whiles – crocheting away at something blue, which she said was for Polly's next baby. No one dared ask how she knew the sex.

Lance and his band of merry men arrived on the heels of Mrs Maggs and set about making life difficult for everyone, clanging here, pounding up and down the stairs and shouting instructions there. Lance said that Lennie's work had left something to be desired but, with a tweak here and there, they could be out of the place in a couple of days.

Lennie rang in to say he was sick but that he'd completed his part of the contract, he was making out his invoice to be paid immediately, together with his expected bonus. Julian said that when Lennie was better, they must meet to discuss the situation.

Big Teddy took Bruno for an early morning run.

Mr Colston requested a little peace and quiet, if you please . . . and didn't get it.

Julian ate painkillers and limped and crutched around, finally settling in the old library, which still had dust sheets over the furniture. The table and some chairs were unveiled, and coffee provided. This became the new hub for operations.

The police withdrew their sentinel from the wrecked room, and everyone crowded around to look at the mess within. Glass sparkled everywhere, piercing furniture and carpeting the floor. There was no way the family could move back into their old quarters.

Rosemary suggested no one but she should enter for the time being. She said she'd wear protective clothing and would retrieve whatever was needed.

Teddy would ferry everything from the 'incident' to the kitchen to be returned to its owner, including whatever paperwork hadn't been shredded in the blast.

She brought out changes of clothes and toiletries first thing. Clever girl. Bea got her handbag back; with great good luck, she found her keys and her smartphone still in it, but Julian's and Polly's smartphones remained in the possession of the police for the time being.

Bea changed into a sweater and good trousers, topping off with a waistcoat which had pockets in it. She was not going to be parted from her smartphone again in a hurry.

Imran had used his initiative and brought a couple of burner phones for Julian and Polly to use temporarily, so that they could reconnect with the big wide world outside.

As soon as Bea got her smartphone, she rang Piers. He was annoyed she hadn't picked up when he'd phoned her the previous night. He didn't listen to her excuses, but said he was in a hurry but still hoping to see her that weekend – and then he rang off. Now that was good news, though it would have helped if he'd given details. What flight was he supposed to be on? Was she supposed to meet him at the airport? Or was it another lot of chitchat to confuse anyone listening in?

Her call to the agency also brought good news. All was sweetness and light and Bea could hear all about it on Monday morning.

Another blessing was that the landline phones for the Hall were still working. There was an extension in the library and, with that and the burner phones, they all set about trying to work out what needed to be done, to whom, by whom and in what order. The number of organizations which needed updating ranged from solicitors to British Heritage to the local council to the press breaking the news about the priest hole and so on. And then the press started to ring, asking for details of the 'incident' at the barn!

Polly complained about being told to rest, so Julian and Bea enthroned her in an easy chair at the far end of the library, where she could keep an eye on Pip. He, feeling that he'd been properly fed for the first time for days, started to work out how to crawl and had to be rescued from under tables and chairs as he explored this marvellous new space. Pip liked space.

Rosemary asked for and got a half-hour slot with Julian in the entrance hall from which he returned looking amused. So presumably she hadn't asked him to stand her on her head or throw her across the room.

Lance reported how far along he was; Julian took more painkillers, held long conversations on the phone with his old firm which had, tentatively, some good news for him, if and when and providing . . . and then with the chair of the local society for this and that and . . . and . . . he went from one to the other, making notes, updating Rosemary, taking and making phone calls and generally keeping his cool.

Which was more than Bea was doing. She took on the task of dealing with the press, who wanted details of this and that . . . starting with the local press and working its way up to the nationals.

Mrs Maggs provided coffee and a running commentary on the builders, electricians, sightseers, members of the press who'd got the wrong end of the stick, that dratted dog Bruno who had got under Kate's feet and been told to go out front and scare sightseers away, and was Lady Polly feeling all right, because Jenny had said she should go up and rest on her bed for a bit.

Julian had no laptop, but fortunately Rosemary had a small but efficient office in her mobile home, so she was kept busy running to and fro with this and that, not to mention the other.

Every now and then Julian got up from his chair and crutched himself around the room. Bea grew anxious whenever he went near a window, thinking that if someone with a gun were outside in the grounds and saw him, he'd be a wonderfully easy target.

She kept thinking about those missing guns.

Tension mounted. Because it wasn't over, was it? Not till all those guns had been accounted for.

After lunch Polly took Pip off for a nap, and Rosemary suggested that she and Bea should take some exercise in the Long Gallery. Bea welcomed the chance for a quiet exchange of ideas.

Rosemary said, 'Who's behind all this, Bea? Those two boys, Fred and Lars, are not exactly great brains, and I don't see anyone else around whose got the balls needed for these attacks on Julian, do you?'

NINETEEN

Saturday after lunch

B ea said, 'I agree. It's a puzzle. I'm thinking that perhaps there's no one person behind what's happened, but that one event has led on to another. When Julian told me he'd been shot at in the woods but that the police weren't taking it seriously, I was alarmed. Even more so when he told me about finding the dead body of Dora.

'But I arrived with various misconceptions. Having lived all my life in London, I didn't understand how things worked in the country. I thought that people who looked after animals didn't go round killing them, but of course they do, don't they? They're responsible for the animals in their charge from birth to death. If an animal is suffering, they have to put it down. I'd forgotten that and I'd forgotten that every year a few people are prosecuted for ill-treating and starving their pets.

'Another thing I hadn't understood was that local opinion encourages rumour. Craig had been shooting his mouth off about being the rightful heir and people hereabouts were angry with Julian because jobs had been lost when the Hall closed for business. People out of work were inclined to back Craig and to think badly of Julian.

'At first I thought the obvious suspect for the shooting in the woods was Craig. Oh yes, he probably encouraged people to make life uncomfortable for Julian with a nudge and a wink, but he didn't arrive here until after Julian had been shot at in the woods and his mother had been found dead. Also, I don't think he could have got hold of those guns. Does he look the type to want to use a shotgun? Or know how to? I don't think so.'

Rosemary nodded. 'He's tissue paper masquerading as steel. So how do you think the guns got into circulation?'

'Through a disaffected electrician. The poor creature whom Mr Colston had put in the priest hole for us to collect. With hindsight, it would have been better if Julian had broken Lennie's contract at the beginning and started again with another firm, but Lennie and his men *did* know their way around the Hall, and they *were* getting on with the job, if slowly.

'Judging by the evidence of the footprints we found in the estate office, the man who took the guns was the same as the one who installed the new wiring. And that was Brisket, who believes he's owed a share of some mythical buried treasure which is supposed to be at the Hall. He talked in the pub about the guns and speculated how much they would be worth . . . and the two lads from the rescue centre heard him and took action. I don't know how many guns there were exactly. Did you find any paperwork on them?'

'I've unearthed the insurance details and the inventory for Julian. There's a collection of guns ranging from seventeenth-century muskets, through eighteenth-century duelling pistols to some of the latest shotguns. They're worth a fortune. Fortunately, the insurance is up to date. So how did those two stupid lads from the rescue centre get hold of even one or two of them?'

'I don't really know much about Lars – that's the fair-haired lad – but we do know enough about Young Fred, the bully boy, to conclude he has no liking for the law. He had a reputation for violence. I think he jumped at the idea of getting his hands on some guns, not only for sport but also for money.

'Brisket broke into the cabinet, took the guns and handed them over to the two lads. They'd promised him money and failed to deliver. I feel almost sorry for Brisket. He'd stolen the guns, which meant he couldn't complain when they in turn were stolen from him. I assume the lads kept one rifle and one shotgun and sold the rest on within days? Or are they still at the rescue centre?'

Rosemary said, 'No news yet.'

So the searches at the rescue centre and at Brisket's cottage hadn't turned them up? Oh dear.

'I don't think the boys realized how valuable they were. All they could see was that they now had the means of settling various scores. One of them used the rifle to take a potshot at Julian as he was out riding. I'm inclined to think it was the bully boy, Young Fred. I only met his father Frederick once, but the resemblance is uncanny. Both have a bull-like confidence that they'd always get their own way. He did it partly for fun, and partly because he could. Julian reported the incident to the police, but it wasn't taken seriously.

'What happened next? We were given a hint yesterday, weren't we? The two boys blamed one another for everything under the sun and we all heard them. Hopefully, they'll go on doing that.'

Rosemary said, 'Lars is not local, is he? He doesn't look it.'

'Lars is no relation to the family, though there is a connection. You remember talk of Gerda, Bertram's widow? Gerda used to spend time at the rescue centre after Frederick killed her little lapdog. She's one of those women who adore small animals that she can treat like dolls, but is afraid of anything larger.

'She'd heard the rescue centre was short-handed, and arranged for someone she knew to help out. That person was Lena, who is either a cousin or an old friend of Gerda's, I don't know which. To give Lena her due, I believe she's pulled her weight at the rescue centre ever since. Lars is her son, supposedly taking a gap year before going to university.

'I suppose Dora's death was foreseeable, given what they were like. Probably tanked up with beer, I think Bully Boy taunted Lars with being a virgin and suggested Dora – who was known far and wide as the local lay – might help him to grow up. The fact that Dora was old enough to be his mother was actually a bonus because she'd have the experience to do what was required. I imagine she went along with it so far, and then . . . I don't know . . . perhaps she refused to let him go any further and he got so worked up that he couldn't stop?

'Perhaps she laughed at him, in which case he might well have lost it and taken his frustration out on her? Finding that he'd killed her, Lars panicked. Perhaps he might have gone to the police straight away, but I'm thinking either he called Fred to help him, or Fred was there, watching. Either way, a rope was put around her neck and she was hoisted up in an effort to make it look as if she'd committed suicide.'

Rosemary said, 'But why did they meet at the stables here?'

'Where else? Dora couldn't take Lars to her cottage because that's occupied by her latest partner, with whom she was living in spite of the fact that she was not supposed to sublet it. Lars couldn't take her to the rescue centre where his mother was living; there's no room there for such shenanigans. But the Hall is the local lovers' trysting place. It has an air of mystery with all the recent goings-on and the old rumour about buried treasure. Youngsters probably dare one another to visit. If I'm right, there should be some DNA to place

Lars at the scene. They've got Julian's and found it doesn't match, which explains why they haven't been buzzing him so much lately.

'But he's not in the clear yet. For what the police did have was someone who said they'd seen Julian with Dora that night. I think I know who it was. There's a waitress called Ivy in a café in town who'd lost her job here in the cuts and thought Julian had been rude to her when she asked when jobs would be available again. He probably doesn't even remember her. I'm told that either she or her friend was up there for a spot of the usual and saw someone with fair hair joshing along with Dora. Whichever one of them it was, he or she leapt to the conclusion she'd seen Julian and spread that rumour around.'

Rosemary said, 'She saw Lars with Dora? And persuaded herself she'd seen the unpopular Julian?'

'That's what I believe. Meanwhile, the two lads thought they'd got away with it. They'd killed, they'd stolen, no one suspected them. They were on a roll. They ramped up their plans. One of them – I suspect it was Lars – put a teasel under the saddle on the horse, Jack, which Julian rode, with intent to cause him to take a fall and perhaps to kill him. Julian fell but survived. Poor, frightened Mickey – his groom – either guessed or actually saw whoever it was who'd placed the teasel there but was too frightened to tell anyone.

'The horse was killed and removed. Why and by whom? Why . . .? To hide the wound the teasel had created. Who by? I think Lars might have put the teasel under Jack's saddle, but the efficiency with which the horse was killed and disposed of sounds more like Young Fred.

'I spoke to the old vet who looks after the rescue centre animals pro bono. Tom Potter's his name. To be found in the next town. He's getting on in years and he's getting forgetful. He could easily have mislaid the gun that vets use to kill animals there – or had it removed from his case when he wasn't looking.'

Bea continued. 'To make sure of Mickey's silence, someone . . . or perhaps the two lads working together . . . shut him into his own box while they did the deed . . . and left him there for me to find later that evening. On that same trip – and it gives me goosebumps to realize how close I was to stumbling after them that night as I made my rounds – they left a packet of poisoned meat for Bruno to find. Which reminds me that I must hand it to the police and get them to test it. There might even be fingerprints on the wrappings to give the donor away.'

'Yes,' said Rosemary, 'we need proof. Not speculation.'

'I know,' said Bea. 'Far too much speculation, and if they retract whatever they've said in public . . .!'

'We did find them in possession of those two guns. And if Brisket says they took the guns off him . . .'

'They could say they were just larking about when they fired at the window, and that no one was seriously injured. Have the police enough to charge them? It's all circumstantial, isn't it?'

Rosemary said, 'It all hangs on finding the rest of the guns.'

'Yes. I'm also afraid that there's someone directing events from the background, someone who hasn't shown their hand as yet. We can both taste the tension in the air. It's not over yet.'

Rosemary went off to her mobile home to use her printer, and Bea returned to the library to tackle some of the phone calls and emails that were coming in all the time.

Julian was still there, talking on his burner phone while crutching himself up and down the room. He shot a smile at Bea and indicated the landline phone, which was merrily ringing away. Bea got to it as it went silent. Julian tossed his own phone on to the table, and relaxed into his big chair, rubbing his forehead. He probably needed some more painkillers.

Silence fell over the big room.

'Ah, how golden is silence,' he said. 'I'd forgotten what it was like.'

'Where is everyone?'

'Teddy's taken Bruno out for a run. Polly's resting with Pip at her side. Rosemary's updating the historic associations about the priest hole and fending off the press who are ghoulishly wanting details of yesterday's little incident . . .'

He yawned widely. 'I could do with half an hour's nap! At my age, too! I feel I've lived through a year since yesterday morning. Can you look to see if Polly left me the phone number of someone from the parish council? It's about the timing of the meeting tonight. I promised I'd ring her back.'

Bea riffled through the papers which Polly had left. She heard the door open and a voice saying, 'There you are!'

Bea reacted without thinking, dropping to the floor behind the chair.

Then she told herself she'd overreacted. She peered round the back of the chair and found what she saw to be somewhat alarming. She hadn't overreacted at all.

She reached for her smartphone and messaged Rosemary. 'Red alert. Library.'

First into the room was Jessie, the woman who ran the rescue centre, followed by the Swedish woman, Lena, whom Gerda had brought in to help run the place. Neither of those women's expressions could be regarded as friendly.

Behind them pranced Lance's younger brother, Skinny, and the Young Pretender, Craig.

And behind them, hesitantly teetering in the doorway, came a pale blonde, a whiplash-thin woman of perhaps thirty years of age who was not ageing well.

Gerda; that was the woman's name. Bertram's widow, who was reported to be wild with grief at his death. She had the fixed stare of a fanatic.

Bea drew in a sharp breath. She had wondered, oh yes, it had crossed her mind several times that Gerda might have been a player in this game, but it had been all too easy to dismiss her as ineffective.

Bea had forgotten that puppets are manoeuvred by human beings, and that some of those human beings prefer to live in the shadows and get others to do their dirty work for them.

Julian half rose when they arrived.

Craig pushed Jessie aside to confront Julian. 'Yes. You can get out of that chair. It's mine, not yours.'

Lance's Skinny brother danced around. 'I said you wouldn't last!' He swiped at the table, deliberately sending Julian's phone to the floor.

Bea was halfway through dialling nine-nine-nine to call the police when Jessie shouted, 'There's someone else here!' She rushed at Bea, wrenched the phone from her hand, and back-handed her into the chair.

'You're that office woman, right? This is none of your business. You sit still and keep quiet. Our quarrel's with him, not you, right?'

Bea nodded. She sat very still.

Gerda hovered in the background, scratching at the back of her hand.

Lena leaned over the table to spit words out at Julian. 'You have to tell the police my son did nothing wrong, do you hear me?'

Jessie, still standing over Bea, called out, 'That's right. You tell
him! And if he thinks he can turn us out of the centre, then tell him
he can't, right!'

Julian said, 'This is ridiculous. The shooting incident yesterday
is being dealt with by the police and there's no way I can interfere.
Please leave.'

Craig pulled another chair out from the table and sat, smiling
and crossing his legs. 'You've got no bodyguard today, I see. No
dog, either. I'm so glad you're all alone. This is family business.'

Bea shifted her legs. Jessie swung round on her, fist raised. Bea
stilled. She would have to wait till they were distracted by something
before she moved again. She didn't like the fact that two of the
women were carrying heavy tote bags. Nor that they were there in
the first place. Nor Craig.

Skinny didn't count. He was an irritation, like a mosquito.

Rosemary would get the message and ride to the rescue . . . if
she were not deep in some technical stuff, or already using her
smartphone.

Five people had entered the library who all had cause – in their
view – to want Julian gone. A tense situation. If not actively
dangerous.

In the background Gerda hovered and scratched at her hand.

Julian concentrated on Craig. In his quietest, most reasonable
voice, he said, 'Craig, you really should talk to the family solicitor
about this. It is, as you say, a family matter and, for your own sake,
should be kept within the family.'

'So you say!' A sneer in Craig's voice that he must have been
practising. 'You can't deny Sir Florian paid my mother a large sum
of money, which proves—'

'It doesn't prove paternity,' said Julian. 'Mr Routledge put me
in the picture about various things. I was shown the evidence with
regard to your birth, and I can tell you it doesn't prove that Frederick
was your father. For your own sake, let it be.'

'Ridiculous! Of course it does. What else could it possibly be?'

Julian sighed. 'Ask the solicitor.'

'I'm asking you, and I'm not leaving till I've got you to admit
my claim to the Hall.'

'It's against my advice, but, if you insist on hearing the truth,
you should make an appointment to see the solicitor. He'll put you
in the picture.'

'Out with it!'

'Very well. Your mother enjoyed sex. She had various partners and short-term relationships. She did fall pregnant now and then but none of the men concerned had what she considered sufficient money to give her a good life, so she arranged to have an abortion. Three times.

'Then one day Frederick took an interest in her. When she found out she was expecting again, she decided to keep the child and tell Frederick it was his. Her reasoning was that he'd pay her well for it. Only, by the time the baby was born, Frederick had heard rumours that Dora had been seeing another man at the same time that he was visiting her. He had a DNA test done which proved he was not the father. He beat Dora up so badly that she had to be taken to hospital. The money Sir Florian paid her was in consideration of that beating, and not because Frederick accepted paternity.'

'What! That's a lie! Frederick was my father! Everyone knew it.'

Julian said, 'It suited her to let everyone think so. I imagine she thought it gave her some standing in the community. But it was not true.'

Craig's fists flailed the air. He stomped up and down, up and down. He said, 'She wouldn't lie about that. No way! Would she?'

No reply.

Craig thumped the table. 'Who do *you* say is my father, then? One of the farmers hereabouts? A holiday visitor?'

Julian said, 'When I was growing up, I used to fantasize who my birth parents might be. I stopped doing that in my early teens. They'd given me a gift which would enable me to earn my living as an accountant. I was happy with that. Your father gave you a gift which enables you to earn a living. Be content.'

'*Who the hell is he?*'

'Are you sure you want to know?'

Craig's face had empurpled. He reached across the table and swiped Julian's crutch out of his reach. '*If you don't tell me, now, I'll knock your block off!*'

'Calm down. Very well, if you must know . . . Your father was still a schoolboy at the time, the youngest from a family that subsequently left the village and moved to London. Dora was his first. She liked them young. He wanted to go to art collage but hadn't the money for it, so did bar work until he was old enough to join the army. He died in Afghanistan some years ago. I don't think he ever knew about you. He wouldn't have been able to give you a good start in life, which is why Dora allowed everyone to believe the story that you were Frederick's child.'

'How do you know he was my father, then?'

'Frederick knew you weren't his child, but wanted to be sure Dora could never prove it. So he had someone locate your real father and had another DNA test done. That confirmed it.'

'I don't believe it! You're making it up!' A wail of distress. Craig was beginning to accept the truth. 'No one else believes it, do you?' Craig's plea to his friends went unanswered, which was an answer in itself.

Someone muttered, 'Enough!'

Was that Gerda? No, she still hadn't spoken. She watched, and she waited. The puppets were moving well at her instigation. She had no need to act, yet.

A woman's back view slid into Bea's sightline between her and Julian. The heavyweight, Jessie. She was carrying her heavy tote bag high up in her arms. Why?

Lance's brother, Skinny, jogged on the spot. 'Craig, does this mean you can't inherit everything? You promised us that . . .' His voice rose.

'Yes, I promised!' Craig was shouting now. 'I promised, I thought, Dora said . . .! And it's all . . .!' A change of tone. Grimly. 'I'm going to check, everything he said could be just . . . It's a lie! That's what it is! He's lying! And I'm going to—'

'What are you going to do?' Julian sounded exhausted. He pushed up his glasses and rubbed his eyes tiredly. 'Sue me? For what? You have no case and people would laugh at you for pretending to be something you aren't. Look, I didn't ask to inherit this place. I was content with the life I'd got. But now I have to take responsibility for the Hall and try to guide it through to better days. Don't envy me for it, Craig. Be content that you have a means of earning a good living wherever you go.'

'You owe me!'

'Enough!' A harsh voice. The Swedish woman, Lena. 'I want my son released. The other – Young Fred – I don't give a damn about him. He led my son astray and he should pay for it. But Lars comes home today and no further charges are made against him.'

Julian's voice was even. 'I regret I cannot help you. I believe the police will charge him with the murder of Dora among other crimes, and I believe they have enough evidence to convict.'

'It was Fred who killed Dora, not Lars. My son was there, but he did nothing to harm the woman. He told me all about it. She said she would do this and that for the two of them but what can you expect with that kind of woman? Fred held her fast to stop her screaming and she struggled instead of keeping still. So it was an accident and a murder charge will not stick. It was Fred, anyway. Not Lars. And if you withdraw the charges about him shooting at the barn wall, then he will be freed.'

'That's not up to me to decide,' said Julian. 'DNA results will soon reveal which of the two was responsible for Dora's death, and which of the two fired the shotgun through the window with intent to kill me and my family.'

'Everything was Fred, not Lars. All you have to do is withdraw all charges.'

Julian said, 'You misunderstand the nature of the law here. Whoever tried to kill me and my family will be judged by British law and convicted by it if found guilty.'

A soft voice intervened. 'I told you so, Lena! He will not listen.' Gerda, Bertram's widow, moved forward from where she had been standing in the shadows. She said, 'This man is a monster. He killed my Bertram, and he's going to pay for it.'

Julian said, in a mild tone. 'I never touched him. Bertram did try to kill me several times, and in the course of his last attempt he had an accident which disabled him. As far as I can make out, he died from complications resulting from that accident.'

Gerda took another step forward. 'It's as I thought. You are a typical Marston-Lang. You have no feelings. You are cold and arrogant, just like your grandfather. You turn us out of our home, you send Bertram to prison and he dies there. You don't deserve to live!'

'Steady on, Gerda,' said Jessie. 'We agreed, didn't we, that we must keep a cool head. We give him a chance to right our wrongs and then we decide what action to take.'

TWENTY

Saturday evening

The woman with the broad back moved away so that Bea could now see Julian more clearly. He looked relaxed but tired.

He said, 'What are your wrongs, Jessie? What do I owe you? I haven't dunned you for using the stabling and paddock because I know you've been through a difficult time. I turned a blind eye to Mickey's sleeping on the premises. I assume he fled to you when he left here. I know the police would like a word with him, so perhaps you can arrange for him to make himself available.'

'Mickey did nothing wrong, and you can't prove otherwise.'

'Agreed. So?' He lifted his hands and let them fall. 'What do you think I owe you?'

'You caused me to lose my best horse, and the lads who worked for me.'

'Not I. You did that to yourself. By the way, which of you killed Jack?'

Jessie said, 'I didn't. I wouldn't. But Young Fred . . . probably. I know he didn't like you riding around the place as if you owned it, although I suppose you did, in a way. Come to think of it, you're getting to look more like your grandfather every day.' She resented that, didn't she?

'I take that as a compliment. Jessie, I see no reason to break our contract, provided you make at least some attempt to pay the rent we agreed.'

He shifted to look at the pale woman who had brought the others to this place. 'Gerda, you know why I had to close the Hall down and I'm sorry for your loss. I wish you well, but . . .'

Gerda nerved herself to answer. 'I want compensation for all I've lost! My home and my husband. And I want a decent pension.'

The Swedish woman chimed in. 'And I want my son out of prison!'

Bea didn't like the look of the way things were going, not one bit. Where was Rosemary when she was needed?

Craig burst out, 'For God's sake! If you're going to kill him, do it now, before anyone else comes in! Kill the London woman as well.'

Lance's younger brother didn't like that. 'What? Kill . . .? But . . . No, I didn't realize you meant . . .!'

The whip-thin Gerda concentrated on Julian, moving closer to him. She moved like a snake, smoothly intent on her prey. 'I give you one last chance. Pay me and pay me well, or else!'

Craig, all excited. 'That's it! Get him to leave the place and let me have what's right!'

Julian was sharp, for once. 'Craig, you know I can't.'

'Then we will all be the witnesses to your committing suicide—'

'Before our very eyes!' That was Jessie.

'Hang about!' Skinny didn't like the sound of this. 'You didn't say nothing about killing him. And what of the woman, eh? She's seen and heard everything. You don't really mean you want to do both of them in?'

'Yes, we have to!' That was Jessie. 'She's a witness, isn't she? We make out they were quarrelling and we came in to see them aiming guns at one another and—'

'Yes! They committed suicide by killing one another!' That was Lena. 'Kill them both and put the guns in their hand. We've got enough guns, haven't we? Then we say how shocked we all are that Julian killed the woman and committed suicide before our very eyes because we proved Craig was the rightful heir and—'

'And what of my wife and child?' said Julian, looking amused rather than worried. He put his hands in his pockets, and leaned back in his big chair.

'We'll take care of them later,' said Gerda, turning to Jessie. 'Where's the guns?'

Jessie fumbled in her tote bag to produce a long, heavy box which she laid on the table.

Bea craned her neck to see what was in it. She thought they were all quite mad. Deluded. Who would ever believe their story? The only problem was that they were so far into their own version of what had gone on that they could probably do considerable damage before they were stopped. They might even manage a murder or two.

Gerda opened the box, which looked old. Made of mahogany? She took out . . . was that a pistol? An early Victorian duelling pistol, of the sort displayed in museums? Oh, no!

Gerda said, 'I believe this is a real antique. It's ironic, isn't it, that Julian would use one of his family's collection of guns to shoot himself with?'

'I don't like guns,' said Skinny, sounding worried. 'Where did you get that?'

Gerda said, 'From the boys, of course. They'd heard talk in the pub that there were still guns at the Hall. They told Lena, and she told me. I told the boys I'd sell them and give them half the proceeds, and they delivered them to me within the week. Of course I knew there'd be a fuss when the guns were found to be missing, so I told the boys to keep a couple for themselves and the rest they brought to me in the village. I hid them under my bed in the house I share with Mona and Celine. No one's going to look for them there.

'There's a lot of guns, you know. I took photographs to send to a dealer. I found someone who said he'd put them up for sale one or two at a time so as not to saturate the market. He said the pair in the box were really old and looked to be in perfect condition. He said to watch out, that they might still be loaded, but I haven't checked that. Shall we try one on Julian and see? Who would like first go?'

Julian brought up his hand and swept in an arc from left to right.

An explosion rocked the room.

Bea flung herself at the nearest figure . . .

She felt something wet spatter her hands.

A woman screamed.

Someone shouted, 'No!'

Bea clung on to whoever it was she was clutching . . . a man? Craig? But he was too strong for her and slipped from her grasp.

Shouting . . .!

Panting, Bea rose to her knees to see Jessie and Lena clutch at their faces. They bent over, rubbing at their faces. Gasping for breath.

Gerda screamed, in a thin voice that threatened to fade.

Rosemary sauntered through the open door, and found Craig hurtling towards her. She twisted him round, dropped him to the floor, and told him to stay put. He obeyed.

Skinny, terror-stricken, ran for the door and freedom, shouting something unintelligible.

Bruno bounded into the room, saw Skinny rushing towards him and smelled blood. He went for the man's arm and bore him to the ground. That made two on the ground.

No, three.

Gerda lay on the floor, cradling her right arm, moaning as blood poured out from where her hand had been.

The pistol she'd used lay on the carpet some distance away, the barrel opened up like the petals of a flower. It had been overloaded a century and more before, and never fired until Gerda tried to use it.

Skinny sobbed and stuttered, lying on the floor with Bruno standing over him.

Jessie and Lena staggered around, clawing at their eyes.

Bea fell back against the chair, horrified.

Gerda continued to scream thinly, mouth wide, eyes shut.

Bea could hear people sobbing. Men and women.

Julian leant on the table, breathing deeply. He seemed unharmed, except for a spatter of blood. There was blood on the table, too. And all over.

Julian sank back in his chair and reached blindly for his phone. He didn't find it because it had been knocked to the floor earlier. He said, 'Rosemary? Can you see my phone? We need police. Ambulance.'

Gerda, on the floor, muttered, 'Help me!' She was losing blood fast.

Unlike Bea, Rosemary assessed the situation and knew what to do first. She took a piece of string out of her pocket and tied it around Gerda's right arm as a tourniquet.

Bea started to look around for her own phone. Jessie had snatched it from her, earlier. So what had she done with it? It must be on the floor somewhere.

Rosemary found Julian's phone on the far side of the table. She picked it up and handed it to him. 'You make the call. It will come better from you.'

Julian pressed numbers. 'Yes,' he said into the phone. 'Police. Urgently. And an ambulance. Marston Hall. Yes, I'm Sir Julian Marston-Lang. A woman tried to shoot me with an old gun. It exploded. There's not much of her hand left. The other injuries are minor and don't need hospitalization.'

Rosemary checked to see if anyone was foolish enough to try to leave. She pulled hands down from Jessie's and Lena's faces, and said, 'You'll do.'

Jessie clawed at her eyes. 'For God's sake!'

'Water! I'm dying!' That was Lena, gasping, fading fast.

Rosemary had no sympathy. 'You'll live and be charged with attempted murder.'

Bea forced herself to stand upright. Was she going to fall over? No, she was not! She said to Julian, 'What did you hit them with?'

'The pepper spray which Rosemary very kindly lent me. I must say, I didn't realize it would have such a devastating effect.'

Bea found her own phone on the floor by dint of following its ringtone. It was Piers.

Who was Piers? Oh. Ah. Of course. Her husband. And he was chattering away about . . . what . . .?

'. . . safely on the plane, though I had to leave my easel behind. What an experience! Am I glad to be out of that! I should be back in London about ten this evening local time. I'll go straight home, though, and have a good night's sleep. I'll join you down in the country tomorrow, right? What a story I have to tell you! Bea . . .? Bea, are you there?'

Bea cleared her throat. 'Yes. That's great news. We'll see you tomorrow. I look forward to hearing all about it.'

He rang off as police and an ambulance arrived. Explanations were given. There was no difficulty in sorting the sheep from the goats as they all turned on one another as fast as they could.

Gerda was charged with attempted murder, conspiracy and receiving stolen goods. She lost her hand. The cache of stolen guns was eventually restored to Julian, who sold the lot to defray his expenses.

The others were sentenced according to their degree of involvement in the murderous attempts on Julian's life.

Saturday evening

The news of what had occurred at the Hall that day shot round the neighbourhood, and the result was a packed meeting in the parish hall that evening. The press were temporarily satisfied by a statement issued by the police.

Polly had insisted on accompanying her husband to what might well be a difficult meeting and, though he objected, she carried her point, saying the family should confront the situation together.

Brushing a speck of dust off his shoulder, she said, 'If anyone's going to throw tomatoes at you in your only good suit, I want to be there to throw them back!'

So Rosemary drove Julian, Polly, Pip and Bruno to the venue in the better of their two cars, parking in the space left for them at the front door. There was a formal welcome by the chair of the meeting, who introduced various people of importance in the community before escorting the family to the front and up three steps to sit on the platform.

Bea drove Mr Colston and Big Teddy in her own car to the venue, with Mr Colston sizing up the possible value to him of this village if he decided to move there as they went along. His 'thank you' to her on alighting from the vehicle was perfunctory, but about what she'd expected. She saw Teddy guide Mr Colston in, and then went around looking for somewhere to park.

When she eventually got to the parish hall, she didn't go up to the dais with the Marston-Lang family but took an unobtrusive seat at the back. In the chattering audience, she spotted some of the local gentry who had thought it worth their while to turn up now that Julian had beaten off all challenges to the Hall, plus various interested parties.

She was amused to see that Mr Colston had managed to find himself a seat in the front row, with the assistance of Big Teddy, who was backed up by an outsized woman who must be Teddy's aged mum.

Then she saw Mr Routledge, the family solicitor, who was declining gracefully to sit on the dais, while making his approval of Julian known. He'd brought his stylish wife to be introduced to Julian and Polly. A good tactic.

Lance, the builder, arrived with a bustling wife and took seats up front, while some of his men took seats at the back. Bernie, the taxi driver, had also turned up and brought his wife.

Mrs Maggs was there with her extended family, including bosomy Kylie, all giving themselves airs because they'd been the first to offer wholehearted support to the new man at the Hall.

Buxom Kate, that brilliant cook, was there with an impressive number of grown-up children, all of whom were no doubt hoping for a job in the near future.

Also in the throng Bea spotted not only Jan and Ivy from the café in the next town, but also old Tom Potter, the vet, together with a promising-looking son . . . was he aiming to be the next vet to serve the Hall?

Lurking in the back row Bea spotted Mickey, the groom who'd jumped ship when Jack was killed. Presumably he'd come back to look after the rescue centre till someone else could take over?

There were lots of families with youngish, next-generation youths and lasses, shepherded in by matriarchs, among whom Bea recognized some of the women whom Mrs Maggs had dragooned into helping out at the hall. Among these was Imran – with a capable-looking girl beside him . . . the doctor's assistant from the next town? – and his parents, who must have shut up shop early for the occasion.

Altogether, it was a formidable crowd for Julian to face. He managed to mount the steps to the dais with a little help from his crutch, and had made sure Polly was settled in a chair with the Moses basket containing their son and heir at her feet. And Bruno by his side.

Before he could take a seat himself, Julian was button-holed by a hefty-looking man who wondered if Julian were interested in sponsoring or playing in a cricket match? As and when he was fit again?

The noise level in the hall dropped as everyone wanted to hear Julian's response, which was, 'That's a thought. We must get together about it some time.'

A woman in a dog collar arrived on the platform but had no time to be introduced before a woman with a purple rinse and an impressive frontage tinkled a tiny bell and announced it was time to begin . . . and she would start by introducing . . .

Rosemary slid into a seat beside Bea, who murmured, 'What's the general mood like?'

'A collective decision appears to have been reached to let him present his case, with a slight majority thinking he's made the right decisions.'

Julian showed no sign of nerves when invited to speak. He said, sending his voice without effort to the very back of the room, 'I suppose you're all as surprised as I am to find myself standing here. I'm an accountant by trade and these last few months have been a steep learning curve for you . . . as well as for me.'

There was the very slightest ripple of laughter, and the tension began to drain out of the air.

Julian went on to enumerate the problems he'd faced, the disappearance of the Hall's funds, the poor state of the house and its dependent facilities, and Craig's claim to be a member of the family.

Julian dealt with Craig first. He said that probably everyone knew the truth by now but Craig's father was not a Marston-Lang and Dora had received money from the family for other reasons.

Several people nodded. They'd thought as much. Craig was now in custody and they'd probably never hear from him again.

Julian said that the missing money had been located in the Cayman Islands and was on its way back home . . . thanks to a clue given him by his cousin Mona, who was in the process of moving to London.

There were knowing looks all round. They knew what Mona was like and most of them wished her well. Bea looked around for Celine, but she wasn't there, was she? Ah, yes; she was. And what's more, she was sitting next to Mr Colston.

How about that? Did Celine think the ex-teacher would help her with her writing? No, wait a minute. Celine had that big house in the village and if Mona moved up to London, she'd be living in it all by herself. Suppose Mr Colston moved in with her now that Mona and Gerda had departed? Mr Colston would enjoy being a celebrity there, and Mrs Maggs would provide them with a housekeeper and cook . . .? Yes, it might work.

Julian pressed on, talking about his plans to try to put the Hall back on its feet. He said the electricians and builders had almost finished with the house and they were hoping to reopen to visitors at Easter. He was hoping they could fit solar panels to keep bills down.

He said that the finding of the priest hole would help with publicity; a new brochure would be written, thanks to Julian's father-in-law . . . at which Mr Colston – pleased as punch but trying to hide it – managed to half rise from his seat and bow an acknowledgement.

Julian said Lady Polly had been told not to exert herself too much but was nevertheless anxious to create new displays up at the Hall . . .

There was another ripple of amusement and, Bea noticed, of

approval. They did like the thought of continuity at the Hall, because it stabilized the economy thereabouts.

Polly smiled and nodded but didn't speak.

Julian said, 'As for the farm shop, restaurant and amusement park, this is a good opportunity to announce that Imran will shortly be taking over the management of the farm shop, and Kate will take over the restaurant.'

Kate was blushing and smiling, nodding to everyone on either side of her.

Julian said, 'Both will be taking on staff very soon. We'll be putting up notices as to when and where interviews will take place. Please be patient; it will take time to get everything started.'

Someone in the crowd said, 'What about the amusement park, eh?'

Julian sighed. 'If I gave you free tickets to take your wife and children on the rides in the amusement park, would you use them?'

A long, long moment while they considered the proposition.

Because they wouldn't, would they? They all knew how dangerous those rides were. Poor maintenance and lack of investment would have closed them if Julian hadn't done so.

'I hope,' said Julian, 'that when we've paid all our debts, and got everything running again, we'll be able to look around to see what can be done with the amusement park.'

Someone stamped their feet. One – and – two – and . . .

A couple joined in. One – and – two.

Much stamping ensued. A real sign of approval. They didn't like the news about the amusement park much, but they could see it was the right thing to do. Someone laughed. Someone called out 'Bravo!'

Bruno suddenly ducked his head into the Moses basket, and a faint mewing sound was heard. Polly leaned over the basket to pick up her son, whose eyelids were fluttering awake. He waved his arms and legs, waking up to realize he was in a strange place, with lights above him. His mummy was holding him and he was quite safe but . . . he enquired within, and discovered an empty void. Food. Where was his next meal?

Julian meanwhile had delved into the blankets in the Moses basket, assisted by Bruno, and come up with a baby's bottle. He shook it, checked the teat was working, and handed it to Polly, who applied it to Pip's mouth.

The audience – and Bruno – watched with interest.

Bea wondered what would happen if the baby decided he didn't want the bottle. Would they have to heave Kylie from her seat and get her to take the baby off somewhere to feed? She was sitting behind Mrs Maggs and could easily get up to help . . . but no. Pip was so engrossed in trying to work out where he was and what all those people were doing, staring at him, that he took to the bottle with gusto.

'Now that's another thing,' said Julian. 'I expect there was a room which served as a chapel in the Hall years ago. Perhaps we'll manage to locate it, perhaps not. But I'd like Philip to be christened at Easter, if that is in order.' He turned to the woman in the dog collar for her approval.

She nodded. 'We will speak about it.'

'Now,' said Julian, 'I know that it is traditional for the master of the Hall to invite all his tenants to a feast on that day, but I won't have enough money for it this year. Perhaps we can make a date for Christmas, instead?'

Kate rose from her seat. 'I've got it in my calendar for Easter, and I've started the big cake already. There'll be enough for fifty or more.'

Mrs Maggs bobbed up, too. 'I thought we'd have it in the entrance hall at the house. Trestle tables and chairs we can borrow from here . . .'

'Put me down for a coupla dozen sausage rolls.' A voice from the far side of the hall.

'And I've got some of my home-brewed, nigh on a barrel, maybe. We can borrow glasses and plates from the restaurant, can't we?'

'My daughter-in-law's got this recipe from her granny that's passed, for a syllabub that she wants to try out for the restaurant—'

Mrs Maggs said, 'We can do it, Sir Julian. Everyone'll bring something. We'll put a list in the shop for people to say what they'd like to provide. There'll be enough food to go round for everyone, I guarantee that, and I'll organize some sherry and some sandwiches for those who don't have no jobs but want to drop in to see what you're made of.'

Julian said, 'Mrs Maggs, you're a wonder.'

'So are you, sir. So are you.'

Rosemary and Bea slipped out of the back of the Hall. The sky was darkening. The moon was rising. The air was cool but not chilly.

Bea said, 'Job well done, Rosemary. Will you stay on for a while?'

'For three months, perhaps? He knows how to protect himself now but the paperwork needs attention. You'll find me someone to train up to look after him?'

'I can do that.' Bea began to laugh. 'Piers is back tomorrow, full of his little adventure abroad. Just wait till I tell him what we've been going through here!'